HIGHLAND PRODIGY

WILLA BLAIR

OLIVER
HEBER
BOOKS

For Lisa Benton-Short and Laura Glueck, the best Beta readers an author could ask for. You're Alphas to me!

ACKNOWLEDGMENTS

For my first new novel in—ahem--a few years, I'm honored to thank Tanya Anne Crosby and the staff of Oliver Heber Books for supporting me and giving me such a wonderful boost as I attack my keyboard with new ideas and new energy. A new book! A new series! I love new beginnings, and I'm thrilled mine is happening with you.

PROLOGUE

SCOTTISH HIGHLANDS 1521

Aileanna Lathan hiked up her skirts and chased her four-year-old son across the flower-strewn ground. Spring was turning to summer, filling the glen with color. She welcomed the perfumed air after the stench of people and animals inside the keep, and the hum of bees replacing the clang of the blacksmith's hammer.

"Come back here, ye wee scamp!" Butterflies scattered in wee Jamie's path, forming a dancing cloud around his narrow shoulders, a sight Aileanna never tired of seeing.

This chase was a game they'd played often in the meadow below the Aerie, their home, since wee Jamie learned to walk—and to run. Aileanna cherished the time she spent with each of her children, the set of triplets Jamie belonged to and a younger set of twins. She was determined to give them the individual attention any singly-born babe would have. With wee Jamie, the time they spent in the glen formed a special bond between them. Yet she could not coddle her youngest of the triplets—not for much longer. He and his siblings were growing so fast!

Aileanna sighed and glanced around. From the edge of the

nearby wood as well as from the Aerie's ramparts, her husband Toran's men guarded her and her son. They were safe, the sun gilded everything, and wee Jamie's laughter rang out as he turned and danced from one foot to the other on his short legs, waiting impatiently for her to catch up, making Aileanna grateful for the happy perfection of her life.

"I've got ye now, laddie!" She scooped him up in her arms and twirled him around, grinning at his squeals of delight. When she set him down, he held out his hand for her to take, and they walked companionably back toward the trail that led up the tor to the Aerie's gates. Along the way, she pointed out different wild flowers and named them.

When they reached a clump made up of several different shades of blooms, she asked, "Which do ye favor?" The lad was showing signs of a strong personality, and she wondered if he'd begun to develop preferences beyond the scope of what he liked to eat or to wear.

"That one," he said, pointing.

Ah, bright yellow on stalks, some to his waist, the vetch caught his eye.

"Why that one?"

"Ye used it to make Lianna stop coughing."

Aileanna's eyes widened at that. His triplet sister had been sick months ago. Jamie should still be too young to recall that so clearly, much less what she'd used to help her second-born get well. "Very good, my wee laddie. Ye have the right of it."

"Does it have a name like I do?"

"'Tis a vetch," she told him, maternal pride spreading warmth through her at his interest, yet a touch of sadness hollowed her belly as well. She used the lore to treat the sick and injured as they would expect from any healer, with herbs and poultices and tinctures and the like, yet she often sped their recovery with her talent, especially if she needed it to save their life. If her son learned the lore of herbs and other plants from her, perhaps he would one day become a healer, even without her talent.

Could Jamie become a male healer? Or should she forget such a fanciful notion and give him over to Toran when he came of age, to train as a warrior and to foster away from the Lathan clan? Wee Jamie would never be the healer she was and that Lianna and Eilidh could be, though she did not expect to see signs of her ability in her daughters for years, not until they shed the first blood of womanhood. But their ever-curious brother Jamie could still do good in the world. There were men enough to fight and kill. Perhaps this son could help balance against them.

She showed him a few more flowers and told him what they were called and how she used them, surprised when he identified another on his own. If he recalled her lesson of today, she'd think seriously about how best to train a lad in a skill mostly held by women. Other than her mother, Aileanna had yet to meet another with her talent, but village women passed healing wisdom from mother to daughter, as her own mother had done.

She knew better than most that all fighting forces needed healers during and after a battle. It was why she'd been kidnapped from her village and carried along with the lowlander army until Toran rescued her, defeated the invaders, and made her his bride. Aye, Jamie must learn to fight, but he could also learn to care for the wounded, as much as he could without her talent. She'd let wee Jamie's curiosity and interest guide her decision. Unlike her eldest son, Drummond, Toran's heir, wee Jamie had years yet before his future would be a set path before him. Indeed, she realized, he could train as a warrior *and* a healer, if he wished. That decided, she looked up and realized he'd wandered away from her, chasing butterflies again.

"Come, Jamie," she called. "'Tis time to make the climb and find yer supper."

Instead of moving toward her, he turned to face her and held out a hand. "Mama, come look."

"What have ye found, Jamie?" She hurried toward him, not so much concerned as curious. Save for a bee sting, little could harm him in this glen.

When she reached him, she was not at all surprised to see a common meadow brown butterfly resting in his open palm. "'Tis pretty, laddie," she told him.

He shook his head, his expression going stubborn. "'Tis no'. 'Tis hurt, like the one ye found the last time we came here."

"Hurt?" She hadn't noticed until he mentioned it. "Let me see if there is aught I can do."

He pulled his hand back with a frown. "Nay. I watched ye. I can do it, too."

Aileanna gave him a sympathetic smile. "Nay, Jamie, I dinna think ye can do what I did for the wee thing. See?" She traced a finger along one wing. "'Tis broken, right there. I'll mend it." One wing was indeed folded in half, the clean break meaning the beauty would never fly again. A death sentence, certainly.

"Nay, Momma. I ken what is wrong. I'm old enough. I will do it." He touched the wing with one finger.

"Gently, lad," she murmured, her fists clenched in her skirts to control her impulse to take the butterfly from him before he did it more harm. He wouldn't mean to, but delicacy was usually beyond a child so young. Surely once he looked more closely at the wing, he'd give it to her.

She watched with pride the concentration on his face as he softly unfolded the wing, then cradled the break between his thumb and forefinger. His eyes closed and his lips compressed.

"Dinna crush it," she cautioned.

After another second, time enough for her to wonder if the butterfly objected to its injury being handled by her child, no matter how carefully, Jamie opened his eyes, lifted his fingers away from the butterfly's wing and held it up on his palm.

"See, Mamma?"

Aileanna's mouth fell open as the butterfly shook out its newly healed wing and took to the air, joining the fluttering mass circling near her son. How could he have her talent? A lad? And at such a young age? She took a deep breath, to calm her suddenly racing pulse.

"I did see! 'Tis very good, Jamie." She bent and hugged him to her, whispering, "That butterfly owes ye its life," then released him as he squirmed away.

She lifted a hand to her pounding chest as he turned to watch the creature he'd helped, certain he knew exactly which one it was. Her heart nearly burst from her, whether in shock or delight, she couldn't yet decide. Likely both. She would have much to do to teach her son as she'd been taught, to bear the burden of healing as she did, but even more, to keep him safe in a world that distrusted anyone with her talent. Some might call her a witch, though none among the Lathan clan or their allies would do so. What would strangers think of a lad who could do the same?

"Come along, now. 'Tis time for supper. And I wish to speak to yer da."

"Will ye tell him I mended the butterfly? Will he be proud of me? Can I tell him? He's proud of ye and ye can do it."

"I will, aye, and he will, and ye may tell him in private." She knelt and captured his gaze. "But ye must tell no one else. 'Twill be our secret for now. Can ye do that?" He'd shown maturity beyond his years. Could she trust him?

Jamie stuck out his lower lip.

Ach, her four-year-old was back. She stood, took his hand, and started up the path that climbed the tor to the Aerie's gate. "I'll see if Cook made any of yer favorite sweets. Will that be reward enough for yer brave deed?"

"With honey and cream?"

"I suppose ye have done well enough to deserve them, too, aye, but only if ye dinna tell anyone save yer da."

He nodded somberly. "Aye, that will do."

In that moment, she knew her wee lad would grow faster than she wished, but that he would be all the man she could hope for—and more.

1

SCOTLAND, EARLY SPRING 1536

The clang of heavy broadsword blades against shields, halberds, and axes assaulted Jamie Lathan's ears. All around him, men fought and swore and bled. But the deafening din didn't distract him as he thrust through the raider in front of him, pulled his blade free, then raised his shield against another man charging at his side. Calder Erskin, his foster brother and best friend, cut the legs out from under the warrior Jamie fended off, grinned, and turned away to find his next opponent.

Jamie's reputation as a fierce and dangerous fighter was well-earned. He'd learned on the training ground not to touch an opponent's skin, else the urge to heal would overwhelm the battle rage that protected him. He fought with sword and shield, dirk and mace at close quarters, and never with bare fists if he could help it.

Calder matched him in size, strength, and skill. They made a formidable fighting pair. No one could get inside their defenses, and all who tried, died.

Now that he had a moment between opponents, and despite the damage he and Calder had done, he realized the

MacKyries had been pushed back toward the pass they guarded. Something about this battle felt wrong. Dressed simply and without clan insignia, the raiders had ambushed Jamie's patrol just outside the pass leading into the MacKyrie glen. In Jamie's experience, raiders like these usually turned tail and ran after they lost enough men to convince them they could not win. But fighting had been going on longer than usual.

Keeping one eye on potential adversaries, Jamie searched for his foster father. There! Though Donal was older than Jamie's father, Toran, he wielded his sword as though it weighed nothing, and he was fresh to the battle. His years of experience stood him in good stead. Few men could challenge Jamie, and none save Donal MacNabb had ever bested him.

A sudden cry rent the air just behind Jamie. He spun to see a raider's sword pierce Calder's belly. Jamie lunged and cut the attacker's head from his body, but he'd inflicted terrible damage before Jamie dispatched him. Calder collapsed into a pool of his own blood, hands reflexively covering the wound.

"Ye can fix this, aye, Jamie?" Calder gasped. "God, it hurts!"

Jamie dropped to his knees by Calder's side and let his sword fall to the ground beside him. His attention split between his instinct to protect his own life and saving his friend's, he fought for the calm he must have to extend his hidden healing talent into the wound. He took a deep breath and placed both hands on Calder's abdomen. The energy started to flow as a warm tingle, until he pushed Calder's bloody hands aside and touched the severed flesh. The reflected pain seared his belly, doubling him over. He gritted his teeth, fighting to ignore the agony.

Jamie's talent did not allow him to block anything he treated from transferring to him. In other battles, he'd learned to withstand the effect, but Calder's wound was the worst he'd tried to heal. The blood loss was bad enough, but the bowel was cut, spilling poison into Calder's body, mixing with the blood Jamie needed to save his life.

He swore he wouldn't quit, no matter how he suffered. He had to stop Calder's bleeding before he tried to move him away from the fighting. They were vulnerable to attack, but Calder needed his help here and now.

Vaguely aware of Donal and others surrounding them, forming a defensive ring, Jamie focused on his friend. He was slipping away, and Jamie could not work fast enough to get ahead of the damage.

"Calder! Stay with me, damn ye. Why did ye let him get inside your guard?"

"Save me," Calder mouthed, voiceless in the din around them.

If Jamie hadn't been looking right at his lips, he never would have known he'd tried to say anything. Then he slumped, unconscious, before Jamie could take his face in his hands, to tell him he would save him, and make him understand.

Jamie didn't know whether Calder passed out from shock or the loss of so much blood. He needed to focus, but battling for Calder's life made him weaker and weaker. The world around him kept fading to black every time he touched his friend.

A rough hand gripped his shoulder and pulled him off of Calder's body. Jamie retained the presence of mind to whip around and slash with his dirk. But Donal MacNabb was too well-seasoned a fighter to fall for that. He danced out of the way before Jamie could finish the turn. Jamie's view of his foster father and the battle raging around him spun.

"Leave off, lad. He's gone. Ye canna save him and ye'll get yerself killed. We've kept the bastards away from ye, but we canna stay any longer. We're pulling back into the glen. Come away."

"Nay. I'll no leave him. He's still alive." He reached toward his friend and extended his healing sense again, even though he feared he was close to losing both Calder's life and his own.

He heard Donal swear, then something hit the back of his head. The world went black and stayed that way.

JAMIE WOKE UP. He lurched up, reaching for Calder at the same moment he realized where he was—in his chamber in the MacKyrie keep. Not at the battle. Not at Calder's side. Instead, in a chair across the chamber, his foster father sat, regarding him.

"Ye decided to rejoin us, aye? Good. Yer da would never let me live it down if I'd let ye die on the battlefield trying to save another who was as dead as makes no difference."

"Where is he?" Jamie sat up and swung his legs off the bed, determined to find Calder. The room spun. He became aware of a throbbing ache on the back of his head. He reached back and found a lump. "Ye hit me!" He forced himself to his feet, gratified to see Donal do the same.

"Aye. Ye nearly killed yerself over Calder Erskin, and ye were about to take the rest of us with ye. The raiders saw us protecting ye and were circling, getting ready to come at us from all sides. We wouldha been cut off from the pass. Whoever leads them is nay fool."

"So ye let Calder die?"

"He was gone, lad. Ye ken that, or ye will once ye stop and think."

"Ye let him die," Jamie repeated, advancing on Donal. "I could have saved him."

"Ye are more like yer mother than ye want to admit," Donal said in an aggrieved tone, refusing to give ground as Jamie advanced.

"I've heard the tale. This is no' the same."

"'Tis exactly the same," Donal insisted. "Yer da had to pull yer mother off of her brother or his death would have taken her, too. Ye ken that, and yet ye nearly did the same daft thing."

"'Tis no' daft to save the life of a friend. A brother."

"I ken it, lad, and I'm sorry. He was yer friend... but ye ken he was gone."

Jamie's throat filled and he fought down tears. "He told me to save him."

Donal looked away and swallowed. "Nay lad. He kenned he was done for. He didna want ye to risk yer own life and the rest of our men." Donal's jaw tightened, and his gaze dropped. "He learned that lesson better than ye, lad."

"Sorry to disappoint ye," Jamie growled, his grief turning suddenly back to fury. He wasn't sorry at all. Grieving would have to wait. First he needed to punish the man who'd let his friend die. He clenched his fists over his belly, unsure whether the stabbing pain there came from the fury that painted Donal in a red haze, or remnants of Calder's injury. "I should flatten ye."

Donal glared at him. "Ye could try, but ye willna win, and ye ken it. I trained ye. Dinna try me, lad." He gestured toward the bed. "Sit yerself down and use that pounding head of yers before I have to knock more sense into ye."

Instead, Jamie pointed toward the door. "Get out, ye bastard."

"Ye havena earned the right to call me names. Sit." Donal shoved Jamie's chest, forcing him back until the back of his knees connected with the edge of the bed and he sat.

But he didn't stay there. He surged up and swung, intending to catch Donal under the chin with his fist. Donal's head snapped back out of the way, and for a moment, Jamie thought he'd succeeded in knocking him out with one punch. He should have known better. Donal shoved, and Jamie's equilibrium deserted him. He fell.

Before he knew it, he lay flat on his back on the bed, waking up for the second time. He didn't know how long he'd been out, but it couldn't have been long. Donal sat where he'd been when Jamie woke up the first time.

"Despite that temper of yers, ye are one of the best fighters I've ever trained," Donal said, rubbing his chin, "But swinging at me when ye are half out of yer head doesna work. Ye missed me."

"I'll get ye next time."

"Never forget, I'm better. But if ye still want to fight me once ye have given it some thought, find me." Then he stood and left the chamber.

Jamie pushed upright, but his head spun. When he tried to stand, his legs gave way. Instead, he sat and thought about the battle and recalled things he'd been only dimly aware of as he tried to save his friend. The circle of defenders around them. The battle raging only a few feet away. Jamie had to admit Donal was right. They would have been cut off from the glen. With no help nearby, they would have been slaughtered.

Jamie forced himself to take deep breaths to slow his pounding heart and ease his aching head. Donal had done what he deemed necessary to save the most lives, even though he knew what leaving Calder would mean to Jamie, and how it would damage their relationship.

Donal's connection to the Lathans went back most of his life. He'd fostered with Jamie's grandfather and stayed as Lathan's arms master at his request. Donal was there when Jamie's mother lost her brother in the same way Jamie lost Calder. She had hated Jamie's father for a while, but had come to see that he'd saved her life.

Jamie heaved a sigh. Donal had saved his, too. And Donal got his men back into MacKyrie territory where they knew every rock, rill, and hollow, and where his men could pick off the raiders if they dared follow.

Jamie got to his feet, finally steady. The best thing for the sensations filling his body at the moment was another good fight. He'd go to the training ground and work off his anguish there. But not until after he got rid of the lump on the back of his head and the pain in his head and belly. He was about to use his healing talent to take care of himself when someone knocked softly on the door. "Come," he called out and reached for calm he didn't yet feel. Only one person would dare his temper.

Ellie, Donal's wife, the MacKyrie laird and Seer, opened the door and stood, leaning on the frame, studying him. Her long dark hair, bound to the side, trailed down to her hip against the wooden doorframe. Silver streaks glinted that had not been visible when he first came to foster, all those years before.

"Ye ken he's right." Her voice was soft and sure.

Jamie always pictured velvet over steel when he heard her speak. This woman could make him more nervous than going up against her husband Donal, but remnants of Jamie's anger still burned in his blood, making him bold. "Ye would say that."

"Aye. But he is." She stepped into the chamber. "Ye'd be dead with yer friend and more of our precious few men." Her serene expression slipped for a moment as she glanced aside. "Even him."

The thought of the Seer knowing and grieving the hour of her beloved husband's death froze the blood in Jamie's veins. "Ye canna ken that. Ye werena there." Despite his earlier fury, Jamie knew he would grieve him, too, and hoped that day was long in coming.

"Ye forget who... and what I am."

Jamie lowered his gaze to her hands, now clenched at her sides, and watched as she forced them open. "Never," he told her. No more than he could forget who and what *he* was. Or what his own mother was.

"Then hear me. This is a turning point for ye. Ye will go from here—angry, aye. Grieving. Of course. I ken that. But ye will find another path when ye do. Another way to be of value to those ye care about."

"What does that mean?"

"Live yer life, Jamie Lathan." She turned back to the door, then looked over her shoulder and smiled at him for the first time. "Dinna be so certain ye ken who ye are. Ye will find out as it happens."

HE LEFT THE NEXT MORNING, after the last handful of dirt had been dropped onto Calder's grave.

The Seer had begged him to stay another day to rest his head and his temper, then told him if he was careful, he would not encounter any of the men they'd fought the day before. Jamie believed her. He'd never known her to be wrong in all the five years he'd fostered with them, nor during the visits since for holidays or battles.

Donal approached and grasped his forearm before Jamie finished checking the contents of the packs on his horse. "I'm sorry to see ye leave us like this," Donal told him. "But Ellie tells me 'tis for the best, and if ye keep yer temper under control, ye will do well."

"I'm sorry, too," Jamie told him, and meant it.

"Tell yer da I'll pay a visit when I can. And kiss yer ma for me. For us," he added, pulling the Seer to his side and wrapping a muscled arm over her shoulders.

She smiled up at her husband, then turned the smile to Jamie. "Safe travels, lad. Ye are yet a young man. Ye will learn much in the next few years."

Jamie nodded and tied closed the last pack while he tried to come up with a response to that. Ellie MacKyrie had not stinted the supplies for his long journey home, but he knew better than to ask for more detail in her foretelling. Still, he appreciated her attempt to send him off with good wishes.

Instead, Jamie mounted and rode away from the keep before the lump in his throat could grow any larger. Once he got into the trees and out of sight, he wiped his eyes, annoyed that his emotions could betray him this way, first with anger, now with regret. He took a deep breath. The Seer's promise was still vague, but perhaps more specific than her usual pronouncement. Jamie pictured her. Would she have smiled when she delivered it if he didn't have much to look forward to in the next year?

Days were growing longer, so he rode hard, stopping to make camp and quiet his mind through the short nights, resting himself and his mount against the next day's long road. Finally, he got a glimpse between some hills of the Aerie on its high tor. Home.

He reined in and just looked, thinking about the people he loved there, and those he'd left behind.

Would the Aerie be home for much longer? The Seer's words stayed with him. What other path would he find? And how would he be of use? As usual, her words were cryptic, as though she forbore giving anyone too much information about their future. Would their path change if she did?

Her talent, like his mother's and his, could not be explained. Only used, something Jamie did as seldom as possible. He was a warrior, not a healer, except when a life was at risk on the battlefield.

Like Calder's.

The image remained as clear in his mind as if he still leaned over his friend, fighting to save him. He'd never forget it. Never lose that sensation of life slipping away faster than he could stop it bleeding out of Calder's body. He'd saved Lathan lives on many battlefields, and when he could safely do so, those of their allies. But he hadn't been able to save Calder's.

He vowed never to use his talent again. He was and would be a warrior—one of the best. Nothing more.

Though his fury had abated, he had not forgiven Donal that blow to the back of his head. The Seer's words made him wonder if the next time Donal called for men to fight MacKyrie's battles, would Jamie be among them?

Was that what the Seer meant?

He kicked his mount into motion and headed for home. Perhaps he would find answers there.

2

SCOTLAND, SEPTEMBER 1537

From his position on the Aerie's wall walk, Jamie Lathan spotted a swirl in the morning's heavy mist filling the glen below. It moved closer, then lifted onto the long path up the tor to the Aerie. The mist thinned and revealed a galloping horse, its rider bent low, clinging to its mane. As it neared the Aerie's gate, he recognized the rider. Rabbie! Alone? Where were Niall and Fearchar?

"Open the gate! Lathan rider!"

Jamie ran from the wall walk down the steps to the bailey just before Rabbie burst through, the gate open just wide enough for his horse. He pulled hard on the reins, his mount's hooves kicking up dirt as it struggled to stop at the keep's doorway.

Rabbie leapt from the blowing horse to crumple in front of Jamie's mother, Aileanna, the Lathan healer. She'd come out just as Jamie's call rang through the bailey, and waited on the threshold steps.

Jamie reached them in time to lift Rabbie from the dirt where he lay panting and trying to force out words between gasping breaths. Rabbie grasped his hand and Jamie's chest immediately tightened. He pulled his hand free, and Rabbie bent forward, hands on knees.

Despite his mother's pleas, Jamie had not used his talent since leaving MacKyrie eighteen months ago, choosing, as he'd vowed, to train at arms. Yet, he knew Rabbie had suffered gasping attacks as a child and might not regain his breath quickly on his own. "Are ye injured?" Jamie lifted a hand to touch him again, a habit he'd fought to break, but stopped when Rabbie shook his head.

Rabbie lifted his head to fix his gaze firmly on Aileanna. "Need ye," he managed to wheeze out. "Niall will lose his leg." He sucked in air, then added, "Or his life... if ye dinna come."

Aileanna descended the three stone steps to the bailey, put a hand to the back of Rabbie's neck and closed her eyes for a moment. "Better now?" When he straightened, she stepped away, her narrowed gaze resting on Jamie for a moment, her displeasure evident that Jamie had not used his ability to help their kinsman. Then she turned back to Rabbie. "Tell us what happened."

Rabbie's chest rose on a deep breath, then, eyes wide, he gave her a nod of thanks. "The daftest thing," he told her, then took a few more deep breaths. He shifted his gaze from her to Jamie. "We were coming back from Dundee with a day's ride behind us. The trail was good enough, but 'twas getting on toward sunset. Fearchar and I jumped a wee rill first, then he. His horse stumbled on landing and threw him into a downed tree."

Aileanna frowned. "How bad?"

Jamie knew she was thinking of all the ways someone could be harmed in such a fall. He was, too.

"A branch pierced his calf all the way through and broke off," Rabbie continued. "I've seen arrow wounds like it, but doubted the branch was as smooth as an arrow's shaft. I feared removing it. He bled little with it in place, so I thought we could make it home in two days hard riding."

"Possibly," Aileanna said, giving him time to draw another breath.

"Even in pain, he could ride, so we continued into the night until I saw him slump over his mount. By then we were near a keep—a minor branch of clan Keith, as it be—so we begged their hospitality and the help of their healer. He was feverish. She removed the wood, cleaned his calf as best she could and got the bleeding stopped, but feared the wound would fester." His shoulders dropped, as did his gaze. "It did." He looked up again at Aileanna. "By yestereve, she'd done all she kens to do. *Thrice.* I rode as hard as I could through the night, to fetch ye. Fearchar remains by his side. Ye will come, aye?"

Aileanna turned her gaze to her son. "I canna. Marcail's time is near, and this babe will kill her without me. I've no one else to send. Jamie, lad, ye must go."

Jamie frowned at her. She knew what she was asking.

His father had fought to keep his mother from being accused as a witch when she first came to them. If strangers discovered he, a man, had the same talent, he could lose his life. The King hunted witches with great fervor. Jamie had no interest in being burned at the stake or dunked in a loch until he drowned.

Yet, here was an opportunity to strike out on his own. He'd proven himself a fierce warrior, yet his mother still wanted to treat him as her apprentice. They'd fought many times since he'd returned from MacKyrie over what she called his stubbornness, but he'd held to his vow and used only methods any village healer could use. Saving Niall, in his own way, he could prove himself as capable as she, especially if he could do it without using the talent they shared.

"What else did the Keith healer tell ye?"

"His fever continues to rise, and the area around the wound

is turning black, and she fears whatever caused it is in his blood. He's in a lot of pain."

Aileanna gasped and met Jamie's concerned gaze with her own. "Oh, my son. I dinna wish to expose ye..."

"That may no' be necessary," he insisted. He hoped Niall's condition wasn't as dire as Rabbie made it sound, or Jamie would have no way to save him except to break his vow.

"'Twill be," Rabbie interjected. He'd benefitted from Aileanna's talent in the past. He was fully aware of what they could do —and what Jamie chose not to do. "And it may already be too late. We'll never ken if we dinna return now."

"Ye have seen similar injuries in battle," Aileanna reminded Jamie. "Ye ken 'twill be needed if ye hope to save his life."

"I've seen penetrating injuries like his, aye, though soon enough after they happened, they were no' as bad as Rabbie describes." Jamie's stomach turned as he pictured what he would have to endure.

Rabbie must have read his hesitation on his face. "Ye *swither* while he suffers? Ye'd let him die?"

Jamie frowned at Rabbie, insulted, then shook his head. He'd do everything he could before employing his talent, but deep down, he knew he would do what he must to save Niall's life. He'd made the vow after failing to save a friend, but it was worthless weighed against the life of another.

Then he turned back to Aileanna. A vision sickened him again of her writhing in pain as her body fought the poison in Niall's blood and the festering wound. "Ye canna go, Mother," he told her.

Surely delivering Marcail's twelfth child would be less taxing. And she knew, above all else she'd asked of him, that he refused to serve as a midwife. It was not natural for a man to know all that happened during delivery from within a woman's body. He could not bring himself to experience that. "Ye stay and tend Marcail. She'll be better served having ye beside her."

"Aye," she told him, though she shook her head at the same time.

His mother knew the source of his objection to caring for Marcail, and disagreed with him. They'd argued about it many times. To her, knowledge was knowledge, and any that helped heal or save a life was worth having.

"She'd be disconcerted to be attended by a man. Even though 'tis ye."

Relieved that she'd agreed, Jamie turned to Rabbie. "Clan Keith, ye say? How do I find them?"

"I'll return with ye. I ken the way."

"Nay," Aileanna objected. "Ye rode through the night. Ye must rest."

"I must go. 'Twill be dark before we near the keep. Jamie will need a guide or he may arrive too late."

Jamie nodded. "Ye rest for an hour while I gather what I need. Then we'll go."

"Very well."

Aileanna crossed her arms. Her frown told Jamie she did not think all was well, but she'd acquiesced, and that was enough.

"I'll tell the stable master to ready three fresh horses," she volunteered and left them.

"Three?" Rabbie asked.

"To carry supplies. And in case we lose a mount. We willna lose time riding double."

"Aye." Rabbie rubbed his face. "I must be tired or I would ken that."

"Go. Find yer chamber and sleep while I make ready."

When he left them alone, Aileanna turned to Jamie. "Ye ken ye canna heal everything. Ye havena learned or done enough yet. Ye must be careful. Niall's wound sounds worse than any ye have attempted."

"I hear ye. I do," he added in the face of her frown. It was an old argument between them. One of many. "'Twill be much like any battle wound."

"Gone bad," she reminded him. "Ye must take care of yerself as well as Niall."

"I will," he assured her, kissed her cheek and left her to gather the herbs, simples, and poultices that he would use to help Niall—or use to disguise how he really helped Niall, if nothing else worked. In a strange clan, they'd be his most important means of concealing the effects of his talent, as well as valuable tools. He couldn't expect the healer there to have everything he used or might need. Rabbie said she'd tried her cures three times and failed. Jamie would not fail.

AFTYN KEITH WASTED no time after rousing from her bed where she'd collapsed for a few hours of much-needed rest. Niall Lathan was in bad shape and getting worse.

Yet when she realized no one had fetched her during the night, she felt marginally better. She dressed quickly and made her way to Niall's chamber, nodded to his companion, Fearchar, who remained with him night and day, and lifted her hand from Niall's brow.

His fever was hotter. The only thing she could do at this point was to continue to wash him down in an effort to cool him. He'd passed out from the agony caused by the dying tissue in his calf, but his friends refused to let her amputate the leg below the knee, though she'd used every argument she could think of to convince them that it might save his life. She'd still consider doing it, save for the man standing by the bed, left here to prevent her. And the promise by his other companion, Rabbie, to ride like the Devil chased him and bring back the Lathan healer. The glowing way Rabbie spoke of her, Aftyn prayed she could save Niall's leg and his life.

If Rabbie had been delayed, or worse, never made it back at all, the man before her would die. She stood, hugged her arms to her ribs and fretted. She'd already done everything she could think of, save for the one thing they refused to allow her to do.

"Where is Neve?" Aftyn had left her assistant and friend, Neve, with Niall last night.

"She went for more water a few minutes ago," Fearchar told her.

She'd asked Neve to search her mother's journals for anything else that might help. She had found nothing they hadn't already tried. Which made no sense. Surely Aftyn's mother had treated other festered wounds. What had she done differently, and why hadn't she written it down? Was the cure something so obvious it was common knowledge and not worth recording? Something she'd taught her that Aftyn forgot? Or something in the many pages filled with unreadable notations and symbols. She racked her brain as she paced, but no helpful memory surfaced.

Ach, Mama, why did ye leave me so soon? I miss ye. And I dinna ken all I need to ken to do what ye did for our clan. For this man.

Niall's groan brought her back to him. He was no cooler, and he'd begun tossing his head like an angry horse. Surely he'd hurt himself if she didn't get him to stop. She placed her hands on either side of his face, holding him still, and spoke to him in a soothing tone. "Wheesht ye, laddie. Wheesht. Ye must rest to be well." His agitation eased with her touch, so she released him and dribbled sleeping draught between his lips. Once he swallowed enough, she continued speaking softly, trying to soothe him. "I'm doing all I can for ye. Ye must help me. Ye can do that, aye? Sleep now." She let him go when he stopped fighting her and settled on a sigh. He seemed to slide deeper into his fevered dreams.

She straightened and turned to the man watching her over crossed arms, muscles bulging. "Fearchar, can ye trust me with him long enough to find Neve and help her? I need that water now. He's burning up."

He looked as though he would refuse, but they both knew there were no blades in the chamber save the ones he carried. He gave a curt nod and left the room.

Aftyn stroked the damp hair off of Niall's forehead, fighting the urge to cry. Or scream. She hated feeling helpless, and being treated as untrustworthy by these strangers made her feel worse.

The laird's doubts about her were growing, and losing a visitor from another clan would convince him that his illegitimate daughter was not worth keeping in any capacity, much less as the clan's healer. She remained with the clan only because she'd been able to save his heir's life by continuing a treatment begun by her mother before she died. Since then, she'd lived in fear of Braden having another spell, gasping for air, but so far, nothing had happened.

Now, for this man, nothing Aftyn tried seemed to help. Maybe her father was right. She was worthless as a healer.

She sank onto the hearthside stool and let her tears run down her cheeks. Niall would not see them. And even if he did, likely he would not live to speak of them to anyone else.

THEY REACHED the Keith keep long after dark. Jamie was glad of Rabbie's company, and of Bhaltair's, another Lathan guard Jamie's father had insisted accompany them. Rabbie's shout to the gatekeeper got them into the bailey. He led them to the stables where a lad took charge of the horses, then into the keep.

The great hall was empty of all save a few servants cleaning tables. Rabbie led them to a set of stairs. "I ken where Niall rests," he said as he headed up.

Jamie followed, Bhaltair on his heels.

"Where is everybody?" Bhaltair looked around with a frown. "I've never seen a keep so quiet."

Jamie's chest clenched at that. Was Niall dead? The lack of activity in the hall might mean they kept a respectful peace until his kin could claim his body. Or they'd buried him today and now mourned, since his clan was not here to do it for him.

Rabbie led them down a hallway, dark save for one sputtering torch in the middle, pushed open a nearby door and stepped inside. Jamie's breath left him when he saw Niall, his head moving fretfully on his pillow. He lived! Then Jamie took a breath and wished he hadn't. A frisson of unease shivered down his spine as the stench of sickness and rot invaded his nose, sweet and grating over the earthy scent of the peat fire burning low in the hearth. A young lass sat dozing near it.

"Neve!" Rabbie hissed. "Wake up."

The lass blinked and sat up. "Rabbie! Ye're here! Ach, Aftyn will be so relieved."

"Where is she?"

"Asleep, I hope. Poor lass. She's barely left this chamber the entire time since ye left. I chased her out a few hours ago to eat and rest. Fearchar, too."

"The hall was all but empty. Where is everyone? And how is Niall?"

"Ye do ken how late it is? They're all in their beds." She stood. "Niall, well..." she said, paused, and turned her gaze to him. Then she looked back at Rabbie and continued, "I'm glad ye have arrived. He's worse." Her gaze moved to Jamie and Bhaltair. "Which of ye is the healer? We expected a lass."

"I am," Jamie said, his gaze shifting from her to Niall and back again. "I am the healer's son and ken her methods."

"Why didna she come herself?"

"She cares for a woman about to deliver her twelfth babe." Jamie moved toward Niall, the urge to begin healing him

coming on strongly. Even from a distance, he could feel Niall's
distress.

"I hope ye are as skilled as she," Neve said. "Yer friend needs
more care than we could give him."

He wished he could explain to Calder why he had to go
back on his vow. He would have understood better than anyone
why Jamie would have to use his talent. Neve's voice distracted
him and he turned back to her. Jamie frowned. "I will see to
him. Before I do, we've ridden long and hard. Can anyone
prepare some food and drink for us?"

"Aye. Now ye are here, I'll fetch what ye need."

Jamie gestured. "Rabbie and Bhaltair can help ye, then ye'll
need to see to a place for us to rest."

"I have a chamber," Rabbie reminded Neve. "Dinna fash.
We'll use it."

Neve moved toward the open door. "Come with me, then."

Jamie held up a hand to stop her. "Where?"

"The great hall. I'll raid the kitchen," Neve promised.

Jamie gestured them out. "I'll follow ye soon. First I want to
see to Niall." He closed the door after them and turned to his
patient. Placing his hands just above and below the bandage
swathing Niall's lower leg, he closed his eyes and *felt*. What he
found sickened and enraged him. Festering tissue burned and
spread. As much as Jamie wanted to attack it, he knew he
would not have the strength until he ate and rested for an hour
or two. He touched Niall's forehead to put him into a deeper
sleep that would blunt his pain, then took his hand and
squeezed it. "I'm here, Niall. I'll be back soon to help ye."

Reluctantly, he left the chamber and rejoined his men and
Neve in the hall. The food and ale were welcome, and for Jamie
to do what he would be called upon to do this night, necessary.
No one spoke save to ask for more.

They were nearly finished when a lass crossing behind

Neve from the kitchen toward the stairs captured Jamie's attention.

He couldn't take his gaze from her. She glided with the grace of a swan on a still pond. Her skin glowed with each torch she passed, pale as new cream, yet touched with berries on her cheeks and lips. Lashes so lush they hid the color of her downcast eyes added to her air of mystery. She passed beyond their table and fascinated him all over again. Her dark braid ended just at the sweet curve of her bottom and swayed against her back as she climbed the steps. She seemed so deeply lost in thought, she hadn't noticed the strangers in her hall.

Jamie wanted to rise and call out to her, to learn her name and everything about her, but held himself in check. He would discover who she was later. Niall needed him.

3

Aftyn had been away from Niall's chamber too long, but she'd awakened bleary and famished from the nap Neve insisted she take. She visited the kitchen, hoping some food and company would revive her, but no one remained. Even the serving lasses had finished the last cleanup of the day and were gone. The hour must be very late. Most of the clan was asleep in their beds. She ate a little of the food Cook kept out for the night watch, then forced her feet to carry her back upstairs. Crossing the hall to Niall's chamber, she wished she could sleep, too, then chided herself for her selfishness. He needed her, but she hadn't shirked his care. While she took some time for herself, Neve remained with him. They both knew a man in Niall's condition should not be left alone.

She opened the door, expecting Neve to greet her, but she wasn't in the room. Instinct drove Aftyn to whirl and step toward Neve's chamber, irritation building in her at Neve's abdication of the responsibility she'd entrusted to her.

Then she turned back. First, she must check on Niall. He still breathed, and though he'd ceased thrashing from the pain in his leg for the moment, his fever remained dangerously high.

The bowl of water and rags she'd left to be used to cool him remained untouched. Aftyn dunked a cloth, wrung it out, and placed it on his forehead, grumbling under her breath about unreliable lasses while she dunked another and laid it over his throat. Another she used to dribble water over his lips. She hoped the slight part in them allowed some of the water to drip into his mouth. He had to be parched.

Satisfied she'd done what she could for the moment, she gave in to her irritation and went to find Neve. If she was where Aftyn suspected, asleep in her chamber, she'd get a rude awakening.

Neve's chamber was empty.

Aftyn continued down the next hall to the garderobe, but it was unoccupied. She tried the herbal and the upstairs library, but Neve was not there either.

By the time she made it back around to Niall's chamber, she heard unfamiliar male voices within.

"I can do much for him, but the care he has received here…" The voice stopped and a low growl of frustration penetrated the oaken door. "'Twas worse than receiving nay care at all. How can that lass call herself a healer?"

Aftyn blanched, her worst insecurities made real in a stranger's harsh tone.

"Neve said they've done the best they can for him," a second man said. Aftyn felt a moment's gratitude that someone defended her.

Where was Neve? The man spoke of her as if she was not present. These must be Niall's clansmen. Yet she heard no woman's voice, not Neve's and not the promised healer. Only a man railing against her. The Lathan healer was a woman. Rabbie had been very clear on that. Had she refused to come, to do what Aftyn could not—save him—and then to take Niall home?

"Then she is a danger to all," the first man continued. "If even *I* fear I canna save him..."

The voice dropped too low to hear, which was just as well. Aftyn was torn between mortification and fury. A danger, was she? She'd done her best! And they prevented her from the amputation she feared was Niall's only hope.

How was it her fault that her mother hadn't had time to fully train her? And what did he mean, if even *he* feared to save Niall? Why would anyone fear saving Niall's life?

Confused and fuming, she pushed open the door. Her gaze went straight to the bed. Niall lay as she'd left him, cloths still in place. Had anyone changed them for cooler ones? She looked up then. Two men stared at her, a big blond's expression changing rapidly from questioning to smiling. The other one's gaze frozen on her as if in shock.

Aftyn couldn't take her gaze from him. Taller than his companion or his injured friend, he had a warrior's muscles, but somehow burnished long and lean. She suspected he was even stronger than he appeared. His deep brown eyes should look kind, but his current narrow-eyed frown made her unsure. Dark auburn hair and brows caught the firelight and danced with copper glints. What lass could resist that straight, sharp nose or those firm lips? Likely, they had kissed many a lass. She wondered how they would feel against hers—if he ever stopped frowning at her.

JAMIE TURNED at the first sound of the door opening. He was too good a warrior to leave his back exposed, especially in a strange keep. Not that he expected trouble in Niall's chamber, but they were in a strange keep, and among the many lessons Donal MacNabb had taught him, he made sure Jamie learned the consequences of carelessness.

Thinking of Donal did not raise the ire it once had in Jamie, but having his foster father on his mind still made him uncomfortable. As sad as he was to lose a friend, Jamie knew Donal had been right. He had treated Donal unfairly. He'd learned his lesson and hoped never to lose his temper like that again, though seeing Niall's condition made it tempting.

What he saw as the door swung open and light fell on the figure standing there shocked him to immobility. Her! The bonnie lass he'd seen float across the great hall and up the stairs.

"What are ye doing in Niall's chamber?" She demanded before he could say a word.

Her voice resonated with his bone and sinews, making him vibrate with want.

"Are ye his Lathan kin? Where's the healer? And where's Neve?"

Jamie fought down his body's fascination with the lass, recalled his purpose here, and found his voice. "Where's the healer, indeed? She left a festering wound to spread poison throughout this man's body."

The lass reared back as if he'd slapped her, her face reddening under narrowed eyes. Deep blue eyes, the color of a cold loch in sunlight.

"Neve and I cared for him, and we've done all we ken to do."

He yanked his gaze from her and focused on how Niall had suffered since the local healer had gotten her hands on him. "Nought, ye mean."

"So ye say." Fear when she looked at him and sorrow when her gaze strayed to Niall warred for dominance on her face.

Did she fear him? Of course she did. He was big and angry and strange to her. Ashamed, he fought to control the outrage that filled him at seeing Niall's condition. He didn't make a practice of terrorizing lasses. "Lass, I..."

"Ye didna spend days by his side," she continued, speaking

over his attempt to retract his harsh words. "Seeking to comfort him, to cool him, and to treat his wound. Nothing I did worked. And yer men prevented the one thing that might save him. I fear..."

"Nothing *ye* did!" Jamie interrupted her, his intent to apologize forgotten, dismay curdling the food in his belly. "*Ye* are the so-called healer in this clan?" He could not be attracted to the person who had done this to Niall.

Her posture collapsed like a doll suddenly missing some of its stuffing. "I am. Neve helps me, but Niall's care is my responsibility."

Jamie rarely found himself speechless, but the conflicting emotions Aftyn communicated in her expression and her bearing made him hold his tongue.

As if the mention of her name conjured her from the dark hallway, Neve entered. "Aftyn! I was looking for ye. I see ye have met the Lathans."

"No' precisely," she answered Neve, then turned back to Jamie.

"They are Jamie and Bhaltair," Neve told her. "The healer couldna travel. She sent Jamie in her stead."

Aftyn rounded on Neve. "I see ye've been away from the charge I left ye long enough to meet them and listen to their tales. How could ye?"

Neve quailed under the healer's verbal assault. "I'm sorry, Aftyn..."

"Rabbie brought us up," Jamie interjected, fighting to keep his temper under control. She might be a poor excuse for a healer, but she was a lass, and he knew better than to frighten her. He was here to care for Niall, not to cause problems with this clan or upset the lasses any more than he already had. "Neve was here, and took care of us."

"Rabbie's here, too?" Aftyn glanced from Jamie back to Neve. "Where?"

"Resting in his chamber," Neve supplied, "and so is Fearchar."

"Well, then," Aftyn said and rounded on Jamie this time. "It sounds as though there are enough of ye to take over yer friend's care. Especially since ye find all I and Neve have done to be... how did ye put it? Ah, worse than nay care at all. Oh, aye, and a danger to all. Did I hear ye correctly?"

Jamie could feel his face heating and knew it must be reddening. He hadn't meant to be overheard. Despite his dismay at Niall's condition, he regretted his outburst. "Ye did. And we will take charge of his care."

"Very well, then," Aftyn said, her mouth in a grim line. "I havena had a good sleep since Niall and yer other clansmen rode into our keep. I'll leave him to ye." With that, she spun on her heel and exited the chamber.

Neve shrugged and followed her out, closing the door quietly behind them.

Bhaltair frowned at Jamie. "That was no' well done."

"Nay. I ken it." Jamie shook his head, not yet free of the dismay that colored the whole encounter with the Keith healer. "But perhaps that so-called healer needed to hear the truth." And he needed to keep her at arm's length. This was not the place to be lusting after a pretty lass.

"Perhaps more gently," Bhaltair argued.

Bhaltair was right, as much as Jamie hated to admit it. He'd been needlessly cruel, but he could not take the time to soothe the lovely healer's hurt feelings. A patient needed his full attention. "'Tis done, and I must begin to do what I can for Niall." He ran a hand through his hair. "I need ye to guard the door. None may enter until I open it. When I do, I'll send ye for food and drink."

Bhaltair frowned and left without a word, closing the door firmly behind him, as close to censure as he ever came.

Jamie put him out of his mind and turned to Niall, seeking

the calm that would let him heal. He unwound the bandages, dismayed yet again by what he revealed. The healer had not opened the wound track to clean it. Angry streaks of red were being overtaken by the black of dead and dying tissue at the entry and exit sides. The sweet stink of rot, stronger this close to the wound, turned his stomach. Jamie opened the shutter over the window, hoping to clear the air. The room would chill quickly and help ease Niall's fever.

In the meantime, he unpacked his supply of ointments, needles, and knives. He must slit open the wound, remove whatever Aftyn had packed into it, and cut away the dead tissue so healthy, living tissue could replace it. Even with Jamie's best efforts, Niall would always carry a scar, but Jamie meant to ensure he would survive this.

Jamie laid some of the rags Aftyn left by the bowl of water around Niall's calf, dragged over the chamber's single chair to sit on, and placed a hand on Niall's head. "Ye will remain asleep, my friend, and never recall what I do. When ye wake, yer pain and yer fever will be less."

The first step did not require his special talent. He went to work with his sharpest, smallest blade. Once he was certain he'd removed all traces of poultice and the dead and dying tissue, the now-larger wound bled freely, and even more importantly, cleanly. Only then did he *reach* with his talent to stop the bleeding and quiet the throbbing pain Niall would suffer without Jamie's help.

With a sigh, he leaned back and rubbed his own calf where Niall had been wounded. Why must the healer suffer the healing? His mother had never been able to answer that question. She merely bore the pain and persevered. She'd told him many tales while she taught him, but only one really scared him, the one Donal alluded to in pulling him from his dying friend last spring. She'd been too late, her half-brother too close to death, and only Jamie's father's action, pulling her away from her brother's body, had saved her life. Da had forced her to respect her limits, and though she hated him for it for a while, she'd learned her lesson, and passed it to her children. Jamie grimaced. The most crucial lesson, and he'd ignored it, forcing Donal to save him. He still regretted unleashing his temper on his foster father.

Jamie stood and stretched, breathing in the chill air from the open window, giving himself a moment. He still had to deal with the poison flooding Niall's blood. The parallel to Calder's belly wound did not escape him. He had to find a way to eliminate it, or nothing else he did for Niall would matter. He suddenly regretted not spending the last eighteen months learning more from his mother. Jamie hadn't discovered his limits yet, but his mother's tale and his own experience on the battlefield trying to save his friend were lessons he must keep in mind. He'd sworn he would never again come so close to losing his own life. But in the work left to him this night, he might have to risk exactly that.

DESPITE WHAT AFTYN said before she stormed out of Niall's chamber, and despite her exhaustion, sleep eluded her. She'd worried about Niall for so long that she could not simply stop, even though the Lathans had taken over her responsibility and claimed he was now in safe hands. Oh, how that rankled, but knowing she'd failed the injured man hurt worse. She paced from one side of her chamber to the other, working off the anger, hurt, and worry she'd carried with her from the confrontation with Jamie, the Lathan healer—a man! Trained as any healer was trained. How was that possible? And what would the laird do about her when he learned of the Lathan healer's success?

Confusion filled her. When Jamie's deep brown gaze had

settled on her, it pierced her fatigue and she stifled a gasp. She'd never seen him before, but despite what she overheard, she felt an immediate connection, a visceral sense that made her want to go to him, to be wrapped in his strong embrace and comforted. That would never happen. He already held her in contempt. Comfort was the last thing he would give her. He carried a sword, moved like a wolf on the prowl, and when standing still, looked as if he kept every sense on high alert for trouble. *He* was trouble. She just didn't know how much trouble he could cause her.

What was he doing to Niall? Or *for* him? What did he know that she did not? Those questions plagued her until finally, she kicked off her slippers, undressed, and sank onto her bed, spent.

The sun in her face woke her.

Niall! She scrambled out of bed and flinched as her feet hit the cold floor. Then the memory of last night flooded over her. Her knees gave way and she dropped back onto the bed. She'd let last night's confrontation with the Lathan healer convince her Niall no longer needed her. While the clan had been blissfully asleep, she had been forced to withstand Jamie Lathan's withering censure. She dreaded facing him again. He might be one of the most handsome men she'd ever seen, but his good looks did little to balance the angry personality that dwelled within.

Had he treated Niall? Did Niall still live? What could a man do that she had not already tried? She had to know, even if it meant confronting the Lathan healer again. She cared too much about her patient to stay away. She threw on her clothes and raced from her chamber to Niall's door.

Bhaltair stood outside it.

"How is he?" She made to push past him but he blocked her.

"I dinna ken, lass. Jamie is still with him. He'll come out when he's ready."

"He's been in there all night? Please, I need to see..."

"Nay, ye dinna. No' until Jamie himself opens that door."

He looked her over, and Aftyn became aware she'd failed to rebraid her hair and her kirtle sat crookedly on her shoulders.

"Ye should make yerself ready for yer day and go break yer fast, lass," Bhaltair advised. "I dinna ken how much longer he'll be in there."

"I..." Before she could get another word out, the door opened and Jamie stood before her, his skin gray with fatigue, deep creases between his dark auburn brows, and if she read the tension around his eyes correctly, in pain.

"Bhaltair," he croaked.

"I'll get what ye need," he answered, and moved quickly down the hall to the stairs.

"How is he?" Aftyn had to ask, but she feared her next patient would be this man. After last night, she shouldn't feel sympathy for him, but he looked as though he'd exhausted every resource he possessed. Last night, she would have scoffed at the notion, but it appeared he did have a heart in him somewhere, and had used all of his strength to care for his friend.

"Better." His voice sounded marginally stronger than when he said Bhaltair's name. "Ye may go in. But dinna touch anything."

Aftyn frowned and brushed past him.

Jamie fell back against the open doorway to let her by, then straightened, unmoving, watching her.

Since he remained on his feet, Aftyn ignored him and went to Niall. He looked better. In fact, he looked better than Jamie. Against Jamie's orders, she placed her palm on his forehead. He was cooler. The fever had not broken completely, but the raging heat had eased. She glanced around at Jamie, whose gaze had followed her, then back to the table by the bed. She stepped closer to inspect what he had used. Pots of ointments and wicked-looking small blades covered its surface. Near them, she noticed a hint of vinegar and whisky in the air, along with the sickly sweet stench of the putrid-smelling rags littering the floor below Niall's leg, and the metallic scent of blood-soaked bedding.

Despite all of that, the air in the room seemed fresher. Ah, he'd opened the shutter. Sunlight and a cool breeze flowed from it and out through the open door into the hall.

She moved down the side of the bed and bent to see the wound. It was now open, like a glen between low hills, and much larger. Raw, but pink and healthy. It took her only a moment to realize what Jamie had done.

"Ye have saved his leg," she admitted, dumbfounded. Why had she not known to open the wound track instead of trying to wash it out and pack it with poultice? She'd hoped it would close up and heal together, but this way, it looked clean, though it would leave an impressive scar.

"That and saving his life were my purpose in coming here."

Aftyn clamped down on the sympathy she felt for him, but walked to him and studied his eyes. Bloodshot, as she knew they would be. "My purpose, too," she told him, "but I couldna. He's so much better. How did ye...?"

"My methods are my own, lass." He took a deep breath and straightened away from the door. "There is much more he needs me to do for him, but I've done all I can for today."

"More?" She had studied the wound. Surely it would heal on its own now.

Jamie shrugged. "We'll be here a sennight, I think, before he'll be strong enough to travel." He moved carefully past her and began packing away his tools and medicines.

He seemed wrung out, but something else had changed. Was he limping or just exhausted? She didn't recall him having trouble walking last night, but perhaps she'd been so upset, she hadn't noticed anything but the derision he directed at her. Nay, she recalled thinking he moved like a wolf on the prowl. Now he moved more like the wolf's injured prey.

Bhaltair arrived with a tray covered with bread, cheese, and a large pitcher. He glanced at Aftyn. "Are ye ready, Jamie?" His gaze, when it shifted to Jamie, changed to one of concern. "Fearchar is in the great hall. Rabbie is up and will be here soon, so ye may rest in his chamber."

"Aye." Jamie picked up his bag, then turned back to Aftyn. "I'll ask ye to remove the soiled rags, and have some of the lads help ye change the bedding. Ye ken how to do that, aye, without moving him from the bed or touching the wound?"

"Of course. I'm no' completely ignorant."

"I never said ye were, lass," Jamie answered on a tired sigh.

If he didn't look so done in, she'd tell him to go to the Devil. Instead, she clenched her jaw. "Actually, I believe ye did."

Jamie shook his head and moved toward the door. "I'm sorry, lass. I must go. I'll speak with ye later."

She watched him with a critical eye. He *was* limping. And trying to hide it.

Jamie winced as he joined Bhaltair at the door. He gestured toward the bed and met her gaze. "Stay with him till Rabbie arrives, aye? And tell him to fetch me if Niall becomes agitated or wakes."

With that, he left, Bhaltair at his side. Before they stepped out of sight, Aftyn got a glimpse of Bhaltair struggling not to drop the tray and putting a supporting arm around Jamie's back as he sagged.

4

Early the next morning, Aftyn stood in the great hall for the monthly gathering where the laird heard complaints and decided issues brought to him by members of the clan. Important members of the clan, including the war chief, the council, and others the laird invited, always attended, lined up on either side of the approach to the laird's seat, which he placed at the far end of the great hall from the doorway. The Keith believed in showing strength, even to his own clan members. Even before they reached him, some might think twice about airing their complaints.

As the clan's healer, Aftyn's mother had been included among the clan's eminent members, so after her death, Aftyn continued to appear in her place. The laird ignored her.

"Ye dinna have to stay," Braden reminded her, keeping his voice low so as not to be overheard.

"Ye ken why I do," Aftyn answered him in kind. "As long as ye stand by me, I will remain. Even if ye dinna."

"And as long as Da refuses to acknowledge ye, I will remain to show the clan that someday, I will."

They'd started each judgement day the same way for nearly

two years. It hurt her heart that Braden risked their father's displeasure by his show of support for her, but she appreciated it more than she could say.

The morning continued as had many others, with the Keith deciding ownership of three lambs claimed by one crofter and claimed to have been stolen by another. Several more of a similar nature followed. He directed the war chief to take aside a crofter complaining about the theft of cattle from his farm at the edge of Keith territory. If reivers were abroad, at least that tale might have been interesting, but the man now waited quietly behind the war chief for the laird to dismiss them. Aftyn fought to appear alert, glad she was standing. Seated, she feared she would have fallen asleep by now.

Then Agatha, who ran the post house, and her husband, the village stable master, walked forward.

Aftyn's pulse spiked and she became painfully alert. The woman glared at her as she passed. Braden glanced at her and frowned, then turned his gaze back to the laird. They both knew what brought Agatha here. And it was not to sing Aftyn's praises.

"Laird, ye must find the clan a competent healer."

"Must I?"

Those two words, softly spoken, gave Aftyn hope. Her father did not take kindly to being told what to do. Agatha had begun her complaint at a disadvantage.

"That one," Agatha said and gestured in Aftyn's direction, "let my son die not a fortnight past. I stand before ye, humbled and heartbroken over the loss of my wee bairn." She sniffed, then she elbowed the man at her side.

"As do I," her husband added, then cleared his throat.

The Keith frowned at the pair. "Women lose bairns all the time. And their own lives. Why seek remedy for this one?"

"'Twas the only son I've been able to bear for my husband," Agatha said, softly, perhaps realizing the laird was not yet on her side. "His heir. Now he has none. She didna save him. Perhaps she even hastened his death."

Aftyn gasped and tensed as the Keith's frown turned in her direction. She did not kill their son. But Agatha's accusation could turn the village against her.

"We are no' unsympathetic to yer loss, and we are aware of this apprentice's shortcomings."

Apprentice! So that was how he still saw her. Did he also see her shortcomings still existed because of him?

"We will discover whether an experienced healer can be found," the laird announced, frowning in her direction.

At that promise, Aftyn went cold. An experienced healer cared for Niall upstairs right now.

"What will ye do about her? She's no' fit to care for sheep." Agatha stood straighter and looked more defiantly at Aftyn, now that the laird had expressed agreement with her claims.

Aftyn didn't know how much more of this slander she could take. Yet she could not leave. If she ran from the hall, she would confirm Agatha's tale. Thank goodness Braden remained at her side.

"What would ye have me do?"

"She took my son from me. Banish her!" Agatha snarled.

Aftyn paled. Braden took her hand and squeezed it. She glanced aside. His expression took her breath away. His brow furrowed and his lips compressed, he seemed to watch Agatha's theatrics with real concern.

"And leave the clan with an assistant apprentice of even less skill? How many more of yer clan do ye want to die?"

Agatha's shoulders dropped, as did her gaze. "I think only of what will be best for the clan."

"So, ye think only of what is best for the clan? It seems ye seek to replace no' only the apprentice, but the laird as well." His fists hit the arms of his chair and he pushed up to rise.

Agatha's husband chose that moment to bow and then pull

his wife away from the laird. "Nay, laird. My wife still suffers from the loss. Dinna mind what she says." He pulled her out of the hall. The laird dropped back into his seat. His gaze locked with Aftyn's and he jerked his head. She understood his gesture. Agatha's accusation against her embarrassed him.

Conversations erupted into a wall of noise. Gazes all around the hall turned to her. Aftyn knew from the heat in her cheeks that her face had reddened.

"I must leave," she hissed to Braden, who still held her hand.

"Ye must stay," Braden hissed back. "Hold yer head up. Ye didna kill the bairn. Show them."

Aftyn forced herself to stand tall. But inside, her chest hurt and her belly filled with ice. Agatha's tale was damning enough. She did not want to imagine what the laird would have done to her this day if Niall had also died under her questionable care. Guilt filled her that she hadn't been able to do more. And anger that her father refused to send her somewhere to get the training she needed. That his clan needed, as Agatha had just reminded him.

If the Lathan healer told Niall what she'd nearly cost him, she would be disgraced. And if he told the laird? Nay, she would not consider that. The best she could hope for was to be ostracized by the clan. More likely, despite what he promised her for saving his only son, the laird would have banished her. And she knew full well a woman alone did not stand a good chance of survival. How long did she have?

What would the laird do now?

◇

JAMIE CAME AWAKE at the sound of the chamber door opening. Rabbie winced and held up a hand. "Sorry. I hoped not to wake ye, but I need my sword. Neve and I are going riding."

Jamie glanced at the window. The sun's angle told him midday had arrived. "Neve? She isna with Niall? Ye were to have replaced Aftyn in his chamber long before now."

"I havena seen Aftyn, but Neve did. Hours ago. I just looked in on them. Niall is still sleeping."

"Then I must see to him. Who is with him now?"

Bhaltair entered with a nod to Rabbie. "Fearchar is with him. Ye must have more to eat and drink, and perhaps some fresh air before ye go to Niall."

Jamie grimaced, flipped the covers aside, and swung his legs off of the bed. Standing, he still felt lightheaded and his heart raced, vestiges of the poison in Niall's blood. But his leg no longer hurt, though it didn't quite feel as it should.

He'd fallen into bed fully dressed. He needed everything Bhaltair mentioned, but first, a bath.

"Does the keep's hospitality include a tub?" He directed the question to Rabbie, who seemed to have made the most inroads with the local lasses.

"Aye," Rabbie told him with a grin. I'll have one brought up after ye eat."

"Now, Rabbie. Bhaltair can bring food to me here. Likely we'll be summoned before the Keith laird today."

Rabbie left on the run. Jamie was certain he rushed to do Jamie's bidding so he could still meet Neve.

"Aye, ye have been summoned," Bhaltair told him, pulling his attention from Rabbie. "But I told the steward, with the laird's forbearance for yer long day's travel and long night with Niall, ye would meet with him later today."

Jamie nodded. "Good thinking. Thank ye."

Bhaltair left on his errand.

Jamie moved to the window and leaned against the wall. The view gave out over the bailey to the curtain wall and hills falling away to farm land beyond. This should be a prosperous clan. Why, then, did they lack a competent healer?

Jamie left the question for another day as a knock sounded on the door. He opened it to be met by four strong lads carrying a large copper tub. They set it near the hearth and left, but in moments, lasses filed in to fill it with buckets of steaming water. The last one, bearing a stack of drying cloths and small pot of soap, gave him a saucy wink.

"I'd be pleased to bathe ye, my laird," she told him.

"Thank ye, nay. I can do for myself."

"But ye must need someone to wash yer back, at least?"

He gestured toward the door. "I prefer to bathe alone."

She pursed her lips. "Very well. But if ye need anything at all..." She paused as if to let her implication sink in as she placed the towels on the bed. Bending forward and showing off her considerable assets, she set the pot by the tub. Then she gave him a smile and shrugged, making her breasts jiggle beneath her kirtle. "Ask for Maddie," she added. "I'll do anythin' ye wish."

"I'll keep that in mind," Jamie told her as he handed her out the door and closed it behind her. Shaking his head at her brazen offer, he stripped and stepped into the still-steaming tub. The heat melted away the last discomfort in his leg and he sank down as far as he could into the hot water. He dunked his head, then reached for the pot of soap and cleaned himself everywhere he could reach, ruefully realizing he would have enjoyed Maddie scrubbing his back. But he was certain there would have been no stopping her if he'd allowed even that small intimacy, and he neither wanted nor had the energy to spare for dallying with her. Finally, he sat back and let the heat penetrate, knowing he would suffer again when he next treated Niall's leg, so he might as well enjoy this now.

The chamber door flew open and Aftyn rushed in, her gaze flying around the room. "Jamie, Fearchar needs ye. Oh!"

She stopped where her headlong rush carried her, at the foot of the tub, and froze, staring at the surface of the water. No, below it. Jamie grinned and stood, reaching for a drying sheet, amused to see Aftyn gulp and turn her back.

"Ye say ye are a healer. Have ye never seen a naked man before?"

"Of course I have."

Jamie grinned at her back, enjoying her virginal reaction to finding him in his bath. She'd crossed her arms, which pulled her kirtle more firmly against her back and revealed the curve of her waist. Jamie was tempted to reach for it, to smooth a hand over it and down to the lush curve of her arse, but he held himself in check. Not only would Aftyn not permit such a liberty, but his body had tightened at the thought of touching her so familiarly. Without needing to look, he knew a certain heaviness would be entirely visible if she glanced around.

"Ye dinna act as though ye have." Jamie dried his hair, letting the sheet drape over his shoulder to cover the part of him revealing his wayward thoughts. "Face me, lass, and tell me what Fearchar said."

Aftyn glanced over her shoulder, raked her gaze down the sheet covering at least some of the front of his body, gave a small sound suspiciously like an 'eep,' and looked away. "He said Niall is awake."

Jamie swore and stepped out of the tub, drying himself with quick, vigorous strokes, his momentary arousal forgotten. "Why didn't ye say that first, ye daft lass?"

"I... I wouldha," she said, still talking to the door, "but I didna expect to find ye... as ye are. Were. Ye surprised me."

He dug out a fresh set of clothes from his travel pack and donned his léine.

"Ye can turn around now. I'm decent enough."

She sniffed and stayed put. "I'll leave ye to finish dressing. I wish to see Niall, too."

Wrapping the kilt around his middle, he belted it, not bothering to pleat it properly. He frowned, recalling her "care" of his clansman, but he needed another minute. And Fearchar was there. "Go, then."

She wasted no time leaving him alone, not even bothering to close the door.

Jamie pulled on his boots and grabbed his bag as Bhaltair entered with another tray of food and drink. Jamie's stomach rumbled so he grabbed a bite of cheese and swallowed most of a cup of cider. "Niall's awake," he told Bhaltair when he came up for air. "Aftyn just delivered the news."

Bhaltair's gaze strayed to the tub, steam still rising from its surface. "Aye?"

"Aye, she burst in in the middle of my bath."

That earned him a quick laugh as Bhaltair took in the state of his clothing.

"She's gone, so something she saw didna set well with her." He set the tray on the bed and crossed his arms. "Or were ye in such a rush to see to Niall?"

Jamie broke off another bite of cheese. "Both. Let's go."

Bhaltair followed him out, pulling the door shut behind them.

Niall was indeed awake when he arrived. His color looked good, and a quick palm to his forehead told Jamie his fever was much reduced. He dared not use his talent with Aftyn hovering over her, nay, *his* patient, but despite having to stop from exhaustion before he'd completely eradicated the poison from Niall's blood, Jamie would wager Niall's body did the rest.

A few days to finish healing the injury to his leg and to let the man eat and regain his strength, and he'd be fit for the return trip to the Aerie. As far as Jamie was concerned, that day would not come soon enough.

Much to Jamie's surprise, now that Niall was awake, Aftyn lost her aggrieved air. "I'm glad to see ye feeling better," she told him as she took his hand. "And so sorry I wasna able to do more for ye."

He squeezed her hand and said, "I ken ye tried."

His voice was weaker than Jamie liked, but he had responded to Aftyn's apology. If only he knew she'd nearly cost him his leg—or possibly his life. Jamie expected he'd be much less forgiving of her failings.

THE EMOTIONS FLITTING across Aftyn's face fascinated Jamie. Relief had been paramount as she apologized to Niall. Her breathing had slowed and her posture relaxed as she focused on him and smiled the first truly open, unselfconscious smile he'd see on her face. It captivated him. But after that, as she settled back and let Niall rest, he saw guilt and sadness in her downcast gaze. Was she recalling how she'd failed Niall?

Bhaltair was right. Jamie owed her an apology for his outburst when they met. He should tell her he appreciated her efforts on Niall's behalf, no matter how untutored or misguided they'd been. To hear Neve tell it, she'd devoted all her time and effort trying to save Niall. Though he'd blamed her at first for Niall's condition, he found he could no longer. He hated recalling the sadness in her gaze and the defeat in her posture that night. It made him want to comfort her, to take her in his arms—though after she burst in on his bath, his intentions were poised to turn in another direction entirely.

But then she changed again as her thoughts apparently took a new direction. She stiffened and the strangest indication of all, the speeding pulse he could see at her throat, made him watch her even more closely. That and her tightened features spoke of one emotion—one he'd seen many times on the battlefield. Fear.

Fear for Niall? Or for herself? Who would harm her for trying to save an injured stranger? Highland hospitality extended even here, closer to the coast. They would not have turned Niall away unless Rabbie and Fearchar showed hostility to the clan. Niall's injury was the result of accident, not battle. So they'd been taken in and cared for with the best the clan could offer. That best would have been poor comfort to Niall in another day or two, but Jamie's arrival had saved him.

Jamie found himself studying Aftyn and realizing his anger had dissipated as Niall's recovery progressed. But his question remained. Why was a half-trained lass the only healer this clan could summon?

Perhaps the laird would have the answer. Jamie decided then that he would see him before treating Niall again. Aftyn raised questions he wanted answers to, even though they were not strictly Lathan business. Niall's predicament made them his.

He signaled to Fearchar that he would return soon and went in search of the laird's solar.

A big, burly man with a deep voice and gray-shot hair, Laird Keith stood as he entered and welcomed him. "'Tis an unhappy event that brings us together," he said, gesturing Jamie to a seat, "but I'm told yer clansman has improved greatly under yer care."

"He has, and thank ye for yer care of him and yer hospitality for the rest of us. We hope to be gone within the sennight, but much will depend on how fast Niall regains his strength and readiness to travel."

"Of course." The Keith paused and narrowed his eyes. "Perhaps while ye are here, ye will use yer expertise to aid a few of ours for whom Aftyn's skills have proven insufficient."

Jamie's hackles pricked up at how the laird's narrow-eyed expression contrasted with the subtly-delivered suggestion. He didn't know the man, but he recognized an order, even as obliquely delivered as that had been. An echo of his angry vow not to use his talent amplified his sense of disquiet. How much did the laird expect from him? His talent made him a far better

healer than Aftyn ever could be, but he did not know everything. Much he'd failed to learn by turning his back on his ability. At home, he could always call on Aileanna's greater skill.
Here, it had become clear he had the greater skill. The thought
sent him into a cold sweat.

Instead of making a promise he didn't want to be held to, he
temporized, saying only, "I'd be honored to do what little I can
for Keith while we remain." He could use his herbal medicines
without fear of exposing his greater talent. "But I must ask.
Why do ye lack a fully trained healer?"

The Keith's fist clenched and released immediately, telling
Jamie he trod into dangerous territory.

"Aftyn's mother, the former healer, died suddenly..." He
paused and allowed the silence to grow.

"I'm aware. She isna well trained," Jamie said. "Are there no
others who can care for the clan and finish training the lasses
who remain?"

"Such as ye?" The Keith said it with a tight smile that did
not reach his eyes.

A chill skittered down Jamie's back. He was a fool not to
have expected this. "I've already promised to do what I can
while we remain, but a sennight at most is not long enough to
fully train a healer."

"I'm aware," the Keith replied, echoing Jamie's curt
response. "Alas, there are no other healers or midwives within
the clan."

"And neighboring clans?"

"None have ever been available to us."

Jamie didn't like the sound of that. Were relations with their
neighbors that bad? Niall's need had been great enough to seek
help closer at hand. Thank God Rabbie knew Niall's best
chance to survive lay at the Aerie and had ridden for home.
"Perhaps another clan's healer could help if ye sent Aftyn to
them for a time?"

"Leaving us utterly without? Her assistant, Neve, is even less skilled. Nay."

Jamie stood. "I'm sorry ye find yerself in this position. As we travel back to the Aerie, I will make enquiries with the clans we pass. Perhaps another healer can be found, if only temporarily."

The Keith nodded, his gaze assessing. "Perhaps. For now, I leave the lasses in your care."

Out of the solar and away from the Keith laird's penetrating stare, Jamie paused in the great hall to consider what he'd just learned about the man and Aftyn. He clearly saw Jamie as the solution to his problem. Jamie worried that he didn't know the man well enough to know whether the Lathans should leave now, at great risk to Niall and himself, or if they would be safe to remain until Niall was strong enough to travel. Jamie would keep a close watch and alert his men.

How long had they been without Aftyn's mother? He wasn't opposed to giving Aftyn and Neve as much help as he could, but he could not submit to the Keith laird's thinly veiled coercion to stay long enough to see them fully trained, either.

5

Aftyn usually loved the weekly market held in the middle of the village. Today, her mood didn't suit such an outing, but Neve insisted. Now that she and Neve weren't tied to Niall's bedside night and day, they could indulge in a visit. Aftyn finally agreed to go with her. After facing Agatha and her father this morning, she needed the distraction.

Farmers brought the best of their crops, tinkers and tailors came from near and far, and Aftyn always found some herb or flower she needed to add to her mother's—now her—collection. The growers would tell her how to use each plant, whether in food or herbal medicines, and Neve would make a plainly legible note in her journal so they wouldn't lose the knowledge and, unlike what Aftyn's mother had done, would someday be able to pass what they learned on to the next healer.

It didn't take long for the basket over her arm to fill with colorful herbs, roots, and flowers she knew how to use. It gave off sweet, spicy, and earthy scents. She should take it back to the keep, or ask Neve to, but the excitement of the market drew her on. Colorful ribbons rippling in the breeze stirred by the passing crowd caught her gaze and she moved toward them. The front of the stall made her smile, and she'd done little enough of that lately. Bright and cheerful, some ribbons shone in the weak sunlight, others made of velvet looked so soft, she wanted to stroke them.

Neve, at her side, went right to the brightest ribbon, a crimson too pure to be confused with blood. Neve's dark hair and creamy skin would be even more beautiful with it adorning her. "Ye should get it," Aftyn told her. "The color suits ye."

Neve gave it a wistful glance and shook her head. "Nay, I havenae coin enough for it."

"I'll give ye what ye lack," Aftyn told her, hating to see the longing in Neve's eyes as she turned away from the display, and wanting to thank her for helping care for Niall.

"I cannae let ye do that. Ye have little enough coin of yer own."

"Dinna despair. Let me see if the merchant is willing to deal with the clan's healers."

It took only a few words for the man to pull the ribbon Neve wanted from the rack and present it to her. "For a lovely lass who deserves a gift for helping her people."

Neve simpered and took it with thanks.

Then the man turned to Aftyn. "And what color suits ye, milady? I'd nay let ye leave without a gift to complement ye as the red does yer friend."

"I dinna need..."

"Ach," the man said, holding up a hand to interrupt her. "'Tis never about need for a lovely lass such as yerself. And a healer deserves the thanks of all she has helped."

"But I havena helped ye," Aftyn reminded him, pleased to be acknowledged but confused by the sentiment coming from a stranger.

"Nay, ye havena, but my wee daughter still lives, thanks to one of yer sisters."

"Ye have a daughter? Where is she?" Aftyn couldn't see anyone else in his stall with him.

"At home with her ma, thanks to a healer like ye. Because she saved her life, I vowed to give a token to every healer I meet, to express how grateful I am."

Aftyn silently blessed him. After Agatha's accusations piled on top of her failures with Niall, finding someone so grateful to healers lifted her heart.

"Now, milady healer, which of these catch yer eye?" He waved at the fluttering ribbons.

Aftyn's gaze followed his hand and lit on a clear-sky blue velvet that made her breath catch. "That one," she said, reaching out to indicate it. "But I canna. 'Tis too dear. Ye must need the coin it would bring for yer wife and bairn."

"'Tis my pleasure, milady." He pulled the ribbon from the rack and offered it to her. "'Twill be lovely in yer hair or holding a locket around yer throat. Ye must take it."

After hearing his reason for giving such a gift, she couldn't insult him. "I find I cannae refuse ye, sir," she told him and allowed him to drape the ribbon across her palm. The color drew her eye, but when she touched it, she could not bear to relinquish it. The velvet felt as soft and plush as she'd imagined it would. "I will think of yer kindness, always, when I wear it. And yer wee daughter. What is her name?"

"Emma." His smile softened. "She is the joy of my life." Then he held out a hand. "I can ask only one boon more, milady."

Aftyn nearly handed the ribbon back to him, fearing he was about to demand a kiss or something more in payment.

"Simply tell yer ladies to visit my stall. MacGarrity is me name." He laid his hand over his heart and inclined his head. "Will ye do that?"

"Of course," she agreed, relief filling her that he'd not made an improper demand. But he wouldn't. His tale and his demeanor as he told it convinced her he was sincere. She could keep the ribbon as a token of gratitude, as he'd intended. She smiled, grateful to be acknowledged, something that happened rarely. "Do ye come to market often?"

"I'll come more often now that I ken such lovely lasses are to be found here."

Neve giggled.

Aftyn wished him and his family well as she rolled up her treasure. She tucked it into her basket, out of sight, then she and Neve took their leave of MacGarrity.

Neve begged off of seeing the rest of the market, claiming she was tired, and left Aftyn to wander on her own. Only after Neve disappeared into the crowd did Aftyn think to have her take the basket back to the keep. It wasn't heavy, but it made moving through the crowd awkward.

She hadn't gone far when a familiar shape appeared ahead of her. She could not mistake Jamie Lathan, even though his broad back was to her. His dark auburn hair glinted red in the sunlight. When he wasn't castigating her, or wrung out from tending to Niall, his deep brown eyes drew her, his high cheek-bones, full, firm lips, and even white teeth made her want to gaze at him forever. And the rest of him she'd seen in his bath. She'd never met a man who fascinated her as much.

While the other Lathans were also tall and well formed, he moved through the crowded market so confidently, most people parted before him, making way as if for royalty.

But not all. Some, facing stalls and intent on the items on offer before them, jostled each other into his way as they moved along. Reflexively, many held up a hand, making contact with his hand or wrist.

Those fleeting contacts raised Aftyn's hackles and made her watch him even more carefully as she followed along behind him. As though another person's inadvertent touch annoyed him, or angered him, his shoulders would tense as he glanced down and aside with a frown at the clumsy villager, or adjusted his stride to avoid the next person coming too close to him.

Ahead and to his side, a cluster of women and girls bargained with a different stall keeper over brightly colored ribbons. Younger girls moved around them, laughing and plucking at the colored baubles their mothers held up for inspection. An older woman stood to the side, leaning on a cane, her expression disapproving. She stepped around the cluster of women, meaning, Aftyn thought, to leave them to their haggling and make her way to another stall. Jamie tried to give her room, but the crowd of villagers at the stalls on his other side hemmed him in, and she was so bent over her cane, likely she only saw the ground at her feet, not the big man doing his best to avoid her without bumping into anyone else.

The old woman's elbow brushed his arm. She paused and touched his hand, seemingly in apology, as she passed. Jamie twitched so slightly that only someone watching him as closely as Aftyn would have seen it. Then he turned his head to regard the old woman's halting progress. He pivoted and lifted a hand toward her, then clenched his fingers into a fist and drew it back to his side.

Aftyn sidestepped behind a pair of men to avoid being seen as Jamie's gaze raked past her and followed the old woman. She carried on her halting progress, angled away from Aftyn's vantage point. She could see Jamie over the shoulder of one of the men, but he failed to notice her.

Before his expression cleared and he turned back to continue through the market, his lips compressed and his gaze dropped.

Did he feel sympathy for those he could not help? Did that failure anger him? Or was there more she did not yet know, did not yet understand? Thinking back over his reaction to the old woman's touch, she realized there was another explanation.

He'd flinched as though in pain.

It would be simplest to attribute his reactions to the unavoidable press of bodies around them. Aftyn wasn't fond of crowds, herself. But nothing about Jamie Lathan seemed simple, try though he might to convince her otherwise. And she'd seen him limp out of Niall's chamber and nearly collapse. Yet he didn't limp now. Surely he touched the ill and injured who came to him for help. Surely brief contact with fairgoers would make less of a demand on him.

There must be some other explanation. Did he fear cutpurses in a crowded fair? Nay, that couldn't be the reason for his strange behavior. Who would dare a man like Jamie Lathan?

JAMIE DID his best to avoid the crush in the market of villagers and folk from the keep. He would not be here at all, but he hoped to find an herb he needed to make a stronger poultice for Niall's wound. He could manage without it, true, but the sooner Niall was fit to travel, the happier Jamie would be, and the herb would help in two ways. First, because Aftyn would expect to see poultices applied to the wound, and second, they would help disguise the healing effect of Jamie's ability. Though at the moment, he'd happily dispense with his talent.

Every person who touched his skin set off a reaction in his own body. The villagers were rife with pain, injuries, malnutrition, or like the ancient woman who'd passed him a few minutes ago and touched his hand, the infirmities of old age. If he didn't find the herb seller soon, he'd be too weak from battling his discomfort and fighting to keep from using his healing energy to continue. He would have to find the most direct way out of the market and back to the keep, or at least to a place where he could rest undisturbed for a few minutes.

Getting through this market was akin to anything from

being stabbed with an embroidery needle to hit with a mallet, again and again, in his hand, his shoulder, and the length of his spine, his belly, then hip or knee or foot, never knowing when or where each blow would land in his body, depending on what troubled that person. The touches were as unrelenting as they were unintended, and the fatigue from them would soon bring him down. He missed the battle-lust that kept him from feeling anything, even his own pain.

Ah, there. He'd found what he sought. Jamie stepped up to the cart, out of the way of passersby, and inspected the bunches of fresh herbs, leaves, and roots, each tied securely with string, ready to be hung and dried if that was the use they'd be put to. He glanced up at the seller. Did Aftyn know this man? Jamie looked around, hoping to see her in the press of market-goers, but not really expecting to.

Yet there she stood. As soon as he noted her, she turned aside to inspect the contents of a merchant's stall. Jamie had the strong feeling she'd been watching him, and he'd caught her at it.

She was as lovely as the first time he'd seen her, crossing the great hall. Even more so, with the sunlight gilding her dark hair, making it shine like silk and making Jamie want to touch it. He longed to unravel her braid with his fingers and let the soft strands slip over his palms. She wore a simple homespun kirtle of deep blue. Not a healer's color, but still, it suited her. She smiled at the merchant showing her his pottery, and jealousy suddenly spiked through Jamie's belly. He wanted her smile for himself.

She glanced in his direction, but quickly turned back to the potter. So she had been following him. Without thinking, he took a step toward her. If she wanted to see what he was doing here, she could do so at a closer remove.

"A moment, if ye will," he paused and told the farmer before he strolled to Aftyn's side, giving her plenty of time to glance his way again and see him coming. She didn't, but if her skin prickled at his nearness like his did at hers, she fought to keep her gaze on the potter's wares.

"Good morrow to ye, Aftyn."

She spun as if she hadn't known he stood right beside her. But her expression gave her away. In that moment, he realized she could not keep anything from him. She had to have told the truth about her efforts for Niall. He could trust her, but not with everything. His secrets were too important to divulge to someone he'd known only a few days.

"Ach, Jamie, ye startled me. Good morrow to ye, as well."

If she'd spoken smoothly, he might have doubted his judgement in trusting her, but she looked past him and didn't meet his gaze. She was a terrible liar. "I've something to show ye, if ye have a moment," he told her, satisfied with his assessment.

She resisted for a moment, glancing aside at the display she'd used to keep him from being aware she had been studying him. Then she shrugged. "What is it?"

"I found a merchant with an extensive collection of useful herbs. Do ye ken him?" Jamie led her to his find. She shook her head, eyes wide, but not, as Jamie expected, with excitement for his find. Rather, she looked... frightened. Seeing that, Jamie took her arm and led her beyond the cart out of earshot. "What fashes ye, lass? Do ye ken that man?"

"Nay, I dinna think so."

"Then why are ye upset?"

"I'm not upset. I simply dinna need anything he has."

"Dinna need? Or dinna ken how to use?" And if so, why did that make her afraid?

Aftyn covered her mouth with one hand. "How did ye ken?"

"It makes sense, lass. Ye didna ken all ye need, so why would ye ken the less common healing herbs and how to prepare them."

"I have a sufficient supply of the ones I ken how to use."

Jamie nodded. "Perhaps. But ye must learn more. Ye have said so."

She glanced around, then dropped her gaze. "Will ye teach me?"

Why was that difficult for her to ask of him? "I'll do as much as I can until Niall is fit to travel. But I dinna understand yer fear. Has someone threatened ye?"

She paled and a sheen of tears glinted in her downcast eyes. Then her lips pressed into a thin line.

"Ye canna tell me? Or ye willna, Aftyn?"

Instead of answering, she turned back to study the man's cart, then sighed. "I suppose ye will say we'll need at least one of everything he has."

So she would not tell him. Jamie wanted answers, but the midst of a public market was not the place to demand them. He could see that Aftyn had enough problems without him making them worse. She feared something. Or someone. After the way he'd berated her the first night he arrived, he didn't blame her for not trusting him. But a healer afraid to heal was no healer at all.

He should be angry for her sake that her mother's death left her so poorly prepared. She clearly did not recognize many of the tools most healers in Scotland used—even his mother— among the contents of the farmer's cart. But he vowed he would discover the secret behind her fear before he left to return to the Aerie.

"Yer basket is nearly full," he finally said. "Take it home. I will deal with the farmer for his crop and bring it to yer herbal."

She looked up then and met his gaze. He wasn't sure what he saw in her eyes. Sadness? Gratitude? Without another word, she turned and left him. Jamie bargained for the entire contents of the man's cart and carried it all in a fold of his kilt back to the keep. It might serve to get the clan through the winter, until the next growing season would allow Aftyn to replenish any stock she used. He'd show her how to make any common preparations she didn't know and would likely need.

AFTYN PUT her basket down in her mother's herbal. What would Jamie think of it? She'd done little in here since her mother's death save try to understand the journal she'd left behind. Both she and Neve had been over it carefully, and had copied several preparations for poultices Aftyn knew would be useful, but had only managed to recognize one or two symbols from those. Not enough to help Niall. In her urgency to save him, she'd substituted ingredients, timing, even temperature, steeping at room temperature or heating the mixture, all to no avail.

She didn't doubt she'd done something wrong in preparing them, but what? Her ignorance could have killed Niall, had Jamie not arrived in time to save him. She raked a hand through her hair in frustration, then growled as her fingers got stuck in the top of her braid. She pulled them free and looked around her mother's domain. Now hers, at least for the time being.

Bunches of dried herbs still hung along one wall, but all carried fairy tracings of cobwebs, showing how little they'd been used. A collection of pots and vials remained. Aftyn had feared to disturb them, except for a few she had become familiar with before her mother's death. Those she had remade, replacing tinctures and poultices with fresh preparations. The mint she'd used to continue her mother's treatment of the Keith heir was nearly gone. But Braden had survived and now thrived. She ran a finger over the pot and inhaled its fresh scent, grateful its contents gave her some guarantee of a home.

Before long, Jamie arrived and dumped the plants he'd

bought next to her basket. Hands on hips, turned to look around.

Aftyn cringed. What would he think of the dust? The spiderwebs?

Jamie moved to the cabinet that held pots and stoppered bottles, picking one up and sniffing, then another, seemingly at random. He studied the dried herbs and pinched a few leaves between two strong fingers.

Despite the apprehension hollowing her belly over how he would judge what he found, Aftyn found herself watching his hands, not what he touched. He moved with grace and assurance. No trace remained of the limp she'd noticed the other night. She could imagine his hands touching her the way he touched the things in her herbal. The thought made her blood heat and tingles spread from her chest to her fingertips. She forced herself to ignore those feelings and concentrate on why she and Jamie were here. She had no doubt he knew exactly how to use each of those dried-up greens, and how to prepare them. Finally, he ceased his inspection and faced her.

"How long ago did ye lose yer mother?"

Aftyn cringed. He could probably guess from the state of the place. "Nearly two years gone."

"I can tell that in the age of much of what I see. Most will have to be discarded. There are a few things that may remain useful, but only a few."

"I made new batches of the ones I kenned how to prepare." Aftyn's heart sank. As she'd expected, the rest had gone to waste.

"Aye, of course," he answered, his gaze sweeping the chamber yet again.

"Who looks after this if ye are not here? There are dangerous preparations, even some plants, that bairns should never go near."

He was a healer, after all, and a man. What man noticed

dust and spiderwebs? "Any of those that remain are out of reach of wee fingers. The clan respected my mother's skills and did not intrude. I expected that forbearance to continue, and it has."

And the rest? How was she supposed to replace the potions in the entire herbal in the few days Jamie would remain? She fingered the fresh herbs he'd bargained for. She knew a few by name, none by function. This was hopeless.

"I fear ye wasted yer coin," she told him. "There's too much to replace, too much for me to learn, and ye will soon leave."

"We'll set this to rights as best we can, and I will write down all of it. Ye can read?"

"Aye. I have my mother's journal..."

"Ye do?" His eyes widened. "Let me see it."

Aftyn wanted to warn him, but decided he would understand better if he saw it himself. She left him to continue exploring and retrieved the journal from her sleeping chamber. "It is not very useful," she told him when she returned. "She used terms I dinna ken, symbols and such I have yet to be able to puzzle out, that she didna teach me."

While she talked, Jamie turned pages, occasionally running one finger down her mother's crabbed writing, as if that might make it easier to understand.

He nodded. "Some of this, I can follow, some will take some thought. But much of what ye need is here."

"Not in any form I've been able to use." Her frustration turned to embarrassment, then anger. She fought back the tears that still came all too easily when she dealt with anything to do with her mother. "She taught me simple cures, and stitching wounds, which I'm good at," she added, needing him to hear at least that small point of pride in her voice, "but she wanted to wait until I was older for many of the more difficult or dangerous preparations, so she never explained the symbols she used."

"We'll work on it. This journal may save time," Jamie said, clearly unaware of her distress.

She gave a choked laugh. "It has wasted plenty of mine up to now."

He looked up then and met her gaze. He must have noticed the sheen in her eyes that she fought to keep from slipping down her cheeks. He touched her sleeve, never taking his gaze from hers, and told her, "We'll change that, together."

He sounded so sincere. Did he truly mean he would spend the time he had left here to help her? "But Niall..."

"Niall is much better. I dinna need to spend all my time with him. Do ye no' want my help?"

Perhaps she would not have to embarrass herself by explaining how little esteem her father held for her, and how much at risk she remained. She wanted to throw herself into his arms and thank him, but she didn't dare. She opened her mouth to speak.

His gaze dropped to her lips.

Heat sizzled along her veins at the desire in his eyes. What did he think? That she would repay him that way? She took a breath and moved away from him. She gathered her courage, cleared her throat and told him, "Of course I want yer help. I need it."

He pursed his lips, crossed his arms and glanced around. "Do ye ken where Neve is?"

"Aye, she went home."

"Fetch her and we'll make a start."

6

Later that afternoon, Jamie finished the last of a thin lamb stew in the village post house public room, and pushed the bowl away. The Aerie's cook could do better on her worst day, but he couldn't complain. The stew filled his belly and gave him something to do while he waited. He'd promised the Keith laird to do what he could for the village while he remained. Having a meal at the pub where the villagers gathered would help spread news of his presence. He glanced down at the simple robe he wore. It resembled a low-level cleric's garb, and he always wore it over tunic and trews when he went into a village. His satchel of herbs and poultices sat on the floor by his booted feet. He could use them when called for without breaking his vow. Niall was resting easily, Aftyn and Neve were still busy in the herbal, so Jamie took this opportunity to be approachable. Anyone sick or injured would hear and, he expected, seek help, but no one had asked for him yet.

His thoughts strayed back to watching Aftyn and Neve put the herbal to rights this morning. He had become determined to help them.

The more he learned about Aftyn's situation, how bravely

she tried to fill her dead mother's role, and how she had spent day and night at Niall's side, the more sympathy he felt for her. He forgot the fury that had tainted his opinion of her when he first saw Niall. Instead, he now focused on her heart, her beauty, and uncovering the secret that kept her frustrated and afraid.

He knew something about keeping secrets.

While he pored over her mother's cryptic journal after the market, she and Neve had cleared the herbal of all the old preparations and dried plants, and scrubbed every surface clean enough to eat on. Tired but determined, they hung every bunch of herbs and flowers he'd gifted to them, then stood, hands on hips, admiring their handiwork and the change in the sight and the scents of the herbal.

So taken by their efforts, he'd promised to spend the next day with them, making up the dozen or so preparations that any healer used for common abrasions, burns, and the like. Aftyn had been so thrilled with his vow, he thought for a moment she would throw her arms around his neck and kiss him. Or at least hug him, in thanks. He would have welcomed any sign of affection from such a beautiful lass, but he was coming to think of Aftyn differently—as someone who deserved his admiration, not just his lust. He didn't understand how that had happened. She was certainly desirable. But the more he got to know her, the more he admired her.

Instead of showing her appreciation to him in a way he imagined, she declared she wasn't done yet. She began with the handful of concoctions she did know how to prepare, chopping, bruising, heating, boiling, mixing, with a smile on her face.

Inspired, he'd stayed through the midday mealtime and chose several of her mother's preparations to transcribe into something legible that Aftyn could keep and use. That earned him another warm smile before she turned back to the task she'd set for herself.

That smile tempted him to take her in his arms and kiss her. If Neve had not been there, he might have. How would she have met his advance? With welcome? Or would she have turned away? He'd been attracted to her the first moment he saw her crossing the great hall. Since then, he'd learned that she was the kind of person who fought on after tragedy, and he found himself even more drawn to her.

A serving girl interrupted his recollections as she passed by with a pitcher of ale, then paused where he sat and gave him a grin. She moved on when he waved her away. He didn't need that kind of trouble.

A few minutes later, he noticed the post house's mistress berating the lass for taking too much time with certain patrons. Her gaze shifted to Jamie as she said it. Jamie met her gaze, but kept his expression neutral. Arguing with the mistress would not help him—or the lass.

He finished his ale and waited long enough the serving girl gave him another reason to wave her away, then stood. He could do with a walk around the village on his way back to the keep. Except for the market this morning, he'd seen little since he arrived, having spent most of his time in the Niall's chamber or recovering in Rabbie's.

He was met at the door by a breathless young lad, possibly eight years old.

"Are ye the new healer?"

He lifted his satchel. "I am."

"Ye must come with me. I think my mam fell. I found her on the floor. I canna wake her."

Jamie frowned. This could be serious. He should send for Aftyn, but if he needed to use more than herbal cures, her presence would inhibit what he could do. He'd evaluate first, then send the lad for her if he could. "Take me to yer mother, lad."

The lad raced off, then paused to let Jamie catch up with him. They proceeded in this leap-frog fashion to one of the village cottages. The lad shoved open the door and pointed inside. Late afternoon sunlight fell in a broad beam to the body of a young woman sprawled face-down in the middle of the room.

Jamie knelt by her and studied her form. Thin, too thin. Likely too poorly nourished to support herself and keep up a home, a young son and, he supposed, a husband. She'd fainted. He ran a hand over her head, then down her back. He dared do no more with the lad watching. "Fetch healer Aftyn for me, lad, and close the door. Yer mother wouldna want everyone in the village peering in at her.

The lad did as he was told and Jamie went to work. No matter how deeply he extended his senses, he could find nothing wrong to explain her faint. He leaned back. He'd feared she'd hit her head, but found no sign of injury. He could do nothing for her that a steady diet of good meals would not improve. "Where's yer husband, lass?" He debated leaving her as she fell, but decided he could at least make her more comfortable where she lay. He rolled her to her back and straightened her skirt. He found a blanket on a small cot near the opposite end of the room and used it to pillow her head. Only then did he notice the bruising on her face and around one eye. He grimaced over using his talent and breaking his vow yet again, but he had no other means to be sure she wasn't injured. He found bruising on her torso he'd missed by scanning so deeply for the cause of her swoon. Someone was hitting her, and often.

He thought back to when the lad appeared. Had he been bruised, too? Not his face, surely, or Jamie would have seen it in the sunlight, as would anyone in the village.

Was she in pain? Jamie had no way to know whether he should treat her injuries, or if the sudden lack of them would provoke her husband into hitting her again. Then he recalled something his mother taught him about leaving the leaked blood under the surface of the skin, but healing deeper damage. She'd done that while trying to save her half-brother. Jamie did the same for the lass. His face hurt and his eye ached, but they were minor complaints compared to what this lass had been through. He finished just as the door opened and Aftyn rushed in.

"Ach, Mhairi. Again?" She knelt on the woman's other side, opposite Jamie, and studied the woman's face, then met Jamie's gaze. "Where's Rory? What have ye done for her?"

"The lad I sent to find ye?"

"Nay, her husband."

"I dinna ken. And there's little either of us can do. She needs good food more than potions. That and getting away from the person who did that to her." He nodded at the discoloration on her face.

Aftyn sighed. "Rory has a temper."

"Ye kenned he hit her?" He let the outrage for what this woman had suffered resonate in his voice.

Aftyn waved a hand. "The whole village kens. Not that anyone can do anything to help her."

"Would she be better off without him?" Jamie could make him disappear. The thought tempted the warrior in him.

Aftyn grimaced. "She thinks she'd starve, and her son with her, or she'd have left him by now."

"Her son?"

"He isna Rory's lad. He's her dead husband's. Rory doesna want bairns, so he keeps her hungry and ill, thinking that will prevent her breeding. Every time she misses her monthly flux or shows any signs he thinks mean a bairn is on the way, he beats her. She's lost two of his bairns already."

"Keeping her on the verge of starvation could stop her courses. But he's beating her more often than that."

"Probably." Aftyn shook her head. "She fainted, then?"

"That's what I believe. I havena tried to wake her. The lad said she wouldn't awaken for him."

"Likely she's exhausted and sleeping. I'll sit with her."

"What will Rory do when he comes home and finds her like this?"

"Nothing good."

"And if ye are here, ye will be the next lass he hits." Jamie rose and offered a hand to help her up. "Nay. I'll stay and have a talk with him."

She gripped his arm and stood, then stepped back, planting her fists on her hips. "I dinna need yer protection," she insisted.

His gaze snapped back to her face. Aye, she'd noticed. She frowned at him, then looked down at Mhairi. "This is my village. My people. I care for them. I can take care of myself, as well. I dinna need a man to do it for me."

Aftyn's confidence impressed him, but Mhairi's condition gave him a reason to be cautious. "We've already established lasses are in danger from him."

"Perhaps. Or perhaps only Mhairi."

He found himself mirroring her stance, hands on hips, as his irritation with her grew. "Aftyn, I think…"

"Wheesht." She waved an open hand between them. "Ye men are all alike. 'Tis why I swore long ago never to marry. Likely after a month or two of being told what to do, I'd want to stab a husband in his sleep."

For some reason, her vow not to marry felt like a punch to his gut, a punch he couldn't resist returning. "Why do anything so brazen? Poison can be as fast… or as slow, as ye wish." He softened the rebuke with a grin.

And why should he care what she did or didn't do? Her life was here. His was at the Aerie.

"Ach, ye mean to drive me mad, do ye? Go on, leave me."

She waved both hands at him, palms down. "Wait outside if ye must."

Jamie grinned again, willing to cede this round to her. In any case, what he had to say to Rory would best not be overheard by anyone else. He'd await the man just outside his door.

AFTYN KNELT AGAIN, picked up Mhairi's hand and stroked it, hoping to rouse her. Her breathing deepened, probably in response to Aftyn's gentle touch, but she remained asleep. Likely she got little of gentleness in her life. Gentleness from a man like Rory came seldom, if at all.

Even Jamie had nothing to offer her save food and rest. Then again, she was sure he waited outside for Rory, despite what she'd said about taking care of herself and her village, so perhaps there *was* something he could do to help her. Aftyn would be pleased, whether he used persuasion or threats, so long as it worked and Rory treated Mhairi better.

While she waited, she glanced around the cottage. The main room's fire had burned down to a glow. Should she add some peat or leave it be? What would Rory expect when he got home? That Mhairi had worked in the cold, not wasting fuel he claimed for his own, or would he be angry that she had not warmed the house before he arrived, making ready for him? Which would enrage Rory and cause Mhairi more trouble?

She decided it didn't matter what Rory wanted. Mhairi lay on a cold floor, and Aftyn had started to feel chilled as well. She stood and stirred the embers, then added more fuel. In moments, cheery flames leapt to life, and the room seemed warmer, even though she knew the fire had not had time to make much of a difference.

While she was up, she climbed a few rungs of the ladder leaning against the far wall and peered into the loft. It was clean, bedding ordered, and blankets folded and piled nearby. Mhairi kept a clean and neat home. As she climbed back down, Aftyn shuddered to think what the consequences might be if she did not. The main level was as neat as the loft, table scrubbed, pots neatly stacked, clothes not in evidence, so likely they were folded into the chest she'd spied in the loft. Another stood next to the hearth. For the lad? Or spare linens? The cot in the main room must be for the lad. His blanket cushioned his mother's head, no doubt put there by Jamie. It seemed like something he would do. They'd started badly, but she'd come to see there was more to him than his dismay over Niall's condition and his reaction to it. If he'd been warned—and if he knew about her beforehand—he'd have greeted her very differently.

Mhairi groaned and stirred. Aftyn returned to her and took her hand again. "Mhairi, wake up, lass. I'm here. 'Tis Aftyn. We are alone."

"My lad..."

"He's fine. He fetched us."

Mhairi's eyes blinked open. "Us? Rory?"

"Nay. The village now has two healers, at least for a few more days. Ye are too weak, Mhairi. Ye fainted. Ye must eat more."

"I canna," she said as she pushed herself to sitting, then lifted a hand to her face. "Dizzy."

"No doubt. Why can ye no' eat more?"

"The lad is growing. He needs food. And Rory works so hard..."

"He hits ye. Does he knock bread out of yer hand?"

Mhairi didn't answer, but her shoulders slumped.

"Ye should leave him."

"Ye ken I canna. Where would I go? I'd starve for sure. And the lad."

"Why does he no' have a name, Mhairi?"

"He did, once." Her voice dropped to a whisper. "Alastair."

Then she looked up, her voice still weak, but stronger. "But Rory took it away."

"Rory took it... he cannae do that."

"Aye, well, he can and did. He beats me if he hears it. He beat Alas... the lad... near to death once for insisting it was his name. Now the lad stays out of Rory's way." She dropped her head into her hands. "Mostly he hides. I'm surprised he kenned I needed help and fetched ye. Rory would be pleased if he disappeared forever." She lifted her head. Tears glistened in her eyes.

"Ach, Mhairi, this isna right. Ye should no' have to live this way."

"I didna ken what he would be like when I married him," she choked out on a sob.

"We lasses never do, do we?" Aftyn rubbed her back, trying to calm her. In a few moments, the tears subsided. Maybe she should have let Jamie talk to Rory. He sounded ready to pound some sense in to the man. Rory was big, and well-muscled from working the fields, but Jamie was bigger, and something about his shape and the way he held himself, the confident way he moved, told Aftyn he would win any fight that came his way. Or any lass.

JAMIE LOUNGED against the sun-warmed cottage wall, arms crossed over his chest, dirk strapped to his thigh and a sgian dubh in his boot. His longsword was stashed with his other belongings in the chamber the Lathans used in the keep. He wouldn't need it. And walking around the village with it slung on his back did not say "healer." It said "warrior," a message he did not want to send unless absolutely necessary.

Even without the claymore, if Mhairi's husband refused to see reason, Jamie had other ways to drive a lesson home. He uncrossed his arms and dropped his fists to his sides, wondering how long he'd have to wait. The sun was melting into the western horizon. Men should be returning from the fields very soon.

His thoughts went back to Aftyn and what she might be doing for Mhairi in the cottage. It was constructed well enough that he could not hear any conversation or movement inside, but he could picture Aftyn's worried frown as she cared for the lass.

If the MacKyrie Seer had not told him he was bound for a life of service to those he loved at Lathan, he could find himself tempted by the village healer. Yet how could he even think about taking a wife? He was trained to fight and to heal. His skills would always be needed and would often take him far from home, even if he refused to use his talent.

He hadn't been very successful in keeping his vow since he arrived here. To be wed to a lass with a healer's knowledge of herbs and potions and all their uses, he would have to guard his talent even more closely than he already did. She would soon realize he relied on more than potions to care for the ill and injured. He didn't want to think about the consequences of having his talent exposed.

His elder brother was the heir. It would fall to him to marry and provide for the future of the Lathan clan at the Aerie. His younger brother, one of the twins, served as the spare. Jamie was free to make the best use of his abilities, no matter where he roamed or what battles he fought. One day, he expected to become the Lathan arms master. His youngest sister would become his mother's replacement. And though the Seer hadn't said any more, he was certain she meant he'd use his prowess in battle, not his mother's talent, for honorable service to his clan.

Yet he could not get Aftyn out of his mind. Her beauty had captured his attention at first, but she was so much more. Aye, not yet the best healer a clan could hope to have, but she led with her heart and did her best with what she knew. Any man would be lucky to have a lass like that to care for him. To love him.

He shifted his stance as two men appeared on the track into the village, then one more. They passed by with a nod, which Jamie returned and settled back to continue waiting, letting his thoughts wander to Aftyn in his arms. Aftyn in his bed, her hair unbound and spread on the pillow, her body bare for him to see and enjoy.

Another handful of men approached. Jamie reined in his fantastical imaginings and nodded as they passed by. In moments, one lone man coming up the track spotted him and increased his pace.

That must be Rory. He was shorter than Jamie expected, yet significantly bigger than his slip of a wife. Still, size did not make the bully, actions did. His glare as he approached didn't invite explanations. Jamie let him get close, then to be certain, asked, "Ye are Rory, Mhairi's husband?"

"What's it to ye?" The man stood with fists on hips. "Get away from my door and go on yer way."

"Or?"

"What have ye been doing with my wife?" He pulled the door open and took a step forward. "Mhairi, where are ye?"

Jamie grabbed the edge of the door and slammed it shut in his face. "Ye'll no' go in there until I have a word with ye."

"I won't, eh?" He reached for the door again.

Jamie could see until he established who was in charge, conversation was out of the question. "Nay." He grasped Rory's shoulder and spun him around his body until he slammed against the wall Jamie had leaned on, his face to the side. Jamie held him there for a beat to let the man's predicament sink in. Then Jamie bent in close to his ear and spoke softly. "Ye have starved yer wife and mistreated her son. Ye have dishonored yerself and yer clan, if ye have one. Where I come from, ye would no' be considered a man, no matter yer age or yer size."

Rory started to struggle then, but Jamie's forearm across his back held him in place.

"Let me be," he demanded. "Ye have nay right to do this, or to speak of my wife."

"I have every right. I'm the healer her son came to for help after she fell and he couldna wake her. I'm the man who's going to kill ye... slowly... if ye dinna care for her as a husband ought. If I hear any word at all that she's hungry, or that ye have hit her or the lad, I'll be behind ye so fast ye'll never ken the first blow is coming. But ye'll feel the rest, and ye'll die begging me to finish with ye." Jamie applied more pressure across Rory's back, then dug his thumb into a point on the man's shoulder he knew would cause excruciating pain. "That's just a taste of what I can do to ye with no effort at all," he promised, as Rory bit down on a cry. "I ken many more places just like that on a man's body. And unlike ye, I never leave a mark—until I want to. Ye'll be sobbing like a wean before I start cutting parts off of ye. Long before ye breathe yer last."

He let up suddenly and stepped back, gratified to see Rory's knees buckle.

The man clung to the wall for a moment, then straightened and rounded on Jamie with his fist. Jamie blocked the punch with his forearm before he realized Rory held a blade in his other hand. Jamie danced away as the point caught in his léine. He twisted clear and grabbed Rory's wrist, intending to force him to drop the blade. Rory swung with his fist and missed Jamie but managed to stab himself in the arm. Jamie had enough. He hit Rory on the point of his chin, snapping his head back.

Rory went down like a tossed bale of hay.

Jamie rolled his shoulder and rubbed his chin with the inside of his arm where echoes of Rory's pain pulsed. Some men had no sense. Then he knelt to check Rory's wound which was bleeding freely. His sleeve was sliced and he had a deep score down his forearm. Jamie grimaced, looked around to make sure he didn't have an audience, then bent to close Rory's wound. In moments, the bleeding stopped. Jamie stopped knitting the tissue back together just below the surface, leaving a long scratch to explain the blood. Then he stood and rubbed the soreness from his own forearm.

Rory didn't move.

Jamie opened the door and peered into the dim interior. "Are ye lasses all right in here?" His eyes adjusted quickly from the fading sunlight outside and he spotted the two women sitting at the table.

"What's been going on out there?" Aftyn demanded. "I thought I heard a thud."

"Just a moment." Jamie slung Rory over his shoulder and carried him inside, glad to see Mhairi drinking from a clay mug. Crumbs littered the table's surface. So Aftyn had found food and convinced her to eat. Good.

"What..." Mhairi's shocked expression, eyes wide and mouth open, didn't surprise Jamie. But then she narrowed her eyes and pressed her lips together. "Ye can leave him to sleep it off outside," she stated firmly. "Preferably behind the cottage."

Aftyn grinned and patted her on the shoulder.

Jamie's feet wouldn't move. He was transfixed by the expression on Aftyn's face. He'd seen her sad, scared, and angry, but this grin was new. He liked it—a lot. It revealed a certain spirit the lass had kept hidden. She released him from thrall by glancing down at Mhairi.

Jamie had been headed for the wee cot he spied at the back of the room, but he nodded and hid a grin, pleased that Aftyn had revealed more of herself. And had made such a difference in Mhairi's spirit, too. "As ye wish, milady. Ye can see we've exchanged a few words."

"Wait. He's bleeding," Aftyn exclaimed. "Let me look at him."

"'Tis just a scratch," Jamie told her. Then he turned his gaze to Mhairi. "I expect ye'll have nay more trouble from this man. But if ye do, and I hear of it, he kens what will happen to him." With that, Jamie did as she bade and dumped Rory behind their home, not surprised to find that area as tidy and well-kept as the front. Mhairi did not deserve a man like Rory.

Aftyn repeated that she wanted to stay with Mhairi until Rory woke up, but Jamie dismissed that idea and took her arm to encourage her out. Aftyn objected, but Mhairi told her to go, which might be the only reason Jamie wasn't doubled over from a punch to his privates.

In apology, he escorted her to the public room for an ale. "I didna want ye there when he wakes, in case he blames ye. Let him try anything and I'll be nearby. All she has to do is scream, or send her lad running to the keep."

"I dinna think she'll need to send the lad," Aftyn said. She'd seemed nervous when he led her to the public room, but was calmer now that they were settled at a table, ales in hand. "Alastair."

"Who is Alastair?"

"The lad's name. Rory would not let either of them speak it."

Jamie shook his head. "I've never heard of such."

"Nor I, but he terrorized them into complying. Alasdair has been 'the lad' so long, I wonder if he recalls his own name."

7

An hour later, Aftyn looked up from the pot she was stirring when she heard Jamie's "ach." He was bent over her mother's journal on the table across the herbal, and apparently something frustrated him. "Can I help?"

He shook his head. "Nay lass. I thought I had one symbol solved, but when I find the same notation in other remedies, it canna be what I first thought it was." He rubbed his chin, but never looked up.

She nodded, knowing he wouldn't see her, but urging him on in spirit. Jamie had made so many things better in a few short days. She appreciated his help with Mhairi, and hoped the lesson he gave her husband stuck so that both Mhairi and Alastair had a better life. From what she'd seen today, theirs couldn't get much worse.

He'd saved Niall, and now, he was straining his eyes and, probably his back, the way he slumped over the journal in concentration. But if he could take her mother's journal from a source of frustration and tears to something useful, she could build on what she found there. And pass her knowledge on to others.

"Ach, that's what ye mean," he muttered to himself, and straightened up from where he bent over the journal. "Another symbol sorted," he announced to her with a smile.

She moved to his side and looked where he indicated. He'd drawn the symbol her mother used and identified it, then listed several uses for the plant it represented. "Another mystery solved," she said. "Ye must ken how grateful I am. Yer notes will make it possible for me to become the healer I would have been had mother lived."

Jamie took her hand in his. "Yer mother still lives in her journal."

Aftyn's throat closed and she clung to that sentiment. "Ye are right," she choked out. "My best memories of her are wrapped up in the care she gave the sick and injured."

"She meant her journal to preserve her methods," Jamie told her. "We just have to understand it." He stroked the back of her hand with his thumb.

Aftyn suddenly realized other than Niall, she had never seen Jamie willingly touch another person's skin.

His kindness warmed Aftyn to her bones, but his touch heated her in an entirely different way.

He'd been harsh with her when they first met, but he'd been right. She'd had no business treating Niall. In retrospect, she could admit that just because she was good with stitches did not mean she was competent to cut off his leg and keep him from bleeding to death. "I owe ye and Niall an apology," she said, reluctantly pulling her hand from his and crossing her arms. This was so hard. Her future might depend on whether Jamie accepted her apology. "I should never have thought to remove his leg. It was foolish of me to contemplate it. And dangerous. I wanted to save him, but I could have killed him with my ignorance." She shuddered at the idea of what might have happened had his companions not been able to argue against her plan, and leave Fearchar there to protect him from her.

"Ye meant well, lass. I see that now. I'm sorry too, that I was so angry with ye. I didna ken..."

"Nay, ye were right." She interrupted him, not wanting to discuss what he didn't know about her situation, for that could lead to even more revelations she did not wish to make. "I never should have been so hot-headed with ye the first night. I kenned what it cost Rabbie to bring ye so quickly, and that ye had to be wrung out before ye even started to treat Niall. I... my anger was inexcusable."

"Mine, too, lass."

"And I want ye to ken how grateful I am to ye. I have come so far with yer help, yer guidance. Ye will leave me a much better healer than when ye arrived."

Jamie had worked miracles, and the thought made her brow crease. She still did not know what he'd done to Niall's wound for it to improve so rapidly.

There was so much to learn, and so little time before Jamie left. The task before her might as well have been a mountain, reaching to the sky, steep and impossible to climb. She'd never scale it. No one could learn all she needed to know in time.

"What fashes ye, lass?"

Jamie must have noticed the dismay on her face. "Nought," she lied, then thought better of it. She might wish he would stay longer, but her father's threat still hung over her head. "There's so much I dinna ken. How ye saved Niall's leg, for one."

"Ye saw the tissue I cut away. It would never heal the way it was. Each day, several times a day, I rinse the wound with a weak vinegar solution."

"I smelled whisky, too."

"Only at first, and only while Niall remained passed out. It... burns. Vinegar does much the same with less pain."

"What else?"

"The poultice ye ken. Yers was too old and the wound track too contaminated with lichen and soil from the forest. Dry as much of these," he said, waving at the bunches hanging along the wall, "as ye can, then use them as ye need. Some of these preparations will keep for a few weeks, some longer, some only a short time. I'm writing down everything for ye, including a new one I want for Niall."

With Jamie's notes, she could use her mother's journal as it had been intended. She would always have the pages he wrote for her, his handwriting a constant reminder of their time together. But she wouldn't have *him*. She would miss him. She turned away to fuss with a bunch of herbs, hiding her face from him. Surely her expression would reveal her sense of loss.

"Now, I have a question for ye," Jamie continued, clearly unaware of the path Aftyn's thoughts had taken. "Can wee Alastair be found, do ye think? I would like to be certain he has no wounds or broken bones suffered at Rory's hands. The lad is quick and may be unhurt, but I'd like to ken that before I leave."

"I'll send Neve to find him." Aftyn's heart swelled that Jamie would care about the wee lad, but the thought of Jamie leaving made her chest ache. "If he isna home with Mhairi, someone will ken where he bides."

"Good. Are there others in the village ye wish me to see? Those who havenae gotten better after days or weeks of care? Ye ken the laird asked me to help ye with such while I am here."

Aftyn frowned. She wasn't surprised at that news, but it hurt, all the same. Jamie must have noticed her reaction.

"Ye didna ken?"

"Nay." She couldn't tell him why it bothered her. Still, as much as she hated to admit it, even to herself, her father was right. They should take advantage of Jamie's expertise while he was here. And she knew whom she wanted him to see first.

"There's a woman with a wasting disease. She's terribly ill. Lately, she's started having trouble breathing. I fear she will not survive much longer, but perhaps if ye could do something for her, or at least make her passing easier…"

Jamie frowned. "I will see her, and do what I can for her, but I will no' kill her."

"Nay! 'Tis no' what I meant." Of course, he wouldn't. He had too much compassion to take a lass's life. "If ye think she canna be cured, then if ye can make her comfortable, make a preparation I can use to dull her pain, help her breathe, something, until she leaves us. Her husband has suffered along with her. For his sake, and for hers, to ease her suffering would be a blessing."

"Where is she?"

"The farm is on the far side of the village and up the hill. 'Tis a good walk from the keep."

"Then we will go in the morning to see her."

"Do ye want to see Alastair first?"

"Aye. If he's been harmed, I dinna want the lad to suffer, either."

And there, she thought, was Jamie—the Jamie she was coming to know. Caring for women and children came as naturally to him as curbing a bully's worst impulses. The healer and the warrior. She'd seen both, and both impressed her.

Niall was asleep when Jamie finally got to his chamber. Neve nodded in her chair and Jamie hated to wake her, but he needed to tend to Niall before he could sleep, and he could not do what he needed to do with her there.

"Lass," he whispered. "'Tis been a long day. Go to yer rest."

Neve blinked and covered a yawn with one hand. "Will ye also? Ye need to rest as well."

"Aye. I'll be here only a wee while, then Rabbie will stay with Niall through the night. Ye and Aftyn will be busy in the herbal tomorrow. I left notes for several of her mother's potions for ye to make. But first, Aftyn wants ye to find Alastair in the morning, so we can be certain he's taken nay harm."

Neve, nodded, stood, and softly bid him goodnight as she closed the chamber door behind her.

"She's been taking good care of me," Niall said, surprising Jamie.

"I thought ye slept."

"Nay, only feigned sleep since Neve expected it."

"She's a good lass."

"Aftyn, too." Niall narrowed his eyes. "I heard what ye said about her the night ye arrived."

"Did ye also hear she nearly killed ye? Rabbie got to the Aerie and back with me just in time."

"Aye, and thank ye for saving me from that," he added on a shudder, then he shrugged. "Ye also ken she stayed with me..."

"I do. The lass has a big heart. She did the best she kenned to do." And touching her hand, earlier had soothed both her and him, but hadn't brought out his healing response. What would happen if he did more, like kiss her? He'd often wondered if the arousal he felt with other lasses was the same as his battle fury, suppressing his healing response. Not wanting to hear how she might know the answer, he'd never discussed it with his mother.

He pulled his attention back to Niall. "But now, 'tis time for me to do more for ye. Ye have had food and drink aplenty today?"

"I have."

"Good. Ye will need the strength that gives ye. Tomorrow, yer wound will be bound, and ye will walk—with a cane. 'Twill help ye regain yer strength and get us all home faster. But 'twill no' be easy to bear."

"I'll do it." Being bed-ridden frustrated Niall, as it would any man.

"I ken ye will. Now, settle yerself. Sleep," Jamie added and placed a hand on Niall's forehead, encouraging his body into a healing sleep that would let him remain unaware of any pain that came with what Jamie did to him. Soon, Jamie saw that he was deeply asleep. He moved to Niall's leg and laid his hands on either side of the wound trench, reaching slowly and carefully into the deepest recess of flesh, encouraging tissue growth and blood where he needed it to form. His own leg ached abominably, shot through with hot stinging that felt like being stabbed with embroidery needles, thousands of them. He fought to ignore the agony and kept his focus on Niall, whose heart beat faster as Jamie taxed his body's reserves. The tingling warmth in Jamie's hands became a pulling sensation long before new, pink flesh began to form in the bottom of the trench.

Layer upon layer, he helped Niall's body rebuild the calf. Jamie shook with fatigue by the time he finished and rewrapped the wound.

He rubbed his own leg, trying to ease suddenly stabbing cramps. If he stood to walk off the pain, it would fade away faster, but for the moment, it crippled him. Finally, he forced himself to his feet and limped to the door.

Bhaltair stood outside. "Neve told me ye were with him. What do ye need?"

"Some mead, I think. Then I'll sleep. Guard him and dinna let anyone remove the wrapping."

"Sit by the fire afore ye fall down. I'll be back in moments."

Jamie nodded, closed the door and did as Bhaltair bid. He rubbed his leg with both hands, resentment flaring up in him again that this talent, as his mother called it, carried such a heavy price for its wielder. And she wondered why he preferred fighting to this.

A few hours' sleep would improve his outlook, and tomorrow, he'd visit the villager Aftyn had described, treat Niall again, then, if he wasn't too spent, continue to help her with the journal.

He found himself looking forward to seeing her, wishing she was here. He indulged in imagining her kneeling before him, rubbing his leg. Thinking about where that could lead took his mind off the pain.

The door opened, breaking into his thoughts. Rabbie entered, followed by Fearchar and Bhaltair, with a tray of cups and a jug of mead.

"When will he be ready to travel?" Fearchar asked quietly, as he filled the cups and handed them around.

"I told the laird a sennight, but Niall might be strong enough to go a day sooner. I'll do more with the wound tomorrow, but 'tis nearly healed and must stay covered the rest of the time we are here. No one can see it. Especially not Aftyn and Neve."

They all nodded, understanding what consternation its rapid healing would cause.

"He must start walking with a cane on the morrow," Jamie continued after emptying his cup, "so that he begins to regain his strength."

"What about Aftyn?" Bhaltair crossed his arms, cup in one hand.

"What about her?"

"How much will ye be able to help her before we go? Or will she come with us?"

Jamie tensed and shook his head. The thought of leaving her stung. "She willna leave her home. But her mother left a journal. 'Tis hard to read if ye dinna already ken most of the cures she describes. From the notes I give her, Aftyn will be able to continue learning from it even after we're gone."

"Neve, too?" Rabbie asked.

"Neve, too," Jamie assured him. "We will leave them better off than when we arrived."

His friends seemed satisfied with that, tossed off the rest of their drinks and filed out, all but Bhaltair.

"Wake me if he seems in any difficulty," Jamie told him.

"I will. Now go. Ye need rest, too."

Jamie nodded. "I ken it," he said as he limped to the door. The pain in his leg was less, but still hobbled him. "We willna be here much longer."

"Ye ken Niall has his eye on Neve, but so does Rabbie. And she's not encouraging either of them."

"We'll be gone before it becomes a problem between them," Jamie told him, hoping he was right.

Bhaltair frowned at that, but Jamie didn't stop to ask why. He went to their shared chamber and fell into the cot, asleep immediately.

THE NEXT MORNING, Neve entered the herbal with Alastair clinging to her skirts and looking around wide-eyed. He seemed entranced to be in the keep until he spotted Jamie. Immediately, he tried to run back the way he'd come, but Neve got a grip on his arm and held him in place. "Wheesht, laddie. Ye'll come to nay harm here."

"But the healer is here."

"Aye, I am," Jamie said from his perch at one of the workbenches where he was transcribing from Aftyn's mother's journal. He set it aside and knelt before the lad. "Ye came to me yesterday to help yer ma. Do ye remember?"

"Aye."

"And did I help her?"

"Aye, ye and Aftyn."

"Exactly." Though in truth, Aftyn had been the most help to

Mhairi. Jamie had been pleased to see her sitting, eating, and with the will to have him dump her abusive husband behind their cottage. "I'll see that ye are nay harmed."

"As will I," Aftyn added, coming up on Jamie's other side.

"I'll go fetch ye something to eat," Neve volunteered. "Would ye like that?'

"Aye," Alastair replied, vigorously nodding his head. "We've never enough to eat."

Jamie bit back a curse. "We'll see to that, too, lad," he promised. Alastair was a growing lad and needed good food in plenty, as did his mother.

"I'll see what Cook has ready and bring up a tray," Neve said, directing her gaze and the comment to Aftyn.

"Thank ye," Aftyn told her. "That will make our wee friend feel welcome, aye, Alastair?" She placed a hand on his thin shoulder.

Alastair looked up at her with adoration. "Aye." After a pause, he added, "Thank ye."

Neve gifted him with a smile and left the herbal.

"Ye have fine manners, young Alastair," Jamie told him, thinking after all the time the lad had been without a name, the more he heard it here, the more confident he might become.

"Thank ye, healer."

"Come," Aftyn said, pointing to a high stool. "Let's sit ye there and have a look at ye. Can ye do that? 'Tis a very high seat."

"I can do it," Alastair insisted, and proved it by climbing up and settling himself like a king.

"Good lad," Jamie told him and under cover of studying his eyes, put his hand on the boy's neck, out of Aftyn's sight. He sensed only minor bruising on his torso such as any young lad might acquire on his own, already healing. No broken bones, current or past. The lad had apparently been adept at avoiding his tormentor.

Aftyn joined Jamie and held out her hand. "Let me see yer arms, please, Alastair."

The lad held out both hands, arms extended. She pushed up his sleeves and pursed her lips, then pulled them down again. "Old bruises. Did Rory do that to ye?"

Alastair shrugged and looked aside.

"Ye needna fash," she told him. "Do they hurt?"

"Nay. They're nearly gone."

Jamie caught Aftyn's gaze and nodded. "That's good, Alastair. How's yer tummy?"

"Empty!"

Aftyn laughed and after a moment, both Alastair and Jamie joined her. Jamie's gaze went to Aftyn as she laughed. Musical and sweet, he would never tire of hearing that sound, or seeing her mirth reflected in her gaze, replacing the sadness that so often filled her.

"We'll soon fix that," Jamie said. "Neve will return with plenty to eat. In the meantime, can I see yer feet?"

"They're right there, at the end of my legs," Alastair told him with a cheeky grin.

Ach, good. The lad was responding to them both and showing more personality than Jamie had yet seen. Jamie reached down, grabbed both feet, and pulled off his soft boots. "I see. Shall I set them aside for ye or do ye like them where they are?"

"Where they are!" Alastair looked worried, but his reaction gave Jamie the few seconds he needed to pay attention to the lad's legs and feet. To Jamie's relief, he was unharmed.

Aftyn laughed again, reassuring Alastair, and Jamie released his feet. "I'm with ye, lad. I like them where they are, too."

"Why do ye have flowers in here?" Alastair asked, then turned his gaze to Jamie. "Are ye courting Aftyn?"

Aftyn choked, but covered her expression behind her hand.

Jamie just shrugged, though his pulse kicked up at the thought. If he was, it was a most unusual courtship, since most of what he'd done for her involved her mother's journal. He'd yet to kiss her. And though he'd held her in his dreams, in reality he'd barely held her hand.

"They'll become potions to make ye feel better if ye fall ill," Aftyn answered when Jamie failed to speak.

He noticed she carefully avoided looking at him, and color was fading from her cheeks. Had the lad's question embarrassed her, or was something else behind her reaction? Could she be interested in him, too?

"Flowers? Truly?"

Alastair was full of questions today.

"And those plants, and those bunches hanging by the window, too," Aftyn pointed out.

"What are they?"

"My, ye ask excellent questions, Alastair," Jamie told him with a grin. He wanted to say the lad's name as often as he could so the lad would know he mattered as a person. Then footsteps out in the hall alerted him. "And here comes Neve, I think. Are ye still hungry?" Like any growing lad, he was probably excited at the prospect of food arriving soon.

"Aye!" Alastair was emphatic on that point, questions forgotten for the moment, as Neve entered with a tray laden with bread and sliced venison, cheese, apples, and honey cakes.

"Cook thinks ye should eat as much of this as ye wish," Neve announced as she set down the tray on an empty table. "How does that sound?"

Alastair's eyes widened. "All of that is for me?"

Aftyn looked ready to tear up, her face flushed and her eyes glossy, so Jamie jumped in. "Aye, all of it. But if ye get full before 'tis gone, dinna fash. Ye can take what's left home to yer ma." That might prevent the tummy ache Jamie saw in the lad's future if he tried to empty the tray.

Alastair nodded. "Then I willna eat all of it."

Behind Alastair and Neve's back, Aftyn gave Jamie a grateful smile. He savored it, holding her gaze as long as she was willing. She lifted a hand to her heart, then turned her gaze back to Alastair. It took Jamie a moment to break the spell. What had her gesture meant?

Neve was slicing an apple for the lad, but he went immediately for the honey cake. Jamie couldn't blame him. They smelled buttery, sweet, and delicious. He might have to visit Cook himself once Alastair headed home.

Aftyn went to the lad's other side and encouraged him to try the meat, then spread a bite of bread thick with butter and folded a thin slice of venison and another of apple on top. Alastair's eyes lit up after he took a bite, but his mouth was too full to comment.

Aftyn had a gentle touch with the lad, and it was good to see his wariness around adults melt away under her tender care. Despite their rough beginning, it was now clear to Jamie that Aftyn had potential as a healer. How she dealt with Niall, with Alastair, and her other patients reminded him of his mother's compassion for those she helped. Aftyn could learn the medicines, blades, and stitches, but her empathy came from within.

8

"What are ye doin' to me wife?"

Jamie straightened at the husband's sudden appearance in the croft's doorway. Startled by his outraged demand, for it was surely a demand and not a question, he lifted his hands away from the woman's diseased breasts and stepped back. The man's echo of Mhairi's husband's challenge when he arrived home urged Jamie to rest one hand on the pommel of his dirk. He fought it. He hadn't actually been touching her, though it was clear that distinction had escaped the irate highlander now moving toward him with a murderous gleam in his eye.

While he took measure of the man's height and weight, Jamie told him, "I'm a healer," and gestured toward the typical healer's kit of small pots and packets of dried herbs he'd set out on a nearby table when he arrived.

"Who sent ye here?" The man stopped just out of arm's reach, fists clenched.

Jamie eyed him, not letting down his guard. Big and angry, the husband would be a challenge to subdue in Jamie's depleted condition.

The exhaustion that accompanied each healing session varied depending on its intensity and length, and this one had been extraordinarily difficult. He'd stopped to rest and was stepping away from her as her husband burst in.

Jamie had never seen anything like this woman's condition. He now had a tangible reason to regret spurning his mother's pleas that he accompany her when she went to deal with "women's complaints." She might recognize the wild growth. It had taken over one breast and spread like mold to the other, and into the woman's lungs, causing her body and spirit to waste away. He'd done what little he could to attack the invader, but it wasn't enough. He knew the basic anatomy of a woman's body better than most men, no matter how sexually experienced they were, but this went much deeper. He feared doing more harm than good, and dismay compounded his exhaustion that he hadn't been able to save her life. All the more reason he did not want to harm her husband. She'd need his care, rest, and good food if she was to have a brief respite from the trauma of her illness.

"Aftyn sent me," he told the man. "She meant to come with me but was called to tend to someone else. She said yer wife was very ill. She was right."

Her pain still tormented his own chest. He was having trouble breathing, and prayed the husband didn't notice or he'd jump to the wrong conclusion. Jamie was in no condition to fight a man who thought he'd assaulted his dying wife.

"Aftyn sent a strange man to my wife?"

Where were Bhaltair and their horses? "She's seen yer wife many times but said that she wasn't getting better. She trusted me to try to help." Would the man stop frothing at the mouth long enough to notice the simple robe Jamie wore over trews— though the effect was somewhat spoiled by the dirk slung at his hip and the claymore on his horse, outside.

"Aye? Are ye from the abbey?"

"Nay."

"Well, then, I dinna trust ye. What kind of healer carries a sword?"

Again a demand, not a question. Jamie shrugged, then regretted it when a phantom dirk knifed him in the chest, the residue of what he'd been doing when the husband burst in. How did she stand it? He took a moment before responding, hoping the pain would quickly subside, gathering strength to answer the man. "A healer who often travels through unfriendly glens." If Aftyn hadn't warned him how sick Robena was, he would have walked from the village. Instead, he rode and brought food, drink, and weapons, all of which, except the dirk and the sgian dubh in his boot, remained with the horses Bhaltair attended. "I was a warrior, once," he said, stronger. "When needful, I can be again." He paused to let that sink in.

It didn't.

"Let's see if ye can fight as fast as ye talk outa that mouth of yers," the man challenged and raised his fists. "Step outside. I can take ye. I'll no have ye harming my lass." He backed toward the door, never taking his gaze from Jamie.

Resigned, Jamie moved to follow him.

"Colin, wheesht!" The woman's weak voice stopped her husband in mid-stride.

"Robena? Ye have breath to speak?" He pivoted away from Jamie and knelt by his wife's bedside.

Forgotten for the moment, Jamie watched as the man took her hand and stroked it.

"A wee," she replied, her voice stronger. "The healer helped... ye must no' threaten him."

"What was he doin' to ye when I came in?"

Jamie suspected the man had cause to be jealous. Despite her dire condition, Robena was still a lovely woman, though pale and with threads of premature gray streaking her dark hair. She must have been radiant before succumbing to her illness, attracting the eye of every male in the region. Perhaps, with Jamie's help and some time to regain her strength, she could be again.

"I dinna ken," she told her husband, then smiled at Jamie, "but see?" She took a breath.

To Jamie's eye, she still struggled, but her husband apparently believed her.

Colin glanced around at Jamie and shrugged one shoulder. "Ye have my apology, if ye'll accept it."

"Of course," Jamie told him with a slight nod, his face impassive. Now that the tension had abated, fatigue washed through him like a wave, nearly taking his knees out from under him. He fought to stay on his feet and to answer Colin's questions. A hot meal, a pitcher or two of ale, and a long sleep were what he needed.

Why hadn't Bhaltair stopped the husband from coming in?

He gathered his kit and dispensed his last bit of advice before he escaped to care for himself. "I've done all I can today, Robena." He took a chance and touched her head in full view of Colin's suspicious gaze. "Rest now," he said as he took a moment in what to the husband would look like silent prayer and laid a healing sleep on her. "I'm sure Colin will take good care of ye until ye are again able to do for yerself." He hoped, though he hadn't saved her, at least he had given her a little more time. And if he could treat her again, he might do better. He lifted his hand and turned his attention to the husband whose gaze was fixed on his wife's face. "She will sleep until tomorrow morning. See that she rests as much as she needs." He offered a vial he'd set aside from his pack. "Give her a wee sip of this each evening to help her sleep. Only a sip, mind ye." When Colin accepted it, Jamie continued, "And feed her well, as much as she will eat on her own. Then convince her to take another bite or two. She's lost a great deal of her strength. Food, cider, and mead will help her. Let her rise and work if she is able, but do not push her beyond her wishes or it will be harder for her to recover—if at all." Jamie hated saying the words, but her husband needed to prepare himself.

Colin blanched, but nodded dismissal and turned back to the woman whose life Jamie tried to save. He wasn't used to this kind of illness, this sense of ignorance and failure. He never wanted to experience anything like losing his friend on the battlefield again. But not being able to cure Robena filled him with even more guilt. If he'd listened to his mother—his teacher—and accepted her precept that all knowledge was good for a healer to have at her or his command, he might not be leaving here with the weight of Robena's suffering on his shoulders.

He backed toward the door and left the croft. He didn't see Bhaltair or their mounts. He must have moved them behind the cottage. Pausing outside the door, he sucked in air that, though damp and chill, tasted like wine after the interior's sickbed stench.

To his very great surprise, the door opened behind him and Colin stepped out.

"I dinna ken how to repay ye," he began.

Jamie waved him off, knowing full well what came next. "Ye must save yer coin for yer wife's needs."

"Aye." Colin ran one strong hand through his graying hair and pushed it back from his forehead. He held out his other hand, gaze on his palm. "But she would want to spare at least this. It might buy ye a meal at the post house yonder in the village." He looked up and met Jamie's gaze. "Go with my thanks. Robena... well, I dinna ken what I'd do without her."

Jamie accepted the two coins Colin offered in the spirit the man intended, with honor. He could not spurn a gift so hard-won and so meaningful to the giver. "I will inquire, thank ye. And I hope ye never have to find out. She seems a good wife to ye. I will return in a day or two to see how she is."

Colin gave a gruff nod, eyes downcast as though his thoughts had already returned to her impending death rather than the glimmer of hope Jamie had tried to give her. He pivoted on one heel and went back inside.

Jamie studied the coins in his palm. Though twice nearly nothing was still nearly nothing, it might pay for a meal at a croft or pub on the way home. He tucked away the coins and used his last bit of strength to call out for Bhaltair, who appeared in moments, leading their mounts, a package of food in one hand. With a meal and some rest, Jamie would recover his strength by morning. If only he could say the same for his patient.

BHALTAIR LAUGHED as Jamie described Colin bursting in and demanding to know what Jamie was doing to his wife. The ride back to the keep didn't give him much time to relate how the encounter had gone. "Why did ye no' keep him out?"

"Of his own home? Aye, I suppose I couldha spun a tale to keep him entertained while ye sneaked out the back." He snorted. "But then, I'd have no explanation for why I was there with two mounts, now would I?"

"We thought the husband would be out in the fields, no' coming home for a midday meal," Jamie allowed, his breathing easing the farther they rode from the croft.

"It didna matter in the end," Jamie said, his gaze on the hills in the distance, beyond the village, his chest still burning and his belly in knots. That way lay home, and perhaps help for Robena's wasting sickness.

"What do ye mean?" Bhaltair frowned.

Jamie shrugged. "I couldna help her. She's dying. In agony. And I could only delay it and ease her pain for a time. My arrogance..." He shook his head, regret in every wasted moment of the last eighteen months. "With more time—but I doubt it. Perhaps only someone with the Lathan Healer's skill and experience could save her."

"One of us could fetch her as Rabbie fetched ye."

"Nay. I'll no' risk my mother until we ken more about what the Keith is likely to do. I believe I bought Robena some time. If she survives so long, Aileanna can come then."

They rode through the Keith gates and gave their mounts to the stable lad.

Bhaltair glanced at the sky. "Ye should rest until the evening meal."

"Nay, I'll check on Niall first. I havena finished all he needs me to do."

"It sounds as though ye have done enough for one day," Bhaltair said as he opened the door into the keep.

Jamie followed him in. He was nearly asleep on his feet, but he'd neglected Niall today. Had Aftyn been in to care for him yet? Jamie hadn't seen her all day, either.

He led Bhaltair up the stairs to Niall's chamber. Niall sat by the fire, reading. Once Bhaltair closed the door, Niall stood.

"Have ye been walking today?" Jamie studied his face. His color was good and he seemed comfortable standing.

"Aye, and with a cane, as ye said."

"Good." He gestured Niall to the bed and unwound the bandage covering his calf. "I want to do a little more now, and again tomorrow. After that, ye will be able to ride to the Aerie."

"Two more days?"

"I thought it would take most of a week, but ye are healing well. When did ye last eat?"

"An hour ago. Fearchar brought enough for all of us." He gestured at the tray on the bedside table. "Help yerself if ye want."

Jamie nodded. "Keep on as ye have and we'll be free of this place sooner than I hoped." Sooner than he'd promised the

Keith, but if Niall could ride, they should go. Jamie didn't like the impression the Keith gave him, nor his neglect of Aftyn. He made it impossible for her to succeed. Jamie couldn't imagine why, but the man seemed avaricious—and any laird could be dangerous given the right incentive. His clan needed a competent healer, but Jamie would not be it. Aftyn, suitably trained, or someone else, would have to satisfy the man.

He moved to the tray and sampled the cheese, then cut a slab and put it on a slice of bread. Bhaltair poured cups of ale and passed them around. They ate in companionable silence. Finally, Jamie felt recovered enough to help Niall. This, at least, he knew how to do.

Niall lay back with his head on his hands. "Do yer worst," he jested.

Jamie's belly clenched. He'd done that already today, for Robena. Niall's wound was child's play in comparison. He shoved the despair to the side and put Niall into a light sleep, then placed his hands on either side of Niall's wound, closed his eyes and pictured blood and tissue forming where there was none, filling the wound track with healthy new muscle and skin. His leg ached, then pinched and burned as Niall's wound changed under Jamie's hands. He took his time, ignoring his pain. They were all eager to get home. The sooner he could make Niall ready for the trip, the sooner they'd leave.

Finally, he sat back and sighed, then reached down and rubbed his own calf. Bhaltair handed him a cup and he drank, not caring what was in it. More ale. As depleted as he was, it tasted as sweet as cider. He held out the cup for more and drank that down, too.

Then he woke Niall and wrapped his leg. "Dinna scratch it," Jamie warned. "I'll no' have ye damaging it."

Niall nodded and accepted a cup from Bhaltair. "I willna. I want to be ready to ride the day after tomorrow."

"Walk as much as ye can with the cane tomorrow and we'll see. And dinna let anyone unwrap it."

"Anyone like Aftyn or Neve?"

"Aye. I'm for bed for a few hours," he added and handed the cup back to Bhaltair. "I'll check on ye later."

"Aftyn, where are ye?"

Neve's voice echoed down the hall and jolted Aftyn from the doze she'd fallen into over the herbs she'd been sorting. After an eventful night, she was too wound up to sleep, and returned to the herbal to begin the work she'd planned for the day. She'd missed seeing Jamie yesterday. Their paths had not crossed, even at meals. She couldn't tell whether he'd spent time with her mother's journal yesterday while she was away from the herbal. The table where he worked on it seemed undisturbed. If he'd been here but frustrated in his attempt, there would be no new notes.

She blinked and glanced down to reassure herself she hadn't mixed up any of the herbs she'd divided, ready to be bound and hung to dry or steeped in hot water for teas and tisanes. The herbs that doubled as culinary flavorings were nearest to her, ready to flavor medicines, such as the mint she'd used in steam to help Braden breathe through one of his attacks. But Jamie had given them so much, she'd give some to Cook.

The deadliest, such as black nightshade and foxglove, lay nearest the wall, covered with coarse linen against prying eyes and fingers. Nothing had been disturbed. She sighed and slid off the wooden stool she'd perched on when she began her work. She needed a good night's sleep to recover from delivering Kayla's wee bairn just before the sun rose. She stretched her arms above her head in an attempt to wake herself, then strode to the door and peeked out.

"I'm here," she called back, just as her friend rounded the corner, dark hair flying around her head and covering her face, so fast had she moved. Aftyn put a hand over her mouth to stifle a laugh and stepped back into her workspace.

"What took ye so long to answer me?" Neve demanded as she entered, still shoving her errant strands back behind her shoulders.

Aftyn gestured at the table. "I was working and didna hear ye. Where have ye been?

"In the village. Mhairi was glad of the food ye sent. Rory wasna there, but she said he's been... polite... since Jamie talked to him."

"Good. So why are ye in such a rush? Is there more news?"

"Ach, aye. I stopped by the post house to visit a friend. Ye will want to hear this. Jamie tended to Robena yesterday. Can ye imagine? A male healer! And after all ye have done to help her! Colin told a mate of his who told the stable master. That's where I heard it. The whole glen is talking about it by now. I bet Agatha is in a fine temper."

"Ach, nay! I thought he spent yesterday with Niall. When I was called away to help Kayla, I asked him to wait to see Robena with me. Did Colin say how she is or what Jamie did to her?"

"I didna hear."

Aftyn gave her worktable a regret-filled glance. The tasks she'd planned to do this day would now have to wait. "I must go to her. He may have saved Niall," she said and clenched a fist in frustration. He was a better healer, aye. "But he doesna ken Robena," she said, finishing her thought aloud.

Neve pursed her lips. "Ye have been trying to save that woman's life for months, yet she still suffers. Perhaps he finally put her out of her misery. 'Twould be for the best."

.

Aftyn slashed her hand across the space between her and her friend. "Nay! Never say that. Robena doesna deserve to die."

"She hasna deserved the suffering she's borne, either, but that has been her lot."

"A lot I'm still trying to change." Aftyn muttered, moved to the cabinet of newly finished tinctures and potions she kept closed away from prying eyes, and pulled out what she thought she'd need to help Robena. She could only guess, not knowing what Jamie had done for her. She'd talk to him, aye, when she found him. In the meantime, she'd do her best to help the poor woman.

"Where is Jamie?"

"I dinna ken. If I see him, I'll tell him ye are looking for him, and where ye have gone." With that, Neve left.

When Aftyn finished filling her pouch, she closed the cabinet and grabbed her shawl. Once she saw Robena, she could come back by Kayla's cot and see how she and the bairn were doing today. Then she'd visit Neve and let her know what she'd found. Her friend would expect that, since she'd brought the news in the first place.

Colin was nowhere around when she arrived at the croft. Aftyn assumed he was working an outlying field, or off in the woods, hunting. She let herself in, pleased to see Robena sleeping and breathing easily, more deeply than Aftyn had observed in months. What had Jamie given her? Aftyn must find out, so she could continue to treat Robena, and others who might need similar care. She looked around for anything he might have left, and found a small bottle filled with a liquid that smelled pleasantly herbal, a blend she recognized as a common sleeping draught her mother taught her to make. Surely that was not all Jamie had used, but he must have taken everything else with him.

She settled at the croft's small table to rest before starting back to the village to visit the new mother and bairn. She hoped Robena would awaken while she was here, but did not want to disturb her to speak to her.

The door opening jolted her out of her second doze of the morning. She glanced toward Robena, still sleeping peacefully, and despite her tiredness, could not be jealous. Robena hadn't slept well in months. Then she turned toward the door. "Colin, come to check on yer wife?" She greeted him with a smile. "She seems better."

"'Tis a blessing," Colin told her, as he bent over Robena's sleeping form. "One I scarce deserve." He stood and turned back to Aftyn. "I nearly pummeled that healer ye sent, before my lass spoke to me." He turned his head to look back at his wife.

Aftyn could imagine Colin's surprise—and ire—at finding Jamie here alone. Yet—"She spoke?"

"She breathes better now. I'm ashamed, and thankful, too."

But how? "I'm thankful, as well, Colin." She stood and put a sympathetic hand on his shoulder. "Now ye are here, I'll leave ye to tend Robena and come back to check on her tomorrow. Ye will send for me if anything changes, aye?"

"No' the new healer?"

Pain lanced through Aftyn's chest. She pushed it aside. Jamie had done more for Robena in one day than she had in months. Of course, Colin would want him to attend his wife. "We wouldha come together, save for Kayla's bairn. She had a long day and night. The wee one came before the sun this morning." She covered a yawn, then added, "But we'll both come if ye need us."

9

The next morning, Aftyn dressed, gathered her cloak and a packet of supplies she might need, then went down to the great hall to break her fast. Once she finished, she planned to go back out to Robena's to see how she'd fared during the night. When she got back to the herbal, she'd intended to continue preparing the potions she needed to stock her shelves and be ready for new patients.

She was surprised to see Niall come carefully down the stairs between Rabbie and Fearchar. He gripped a cane in one hand that he used to limp to the nearest table and take a seat, relief evident on his face as he looked around. She went to him and placed a hand on his shoulder. "I'm so happy to see ye here," she told him.

"I, too," he answered with a smile. "I'm glad to see something besides those four walls. No' that I'm complaining, mind ye."

"Nay, ye would never do that," Rabbie teased, and Fearchar rolled his eyes.

"What will ye do today?" Niall asked, then added, "Now that ye dinna have to spend all yer time watching over me."

"I never minded that," she told him, sadness filling her at the lie. She'd minded thinking she'd have to cut off part of his leg. She'd minded watching him die in agony. But Niall didn't need to know that.

"I ken it, and I'm more grateful than ye can ken for all ye did for me."

"I'm glad Jamie got here when he did," she admitted, her throat tight. She cleared it, unable to bring herself to say how close he'd come under her care to dying. "I planned to check on ye later, but ye saved me the visit. I'm headed beyond the village to visit a woman under my care. Where is Jamie?"

"Down in the village. Ye might see him there. He said something about the promise he made to the laird."

Aftyn's stomach sank at the reminder of her father's opinion of her abilities, but she hid her dismay. The only assurance she had against her father's claim he would find someone to replace her was that Jamie fully intended to leave in a few days. "Well, then, I'll be off," she told them, returned to her seat to pick up her belongings, and headed out of the keep. Would she find Jamie as she walked through the village? She had told Robena's husband they would both come to see her today. But she passed through the village without a glimpse of him.

She needed to know what he'd done to Robena while he was there without her. She hadn't seen him since the evening before last. When she did, she'd get the answers she wanted.

She hoped the lovely morning was a sign that she'd find Robena well. The long walk gave her time to enjoy being out of the keep and by herself. And to remind herself that Jamie hadn't gone behind her back to care for Robena. He'd only done what he'd promised the laird. It wasn't her fault she hadn't been able to go with him.

When she entered the croft, Colin was already gone and Robena slept, still breathing more easily than she had in a fortnight. Relieved, Aftyn took a seat to rest for a while before heading back to the village to see Kayla and the new bairn. Watching Robena breathing made her happy, but before long, watching her sleep made her drowsy. She was about to get up and head back to the village when a noise outside alerted her just before the cottage door opened. "Colin?" Aftyn stood, expecting Robena's husband.

Instead, Agatha stepped in, followed by a tall, broad shape Aftyn knew well, silhouetted against the morning light streaming in the door. Jamie! He stepped farther into the room and shifted his stance as he took in the interior of the croft in one glance, then fastened his gaze on her.

She had no time to ask why he had come back here without her.

Agatha's eyes widened when she noticed Aftyn. "Ye! What have ye done to Robena? Is she breathing?" She took a step forward, then stopped and put a hand over her heart. "Or have ye finally killed her? Are ye waiting for poor Colin to come home so ye can revel in his grief?"

Agatha spat her hateful words so quickly that Aftyn had no chance to defend herself. "I came to check on my patient," she explained once Agatha stopped for breath.

"She's nay your patient. Colin said he's a better healer," Agatha added, gesturing at Jamie, who frowned down at her, then moved to Robena's bedside.

Jamie nodded at the bed, then frowned at Agatha. "Yer friend Robena still needs rest. Ye will wake her."

"'Tis good he's here to keep his eye on ye," Agatha continued, pitching her voice a little lower. "Ye can no longer kill her slowly with yer potions and spells."

Aftyn gasped. "Spells?" She did her best not to express her outrage in the volume of her voice. "I dinna use... I havena harmed her," she hissed. "I helped her..."

"Nay, ye havena. Ye let her suffer without doing anything to heal her," Agatha cut in and pointed at Jamie. "He's done more to help Robena in a day than ye have in all the months ye have tended her."

That reminded Aftyn of her most pressing question. "Indeed? And what did he do for her?" She moved her gaze from Agatha to Jamie, fighting to control the agitation that Agatha's presence always made her feel. "She still sleeps. What did ye give her?"

He hesitated, then answered, "My methods, and my medicines, are my own, lass. Ye ken that."

She glared at him for a moment, puzzled, then realized it was true. He hadn't given her anything of his. He'd spent his time making her mother's cures useful to her.

Regret filled his dark eyes, regret she didn't understand.

"I'm the healer to this keep and this village. Long after ye are gone, I'll still have the care of these people. If ye have something more effective than my medicines, my methods, I must ken. I've asked ye before. I'm asking again."

"Dinna listen to her," Agatha snarled. "She kens a wee from her dead ma, but she's no' a real healer."

"Agatha, I've told ye I am sorry for yer wee son, but nothing anyone could have done would have saved him."

Agatha blanched and dropped into a chair. "How dare ye mention my wee bairn? My only son." Her pallor didn't ease as the sheen of tears formed in her eyes. "My husband's only heir, and ye let him die." Suddenly her color came back, along with the wild accusations Aftyn had become accustomed to from her. "Have ye slowly poisoned Robena all this time? Did ye do the same to my bairn?"

Aftyn clenched her teeth. How could she answer such an allegation? It made her heart sore to hear it. "I would never harm anyone." She wanted to cringe, recalling what she'd considered doing to Niall, but she kept her expression impassive.

Jamie put a hand over hers, holding her still, then spoke to Agatha. "How was Robena when ye visited yesterday?"

Agatha cleared her throat, her expression changing from angry to abashed. "She was able to sit up in bed and eat some food I prepared for her. Colin returned home to find her there. He was overjoyed."

"Understandable."

"No thanks to—"

"Dinna say it," Jamie said, cutting her off before she could indulge her anger, leaving her sputtering. "Ye dinna ken what ails the poor lass. Aftyn did everything possible and kept her alive until I arrived."

Agatha sputtered. "I dinna..."

"Ye blame the healer unfairly for a tragedy no one could have prevented," Jamie said, cutting her off.

Agatha's gaze dropped to the floor. "I wish she'd saved my bairn instead of me."

Shocked, Aftyn spoke up. "Ye were never in danger. And the bairn's death had nought to do with ye, or his birth. He simply was no' strong enough to survive."

Aftyn had heard his heart stutter and stop. She'd tried but could not make it beat again. Agatha had lost two daughters to stillbirth. Perhaps the dashed hopes after the joy of a live birth —a son—had been more than anyone could bear. In any case, Aftyn stayed away from both Agatha and her husband, and hoped they never needed a healer again, because they would not accept her help. The day their son died, her future in the glen became tenuous at best, dangerous at worst. If people would not call on her, and she knew some who wouldn't, she remained on her father's sufferance, nothing more.

"What she says is true, Agatha," Jamie told her.

Agatha didn't look up. "How would ye ken? Ye were no' here."

The pain in her voice still tore at Aftyn.

Jamie answered her. "I've seen the like before, and I'm sorry for all ye have been through, but ye must no' blame this lass."

"Dinna tell me what I must no' do! I do blame her."

"Ye always have," Aftyn said, then wished she hadn't. Provoking Agatha was not wise.

"Get out of my sight," Agatha snarled.

"And does that apply to me, too?" Jamie asked, his voice remarkably calm.

"What? Nay, of course no'. Robena might still need ye."

"It does, Agatha. Ye canna see it for yer grief, but ye canna drive away one healer and expect to keep the other."

She crossed her arms and glared at them both. "Then I'm done with both of ye."

"But perhaps Robena isna."

Aftyn held her tongue, letting Jamie's tone of calm reason settle Agatha. Nothing she could say would make Agatha behave any better. She glanced at him for some indication of what he wanted to do.

"This is no place to argue what canna be changed," he said, his gaze on Agatha.

Agatha sniffed, stood, and marched out the door without a backward glance.

Aftyn thought to follow her, to try to explain yet again what had happened to her son. Agatha refused to hear that anything could be wrong with her strong husband's son.

"Are ye no' going to follow her?"

"I'd rather talk to ye. What potion did ye give Robena? She sleeps so long, so deeply. And she breathes after weeks and months of gasping for air when the mist rolls in and the air gets thick and heavy. Did ye give her aught for her pain?"

"I'd tell ye, lass, if I could, but 'tis aught learned from my mother and hers, and is no' mine to share. Ye must rely on all yer mother left ye."

Again, that look of pain pinching his forehead, hooding his

gaze. Did he lie? Or did he truly regret not being able to share his methods with her?

She needed Robena to wake so she could see for herself how much improved the woman was. And she needed Jamie to give up his secrets. She tried a different tack. "Why are ye here again without me? I asked ye to wait."

He glanced at the door as if wishing he could go on his way rather than answer her questions, but she wouldn't take her gaze from him as long as it held him pinned in place. She would use that regret she saw in his eyes against him, as she must.

"I intended to, but I had stopped into the post house and heard Agatha talking about seeing her friend." He nodded toward Robena. "I ken she's abrasive. And I feared she'd do something to upset her, so I introduced myself and came along."

Aftyn fought the urge to stamp her foot. "I need yer help, Jamie Lathan. Ye heard Agatha. She hates me. Her bairn's heart gave out within days of his birth. I could no' save him."

She wrung her hands, then gestured to the sleeping woman on the bed. "I've treated Robena for months, doing all I could to ease her pain, and when it became difficult for her, her breathing. If ye have truly helped her, I must ken how ye did it. She may need the like again in the future, after ye are gone. Others may need the like."

"Lass, I... canna." His jaw clenched as he avoided her gaze.

Aftyn knew she was begging, and she hated it, but she was not begging for herself, but for her fellow villagers. But nay, his expression was resolute. He would not. Aftyn broke eye contact. "Go on, then. I'll wait with Robena till she wakes."

"Nay, lass. Ye must go. Agatha is still out there."

"And I wish to see how Robena fares."

"Ye will. Perhaps tomorrow, without Agatha here to upset Robena."

She moved closer to the bed. "I worry for her. I should wake her."

"She will fare better if ye allow her to sleep and awaken when she is ready."

He'd used the one argument she had no answer for. She would not knowingly harm Robena or anyone else. She could not. She let her shoulders slump in defeat and huffed out a frustrated breath.

JAMIE'S CONSCIENCE niggled at him like a minnow on a hook. Helping these people was not helping Aftyn, yet he felt compelled to do whatever he could for them. How was he to know if he was supposed to help someone, or if death was their fate? He could only do his best and leave the rest to God.

For now, the stubborn lass was in his way, but perhaps not for long. He had used her empathy against her, and could see it working. She'd already canted her body toward the door.

He remained still and quiet, letting Aftyn's own inclinations propel her outside. Once the door shut behind her, he turned quickly to his patient and scanned her as he'd been taught, sensing the slow beat of her heart and the sluggish flow of blood through her veins, the air moving in and out of her lungs, searching for a way to destroy more of the contagion killing her. With Aftyn waiting outside, he didn't have much time, time Robena desperately needed him to spend with her. Time he needed to understand what was wrong with her and figure out how to treat it. He considered making a fast trip to the Aerie and back to consult with his mother. Aileanna would know whether Robena could be cured, and how, or whether the best anyone could do would be to make her comfortable and ease her passing.

Yet knowing Aftyn could never do what he could stopped him.

He knew better than anyone that Aftyn had fought a losing battle with Robena's illness. Nothing she could have done would have saved the lass. But he could not tell her that. He could not explain how he knew, or what he'd done to save her patient. That ability lay within him, an unprecedented gift from his mother. No herb, no potion she could concoct would ever do what he did, no matter how strong or often applied, how well intentioned its use.

His talent, his power, was something else entirely. He couldn't claim to understand it. But he used it. And he guarded it. As hard as it was to hear Aftyn's pleas, he had nothing to give her that would have helped her make a difference here.

But what would happen to her if Robena suddenly, miraculously improved? Would Agatha's accusation resonate within the village? Only two months earlier, the king had burned at the stake the Countess of Glamis for trying to poison him. Jamie had the misfortune of being nearby and saw the smoke roiling above the castle, heard the chanting and the screams. Those screams would inhabit his nightmares for the rest of his life.

If Agatha persisted in saying Aftyn had poisoned her bairn and Robena, it took little imagination to come to a very bad conclusion. Aftyn was in danger because of what he'd done. What she, through no fault of her own, would never be able to do.

Jamie could not leave her, perhaps not even once Niall was ready to travel. Somehow, he must fix this. Time was short. He'd only promised the Keith he'd remain for a week. By then, he must see Aftyn's reputation restored.

During that time, he'd continue to puzzle out her mother's journal and teach Aftyn as much herb lore as he could. He might learn from her, as well.

"Colin?"

Robena's voice startled Jamie out of his thoughts. He turned to her and smiled. Since she had been unconscious until her husband burst in the day before, likely she did not remember him. "Colin is working. I came to see how ye are feeling."

"Who are ye? What are ye doing? Colin? Colin!" Robena's voice gained strength and volume as her panic increased. She sat up and clutched the covers to her chest. "Colin!"

The door flew open and Aftyn ran in, Agatha on her heels. "Robena, ye are awake!"

"What's wrong?" Agatha turned her frown on Jamie as Aftyn dropped to her knees beside the bed and clutched Robena's hand in hers.

"All is well. This man is a healer. He's helped ye. He's made ye better."

"Where's Colin? Where's my husband?"

"Working the harvest," Aftyn told her. "He'll be along soon. He'll be glad to see ye awake."

"How long did I sleep? What did he do to me?" Her glance toward Jamie was accusing.

"How do ye feel, Robena?" Agatha asked.

Robena went silent for a moment, then took a breath and let it out slowly.

Aftyn's smile lit up the room. "See? Ye could no' do that for a fortnight before now."

Robena nodded, color blooming in her cheeks.

"How did ye do that?" Agatha frowned again at Jamie.

"Robena doesna remember me," Jamie said, pitching his voice low and soft to calm everyone, "and that is not unusual. Does her progress displease ye?" He counted on Agatha's temperament to help him avoid answering the question—in her eyes, he was the only legitimate healer in the croft.

"Of course no'. 'Tis a welcome surprise."

"Yer healer laid the groundwork, but it took time for

Robena to feel better. I simply carried on with what she started. And ye see the result. Ye are lucky to have her to care for yer village."

Agatha's suspicious gaze turned to Aftyn. "Indeed? She truly helped Robena? Then why did she no' help my bairn?"

Jamie suddenly knew the scope of his error. Agatha already believed Aftyn had deliberately let her heir die. By insisting Aftyn was as good a healer as Agatha believed him to be, he'd just confirmed Agatha's suspicions.

SOMETHING LIFTED the hairs on the back of Aftyn's neck. She glanced around. Jamie wore a stunned look, his eyes wide, as though he'd just realized something vitally important. She replayed in her mind what she'd overheard him say while her attention was focused on Robena.

Then her gaze shot to Agatha, who twisted her mouth into a satisfied smirk. *Ach, nay.* She fought the urge to rise and run for the door. It would do no good.

Agatha would not forget what he'd said. She'd make Aftyn's life hell for as long as it lasted. Which might not be much longer, if Agatha had her way.

"What's amiss?"

Robena's question pulled Aftyn's attention back to her. Robena had sensed the sudden rise in tension in the room and lifted up on to one elbow, but missed the reason for it. Aftyn cleared a suddenly dry throat and summoned the strength to answer Robena calmly. "Nought, lass. We're simply stunned at how well ye are, and happy, too. Aren't we, Agatha?" She turned her head so Robena couldn't see her expression and frowned at the woman, daring her to contradict what she'd said, and make Robena feel worse.

Agatha's gaze cut to Robena. Her smile looked forced to

Aftyn, but Robena accepted it as genuine and lay back on her pillow even before Agatha spoke.

"Indeed we are happy to see ye so much improved, my friend."

"I'll leave ye to make Robena more comfortable, and return to the keep," Jamie interjected into the silence that followed. "If I encounter Colin, I'll send him home."

"Thank ye," Robena murmured.

But her expression belied her confusion. Aftyn knew she had no idea what the healer had done to or for her, and suspected she wasn't certain how much gratitude she should convey.

As Jamie moved to the door, Aftyn debated following him. Agatha could help her friend bathe and change into clean clothes without Aftyn's assistance. A change of bedding would do the lass good, too. She feared what Agatha would say to her with Jamie out of the room, even more what Agatha would say to Robena once she left them alone. Perhaps she should stay to defend herself.

Jamie made the decision for her. "Aftyn, if ye could join me outside. I'd like to speak with ye."

"Of course." She took Robena's hand. "Agatha will see to ye until Colin returns home. I'll check on ye later."

"That will no' be necessary," Agatha told her with a sniff.

Aftyn frowned but didn't argue. A verbal battle with Agatha would not help Robena, nor would it change Agatha's mind. Instead, Aftyn followed Jamie out the door and closed it behind her.

He stood a few paces away, staring out over the glen, his back to her. She paused to study the way the sunlight glinted in his hair and made it bright with copper, then found herself transfixed by the breadth of his upper arms. He'd crossed them over his chest, which only widened his upper back as well. He spent years training and perhaps fighting to gain that physique.

His thighs, the overall length of his legs, braced apart in a solid stance, spoke of readiness, even willingness, to fight. If she ran headlong into his back, she doubted she could make him sway, much less fall.

Instead, she moved next to him, facing out as he did, then glanced sideways at him. His profile was a strong as the rest of him, his nose straight, high cheekbones betraying some Viking ancestry, and firm lips, not too full, not too thin. The shadow of a reddish beard colored his cheeks and neck. "What do ye wish to discuss?"

He cleared his throat and turned to face her. "I owe ye an apology."

"Aye?"

"I thought only to help ye. Instead, I made your difficulty with Agatha worse."

His admission surprised her. How many men would admit to any mistake, much less one that did not affect themselves? She nodded and kept her tone even. He did not deserve her ire. But he did need to know the consequences of his carelessness. "Aye. She thinks she heard ye confirm that I could have saved her bairn. She'll never forgive—or forget."

"How likely is she to cause trouble for ye?" He turned back to his study of the countryside.

Aftyn pressed her lips together, reluctant to give voice to her fears. But he'd compounded them, so she would tell him how badly. "More than she has already? Very likely. She was never certain, but she thought ye are a healer and I? I only pretended to be." How many ways could she embarrass herself?

He dropped his hands to his sides. "Is she dangerous?"

Aftyn noticed one hand rested on his dirk. "Do ye mean can she sway others in the village to do me harm? I've helped many, so I would like to hope not, but she and her husband, their post house and stables, are important to our village life."

"I could talk to her. Explain about a bairn's weak heart..."

Aftyn whirled, fists on hips, and glared at him, suddenly tired of trying to convince him to stay out of it. Tired of fighting Agatha. Just tired. "She willna hear ye any more than she listens to me. She doesna want to ken the truth. Ye will just make matters worse." She turned away and added the only thing she could think of that would shock him out of the path he seemed determined to be on, no matter how she objected. "Perhaps 'tis time for ye to take Niall home."

Out of the corner of her eye, she saw him shake his head.

"He is no' ready. And I canna leave ye to bear the brunt of my careless words."

He crossed his arms again and took a breath, as if coming to a decision.

"Ye could go with us when we leave."

"Go with ye?" She choked out a laugh, then sobered. "That is no' possible. My reputation would be ruined. Nay."

He shifted to face her. "Is death preferable to a risk to your reputation?"

"She will no' go so far."

"The king did, soon after midsummer. Did ye hear of it?" He dared not describe it to her. "Word of that execution is spreading. What the king does, others will do."

She shook her head. "The royal court is no' the same as this glen."

"Fear and hatred are the same everywhere." He reached out a hand and rested it on her shoulder, tightened his fingers but stopped short of tugging. "Come with me."

She gave his hand a sideways glance, pretending indifference. "Nay." In truth, his touch made her knees go weak and her heart fill with longing. The heat from his hand sizzled straight to her core, and its proximity to her breast made her wish he'd touch her there, or take her in his arms and kiss her. Foolish wishes.

He let go of her and turned back to the view of the glen as

his fingers curled into a fist. "Then to keep ye safe, I must stay. Rabbie and the others can see Niall safely home in a few days."

Really? He would stay for her? The image of being wrapped in his arms she'd had when she first saw him filled her mind again. She dismissed it. Dreaming about this man would not solve anything. "I thank ye for yer concern, but ye are needed at home. Ye said so."

He shrugged. "I'll go when Agatha no longer poses a threat to ye."

He was resolute. Where other men might leave her to her fate, he insisted on taking responsibility. She should be pleased to have the protection of such a man, but sadness filled her. No matter what she felt, the result would be the same.

She pivoted to face him this time and shook her head. "Then ye will never leave this glen."

10

J amie's blood chilled at Aftyn's words. They had the ring of prophesy, but he shook himself and started walking down the rough track into the glen. To warm his blood, he told himself, not because of anything the daft lass had said.

Daft, aye. But also strong, to dismiss his help when she could be in danger from Agatha's rantings.

Or overconfident. She was, after all, merely a lass, poorly trained to care for her people, but trying her best, and unable to defend herself if someone attacked her. Yet she was so much more. She filled his dreams with images of holding her, touching her, feeling her arms go around him and her body press against his, eager to return his kisses. His caresses. In the deepest part of the night, he sometimes dreamt of taking her to his bed, their clothes left on the floor, and making love to her. Those dreams left him hard, aching, and kicking himself for foolish yearnings. On other nights, not all of his imaginings were good.

He paused for a moment, listening for her footsteps following him in the springy ground. But also to force the image from his mind of Aftyn tied to a stake in the village's market square, flames rising around her as a mob chanted, "Burn, witch, burn" and she fought the scream tearing her throat. He had no gift of prophesy, thankfully, just a vivid imagination that helped him see what his talent revealed. The one gift he had gave him trouble enough.

He heard nothing behind him, and turned. Aftyn still stood where he'd left her, staring off into space, her expression unguarded. Worried, if the crease between her brows was to be believed. But not fearful. Not yet.

For a moment, he saw the flames lick around her again. He shook his head and started back up the hill. "Let me escort ye home, lass." It was the least he could do.

"I should check on Robena before I go." She actually took a step back toward the croft.

"Ye should leave her to Agatha for now," he told her. "She'll be better off the sooner everyone leaves her be and lets her rest."

"I could wait for Colin."

Jamie extended a hand. "Colin will see for himself how she fares. Ye dinna need to tell him. Come."

She eyed him, then shrugged, made her way the dozen steps he'd taken down the hill and reached him. Her hips, her stride, made him aware of the number of steps without counting them. Only when she stood just above him did he notice she gazed directly into his face, not up as most lasses did. She could be no more than a hand's width shorter than he.

His gaze fell to her lips, full and moist. Had she been kissed? Surely some man must have given in to the urge filling him now to touch them with his, to part them and explore her mouth's secret recess. To see if her cheek, her throat, tasted as creamy as they looked.

Her eyes, blue as spring bluebells, glinted as though she had a secret. What did she know, or think she knew?

He tried not to frown at the thought, but saw when Aftyn

noted the crease between his brows. Hers mirrored his. "What?"

Aftyn's troubles were compounded beyond anything she could imagine. But he could. He wished he had not been in Edinburgh that day.

Guilt made him press his lips together rather than seek oblivion in her kiss, as he wanted to do. "How long have ye lived here?"

"I was born here. My father fought with the king's men at Flodden Field. He was one of the few who survived that day. My mother, as Agatha so charmingly put it, taught me the little I ken of healing before she died. What of ye?"

"My parents met when my mother, a healer, arrived with an army invading a nearby clan my da visited, nearly three years after Flodden. My father was briefly a prisoner. He took her with him when he escaped back to my clan's stronghold, the Aerie. I was born the next year, one of triplets." He took her arm and started down the hill, Aftyn beside him.

"Triplets! All survived?"

"Aye, and twins two years later, all hale and troublesome."

"So we are of an age, ye and I."

"Close enough." Close enough for what? A family? Bairns of their own? His imaginings were getting out of control.

The track they walked entered a small wood. They were as alone as they ever would be. He took her arm and turned her to face him. "I need to say something... do something..."

A puzzled frown creased Aftyn's brow. "Ye already apologized, and offered to stay to protect me. What more?"

Jamie was done waiting. He bent his head, cradled her cheek in one hand, and kissed her.

Aftyn froze, then leaned away, her gaze locked with his, eyes wide and dark.

Jamie had a moment to fear she would slap him or pull out

of his embrace and run away. Instead, she took a breath, then kissed him back.

"Lass, I..."

"Later, Jamie," she murmured. Her lips parted, allowing him access to deepen the kiss. She tasted sweet, womanly, and even more enticing than he'd imagined during those lonely, sleepless nights he'd spent since he first saw her. He wrapped her in his arms and tangled his tongue with hers. She didn't retreat, but met him, kiss for kiss. Her tongue teased his lips, then she sucked his lower lip between her teeth and nipped it. Hot blood headed downward, filling his cock and making him groan, his body as full and hard as he had ever been.

He slid his hands down her back and gripped her waist, pulling her tighter against him. Her answering moan filled his mouth. He nearly came.

Her fingers raked through his hair, then down his throat and into the top of his tunic. His heart beat so hard against his ribs he was certain she could feel his chest pulse. He put her back against a smooth-barked tree, afraid he'd drop her, then moved his kiss from her lips to her cheek, the shell of her ear, and down her throat.

She arched against him, her breasts crushed against his chest, whimpering with need.

Could he take her? Would she stop him? She wanted him, too. Even here, against a tree in the woods, where anyone might happen by. Like Agatha.

He lifted his head and stilled. "Aftyn, nay. I canna do this to ye."

Panting, she looked up at him, her expression clearing as the haze of lust left her and something else took its place. Fear? Embarrassment?

"I want ye lass, never doubt it," he said as he stepped back, pure torture to his engorged senses, and held her until her feet were steady on the ground. "But I willna take ye like this." He kept her wrapped in his arms, reluctant to let her go, now or ever.

"I... want ye, too," she said and rested her head on his shoulder. Her hand balled into a fist on his chest.

"We must wait. This isna the time or the place. If someone came by..."

"Agatha!" She colored and glanced around him, clearly mortified at the thought of Agatha finding them—finding her —like this.

"The thought of her stopped me," he told her, grinning. "Something ye will thank her for someday."

Aftyn reached up and smoothed his hair, then straightened his tunic.

His body responded to her touch and he fought not to taste her lips again. If he did, he'd be lost.

"A very long time will pass before I thank her for anything, I think," she finally told him and stepped out of his embrace. "We should go."

The path passed through some closely spaced trees, forcing them to go single file. Jamie followed, silent, waiting, expecting her to say he never should have kissed her. Or touched her. But she, too, remained silent until they broke out into another field, this one already harvested.

"That cottage on the edge of the village," she told him, pointing. "My gran lived there. My mother lived with her until..."

"Ye miss her, aye?

"I should be over the grief by now."

"Why? She raised ye. She was everything to ye. Ye have every right to miss her."

She gave him a weak smile. "Thank ye. Most would say 'tis time to get over the loss, find a good husband and make a family but my chances are limited here... oh!"

Her hand flew to her mouth and Jamie hid a grin.

"I'm sorry. I didna mean to be so forward, to imply…"

"I ken it, lass. Dinna fash."

"Ye needna fash, either. I dinna intend ever to marry. Unless Agatha's lies convince the villagers to shun me, my work will sustain me."

Jamie's belly clenched. Did she mean it? She never wanted to marry? He'd thought she jested at Mhairi's when she threatened to stab a husband who ordered her around. And now this? Jamie's thoughts churned. If he was going to leave and never see her again, he shouldn't care. But if he stayed to protect her, she might change her mind. What did he want? His thoughts kept going in circles until they passed through the Keith gates and reached the door into the keep.

JAMIE HAD the look he often wore after seeing a patient, wrung out and at his limit. Why would treating the injured and ill exhaust him? Was it the care, or the empathy she'd thought he exhibited in the market? He didn't appear the same way after making sure Rory hadn't harmed Alastair. Jamie had jested with him, smiling all the while. The lad did not need his care. Was that the difference?

Her conflict with Agatha disturbed Jamie, too. He'd offered to stay here and protect her. Was that why he'd kissed her in the wood?

She led him to a table, her mind on what they'd done there. His body didn't lie. He wanted her. And she'd wanted all of him. But being discovered by Agatha? She couldn't bear the thought. Judging by the set of Jamie's shoulders and the crease between his brows, neither could he. He'd protected her again, from herself this time. How could she let him leave when Niall was strong enough to go? He made her feel wanted. Needed.

Maddie, a serving girl Aftyn had heard unkind tales about,

brought their ales and set them down with a frown for Aftyn and a raised eyebrow at Jamie, who requested food, then looked away. Maddie canted out one hip, then turned and walked away.

Aftyn frowned at her back as she moved toward the kitchen. "What was that all about?"

"Nothing to do with ye, or I miss my guess," Jamie said, and told her about the lass's offer before his bath the first time he met her.

"Ah, the tales about her must be true. So she's *crabbit* because ye are with the likes of me after ye turned her down."

"Probably."

She eyed her tankard. "I'm not sure I should drink this. No telling what she might have put in it."

Jamie shook his head and tipped his tankard toward her. "I watched her pour both from a pitcher on the table over there. She served others from it, too, just before she poured ours, so I'd wager 'tis safe."

Aftyn sniffed, then raised her tankard. "Here's to ye being right, or we'll both be down."

Jamie laughed and touched the rim of his drink to hers, then took a sip. "Tastes the same as I've had before."

Aftyn nodded and sipped. "We're still breathing." She took a larger swallow, suddenly needing fortification. She'd nearly succumbed to Jamie—to her own desires—only a short time ago. She'd wanted him since before she'd seen him in his bath. Kissing him only made the wanting more acute.

"Still," Aftyn said, trying to lighten her own mood as well as his by teasing him about finding him in his bath, "she'd really be put out if she kenned what I saw only a wee while later."

Jamie threw his head back and laughed.

It was the first full-throated, uninhibited amusement she'd seen him express. It thrilled her, and made her embarrassment

over what she'd done today—and what she'd seen that day
—worthwhile.

"Ach, lass," Jamie finally said when he could catch his
breath. He wiped his eyes, still chuckling. "I love when ye
surprise me."

But did he love her?

She forced herself to raise her glass in a silent toast while
she overcame the shock sending tingles down her arms and
legs. Where had that thought come from? Unless he kept his
promise to guard her from Agatha, he would leave in a few
days. She mustn't let herself imagine he had any motive other
than guilt over what he'd said to Agatha. Yet he gave his smile
only to her, and the twinkle in his gaze sent lightning flashing
from her lips to her toes, melting everything in between.

They drank in silence for a few minutes, then Jamie asked,
"What did ye say to Mhairi to put a new backbone into her?
She seemed not at all like a lass Rory had been beating."

So, he also needed to take down the temperature between
them. Aftyn shrugged one shoulder. She understood he wasn't
ready to talk about what happened on the way back from Robena's. "We discussed her future should something happen to
Rory. She's already lost one husband, ye ken. It was hard on her
and she couldn't see past losing another. I reminded her that
she'd stood on her own two feet after her husband died and she
could do it again if she left Rory, or..." She paused and raised an
eyebrow at Jamie, her scrutiny direct and full of implications.
"If something happened to him. I saw the blood. How bad did
ye hurt him?" She let her gaze roam over the breadth of his
shoulders and the bulge of muscle in his sleeves in purely femi-
nine appreciation.

"No' as badly as I wouldha liked. Taught him a lesson he
didna wish to learn, so he came at me with a blade, the fool,
and wound up stabbing himself. I settled him down."

She lifted her tankard in salute. "Aye, ye did." Though he hadn't killed the man, likely he deserved it.

"And ye gave Mhairi the strength to stand up to him." Jamie lifted his tankard in response.

Aftyn felt the heat of a blush rising from her chest to her throat at his praise. "She had her own strength. Likely 'tis one reason she has so many bruises. I hope we have no' made things worse for her," she added to distract herself—and him.

"We'll hear of it. The next time, if there is a next time, will be worse for him. He kens that."

Aftyn shook her head and pushed her tankard away, suddenly despairing. "And when he hears ye have left the village, what do ye think he'll do?" Jamie's assurance irritated her. He didn't live here. He didn't know these people. She would be the one left behind to deal with the results of his actions. Couldn't he see that?

She pressed her lips together, biting down on what she was tempted to say, and after today, what it hurt to think. That he had no business here, and should not feel obligated to stay.

THEIR FOOD ARRIVED JUST as Aftyn's half-brother, Braden limped into the great hall, cradling his arm.

"What happened to ye?" She stood and helped him to a seat.

"Damn Archie hit me in the elbow with a practice sword."

"Well, thank the saints it was made of wood and no' a real one. Ye'd be minus half yer arm, would ye no'?" She carefully pulled up Braden's sleeve and bent to study the offended joint, taking note of the bruised-looking swelling forming above and below it.

"Dinna remind me."

"Can ye move it?" Jamie's concerned expression reminded her they hadn't met.

"Ach, Braden, this is Jamie Lathan, the visiting healer. Jamie, this is the Keith heir, Braden."

Braden nodded to Jamie and demonstrated, shifting his lower arm a fraction of an inch and stifling a yelp as he paled. "The bastard broke it."

"Aye, I fear so," Aftyn told him, sympathy filling her.

"Can ye fix it, Aftyn? Ye must."

"Let me see," Jamie said, stepping close.

"I can wrap it," she said as Jamie, eyes closed and a frown drawing down his brow, touched Braden's arm just above the elbow, then below it. "But first, ye would feel better if ye soaked in the loch. The cold would bring down the swelling."

"And freeze the rest of me, too. Nay, it already feels better."

"Cold water *would* help," Jamie said, stepping back with a grimace.

Aftyn narrowed her gaze. Had he done something? He seemed uncomfortable, but he had before Braden arrived, too. She dismissed her observation as pure fancy. "I'll have some of the lads bring up buckets of cold water. That might serve. Go up to the herbal with Jamie."

Braden nodded and headed for the upper stairs with Jamie a step ahead, making sure no one jostled his arm.

She ran down the stairs and out into the bailey, hailed several lads still on the practice ground and told them what she needed. They hurried off to do her bidding and she went back inside, stopping first by the kitchen to beg a flask of whisky from Cook, who kept several on hand. Braden would need strong drink to dull the pain as she wrapped his elbow.

In the herbal, she poured a cup nearly full and handed it to Braden. "Ye need to drink as much of this as ye can stomach," she told him.

"Ye ken I dinna like…"

"I do ken it, but the whisky will help with the pain," she insisted. And if he passed out, that would be a blessing.

The lads arrived with the cold water she'd requested. She spent the next few minutes directing them where to put the buckets, so she didn't see what Jamie did, but she heard them speaking in low tones. Aftyn turned around in time to see Braden flex his arm, slowly. Jamie did the same with his. Showing Braden how much to safely move it? When Braden cradled his arm, Jamie did, too.

"Good," Jamie told him. "Now do as the healer tells ye, and dunk that elbow." He glanced at the row of buckets on the table top and told Braden, "As the water warms, go to the next, and so on down the line she arranged for ye. By the time ye reach the end, the swelling will be much reduced."

Warmed inside by Jamie acknowledging her to the laird's heir as the healer, Aftyn placed a stool by the first bucket. He didn't know Braden was her half-brother, and she had no intention of telling him. Because of the way the laird treated her, and the fact that she'd kept their relationship secret, Jamie might guess what she was, and that would be the end of any regard he held for her.

Braden did as Jamie instructed, ignoring the cup Aftyn placed in reach of his free hand.

"When ye have done them all," Aftyn said, "I'll wrap the elbow."

"That will help," Jamie agreed. "Ye ken to do it firmly but no' tight, then fashion a sling. And ye, lad, will use that sling for the next three days any time ye are no' abed. No exceptions."

"Will I be able to use my arm after that?"

"Aye, but ye must let it rest for now, or it can swell again, and that will hurt," Aftyn directed.

"Thank ye." He turned to Jamie. "I am grateful ye are here to help my..."

"That's right," Aftyn broke in. "Ye are fortunate to have an experienced healer nearby when ye need one." Jealousy flared at the adoration in her brother's gaze now directed at Jamie, making her belly clench. Had he forgotten she'd once saved his life? "Thank ye, Jamie," she added, determined not to let Braden say any more about who they were to each other. "I can finish caring for him. I'm sure ye have much else to do with Niall."

"I was going to see him when Braden arrived, aye." Jamie nodded. "I'll take my leave, then."

Did Jamie look pale and tired again?

She watched him walk away until he closed the door behind him, then breathed a sigh of relief. She didn't want Jamie to think less of her. She'd already felt his contempt. She would be shamed, and could not stand the thought of enduring that again. Perhaps that was why Braden's adoration of Jamie rankled.

As Braden moved from the first bucket to the next, she shifted the stool for him and asked, "What did he do to yer arm?"

"I dinna ken," Braden said, "and I dinna care. It didna hurt, and afterward, my arm felt better."

"Why do ye spar with Archie? Every time ye do, ye wind up injured."

"All the others avoid him. He's got the coordination of an arrow-shot duck on his best day. And today wasna one of his best."

"Yet ye partner with him."

"'Tis my responsibility as heir."

"To let yerself be battered and bruised and," she said then paused, gesturing at the bucket currently occupied by his elbow, "possibly suffer broken bones, too? I should have a word with the arms master."

Braden sprang to his feet, water dripping from the bunched sleeve above his elbow onto the tabletop and floor. "Nay, ye mustna. How am I, one day, to lead these lads, if my sister complains I'm no' able? They'll be my men, and they must respect me and ken I'll do what I can for them, even if it means taking a few blows now."

"But does it always have to be ye, Braden? Taking all the errant blows Archie can deliver?" She gestured for him to move to the next bucket and pulled the stool along behind him.

"No' for the next three days, nay," he told her and grinned. "Dinna fash, Sister. I'll be more careful."

"See that ye do."

"And I noticed ye cut me off just before I called ye 'sister.' Our guest doesna ken who ye are?"

"The laird's bastard? Nay." And after today, it would be even harder to tell a man who kissed her the way Jamie did exactly who—and what—she was.

"Ye are more than that," Braden insisted, as she indicated for him to dunk his elbow. "When I am laird, ye will be respected and honored. I ken how hard ye work for the clan. How little yer mother left ye to work with."

"Jamie is helping with that, actually." She brought over the journal and a page of Jamie's notes. "He understands at least some of what she wrote, and he's making it plain for Neve and me so we can use her knowledge in the future."

"Good."

"I wish ye had a better idea what he did to yer arm. Did ye notice how he stood when he turned away from ye?"

"Nay. What do ye mean?"

"He cradled his arm, just as ye did, but only for a moment."

"In sympathy for my pain?"

"Perhaps." Aftyn frowned, then nodded. "Aye, perhaps exactly that."

11

"What have ye been doing?" Niall sat up as Jamie entered his chamber. "Ye look fair *forfochen*."

"I am spent, aye. Most recently, from helping the laird's heir," Jamie told him and rubbed his elbow. "Broken in careless swordplay on the practice field."

"Ye are doing too much, ye ken. If ye are no' careful, someone will notice. Someone like Aftyn."

"I was careful. I wasna going to do anything, but Aftyn's determination to help him—even sending lads for buckets of cold water from the loch to bring down the swelling—convinced me I couldna let the lad suffer for weeks. Or lose the use of his arm. He's to be laird, and he will need it."

Niall stood, poured a cup and handed it to Jamie. "Aye, well, just be careful, aye?"

Jamie took a sip. Ah, good, sweet cider, not ale or whisky. "Anything left on yer tray to eat? Somehow I missed another meal."

Niall brought the remains of his meal, a slice of bread and hunk of cheese and a small apple.

"Thanks. That will help."

"How soon do ye think I can walk out of here for good?"

"Bored, are ye?" Jamie took a bite of cheese. "With a cane, this evening. If ye can limp convincingly, ye could join the rest for the evening meal in the great hall."

"For the sight of something other than these four walls, aye. I'd crawl, if need be, but ye are a few hours late. I did that this morning. I was quite convincing, judging by the sympathy I got from the serving lasses."

Jamie could imagine how Niall had enjoyed the female attention. He finished the last bite of bread and held out the cup for a refill, then gulped that down, too. "Did Rabbie find ye a cane? Or a stout branch to make one?"

"He did. He'll be here soon. Ye go get more to eat from Cook, then rest a wee. I can see yer arm still pains ye."

"I will. Yer bandage is secure, aye?" Jamie looked forward to his bed and the dreams that would accompany his sleep this night. Aftyn in his arms, her lips under his, had been even better than the fantasies that inhabited his dreams up to now.

"Aye." Niall tapped it. "And the wound is nought but a shallow trench, well healed."

"I'll see ye for the next meal, then."

Before Jamie could reach the door, it opened. Niall fell back on the bed, then sat up again as Rabbie entered, anxious and out of breath.

"The abbey's roof is afire," he told them, then focused on Jamie. "Ye'll be needed," he added.

Jamie nodded and tucked the apple in his shirt. "I'll get my bag and join ye in the bailey. Niall, ye stay here," he added as Niall stood.

"I could help."

"Nay," Rabbie interjected. "Ye would be questioned. Best ye stay put."

"Very well," Niall answered, but his expression made it clear he did not agree at all. "I'll stay here and count the stones on the wall for the hundredth time. Or more."

Jamie clapped him on the back and left him glowering.

The bailey swarmed with activity. Jamie quickly spotted his men on horseback, ready to go. His mount was saddled and waiting with them. He mounted and nodded to each, acknowledging their good work. "Let's go."

They followed some of the Keith warriors through the gate and the nearby woods for a mile, coming quickly to a glen with stone structures built near a burn. The smell of smoke and the sound of men shouting to be heard over the roaring fire assaulted him. The kirk's roof still burned, flames shooting into the sky. Acolytes in loose robes risked catching fire themselves. They climbed to the surrounding roofs to pour buckets of water on them, trying to keep flaming bits of thatch that flew through the air from spreading the conflagration. Others passed up filled buckets as the men on the roofs tossed down empties. A line of younger acolytes passed buckets from the burn. Billowing smoke briefly blocked Jamie's view, then he saw several clerics run out of the burning kirk with holy objects, parchment rolls, benches, and anything else they could carry.

Jamie's gut churned at the thought of what might happen when the kirk's roof came down. As it surely would. "Tell them to stay out of there!" He shouted to the Keiths ahead of him. "The roof willna last much longer."

One of the Keiths waved and Jamie took that to mean he'd heard and understood. By unspoken agreement, several of the Keiths and Lathans climbed to nearby roofs to relieve acolytes doing the wetting down. Jamie found the abbot directing his men.

"Are any of yer people hurt?" Jamie asked, skipping the usual protocols for addressing a high kirk official. "I'm a healer," he added.

"Aye, I've had them moved over there." He pointed to a spot

near the burn but out of the way of the men passing buckets hand-to-hand.

"I'll go make myself useful," Jamie told him.

"Bless ye, lad," the abbot said and made the sign of the cross over him.

Jamie bowed his head, then moved to the injured. He was relieved to see only a handful of men sitting or lying on the springy turf. He checked each one, but all had superficial injuries, surface burns, scratches, and a few deeper gouges, and most had dark rings from smoke and soot smudged around their noses. None appeared life threatening. He did what he could with his store of poultices and bandages. He dared not do too much until everyone was safely on the ground and the kirk's roof collapsed. There might be more serious injuries to deal with later that would require more of his skill and energy.

Rabbie came by when he finished. "Are ye well?"

Jamie nodded. "So far, but I'd be happier to see them," he said and indicated the loose-robed acolytes, "away from the flames." He looked around, and noticed Aftyn and Neve arriving with more of the Keith's men. Good, they could take over the care of the lesser injuries. He gestured toward her. "Get the lasses over here," he told Rabbie. "I may be needed soon for worse than these."

"Aye." Rabbie ran over to where Aftyn and Neve were dismounting. Jamie was glad to see she'd brought more supplies, judging by the packs one of the Keiths took off of the back of their horses. Rabbie pointed toward Jamie and everyone started his way.

"'Tis good ye are here," he told Aftyn as soon as she got close enough. She looked so fresh, so lovely, she seemed entirely out of place. Yet she could help. She and Neve. He pulled his gaze away from Aftyn. "These men need little care, but worse may follow. Stay near the burn, aye?" He would worry about her. If the fire spread, everyone would be in danger.

Neve knelt among the men, checking on them and speaking to each.

Aftyn regarded the burning kirk, arms crossed and brow furrowed. "Is this everyone?"

Men still passed buckets as fast as they could, but Jamie hadn't seen anyone come out of the kirk in a few minutes. Perhaps by now they'd removed everything they could. "So far."

"How did this happen?"

Aftyn's question pulled his attention back to her. He'd been wondering the same thing. "I dinna ken. When we arrived, everyone went to help. There wasna time to ask."

The height of the fire suddenly increased. With a booming crack and a roar of flame and wind, crashing filled the air, drowning out shouting voices. The kirk's roof caved in, shooting sparks into the sky.

"Please, God, dinna let anyone be in there," Aftyn said in a fervent tone.

"Damn," Jamie swore as one man stumbled out, robes afire, pulling his cowl away from his face with one frantic hand, a large gold crucifix clutched in a wad of cloth in the other. Jamie ran for the man, as did several others. In seconds, Jamie knocked him off his feet and others poured water on him, dousing the flames.

"Father Bertram," the abbot cried as he joined them. "How bad...?"

Jamie knelt and extended his talent under cover of adjusting the man's burned clothing, searching for injuries. Then he shook his head. "Bad enough."

～

Aftyn gasped as Jamie charged into the burning man, knocking him off his feet. Buckets of water poured over him soon put out the fire. Aftyn feared Jamie had hurt himself, and that the man would not survive the injuries he must have.

She approached the group surrounding the man on the ground, Jamie kneeling by his side. She heard what he told the abbot, and clasped her hands over her belly. She needed to do something to help, but had no idea how.

"Let's move him near the others," someone said. Jamie stood and moved out of the way as several men bent to lift Father Bertram's still form and carry him by his arms and legs, clasped wrists supporting him under his torso.

Jamie watched for a moment, then took a step to follow.

Aftyn reached him and put a hand on his arm. "Are ye hurt?"

"Nay, the lads dumped water on us so fast, the fire barely touched me."

Thank God. She gestured toward the priest being carried closer to the burn. "Is he alive?" She hated the thought that filled her with cold dread. He might be better off if he died.

"Aye, for now he is. I'll do what I can." He started toward the injured man.

"How can I help?" She kept pace with him as he followed the group carrying the injured man.

"Find Rabbie or one of the other Lathans and send them to me. Keep the others away. Ye and Neve help anyone else who's hurt. I... I will do what I can for the father."

Aftyn nodded and ran to find another Lathan. She spotted Fearchar carrying two buckets toward the kirk. "Jamie needs ye over there," she told him and pointed. Without a word, he handed the buckets to two other men and went.

Aftyn watched him for a moment, then turned to study the remaining structures. So far, everyone else seemed unharmed, but men still stood atop thatched roofs and ran between buildings, putting out small fires. Now that its roof had collapsed, the fire in the kirk was dying, and smoke drifted across the entire abbey. She noticed some of the men dousing rags in the water buckets and tying them over their faces. Aye, that would help them breathe and keep out some of the soot, but not all. Some would develop terrible coughs, she feared. But the worst seemed to be over.

She turned and walked back to where Neve tended a young man. He smiled at her, as though he saw Neve as his guardian angel. Black-ringed burns dotted his robe, but Aftyn didn't see any serious injuries. The abbot had sent a few more men to their care. One of them groaned. Aftyn dropped to her knees beside him and went to work.

It seemed hours later when she glanced up and thought to wonder about Jamie and the father from the kirk. All her charges were resting quietly. The sun had set and a cool night breeze blew the last of the heavy smoke away from where they lay.

She stood and stretched, then walked toward Jamie. In the dim glow of embers, she saw him, still bent over the burned man, Fearchar, Rabbie, and Bhaltair forming a ring around them, keeping others away. She could see a small pile of burned fabric that must be from the man's robes. Jamie's case lay open beside him. Several jars were open, and he smoothed on unguent. Aftyn knew Jamie was a healer of great skill, yet she had to wonder how long the priest, in his condition, would remain alive.

She approached Rabbie, but he waved her away. Stung, she paused. "I have medicines. Do ye need aught?"

"Jamie will send one of us if he does," he answered quietly. "Go rest. I dinna ken how long we'll be here."

Aftyn paused to study Jamie. He seemed fully absorbed in caring for his patient, but all right himself. She nodded and moved away, her gaze caught by the abbot and several of his priests kneeling together, praying. For the injured? For their losses? She hoped it gave them comfort.

JAMIE FOUGHT. After Calder, he had a better sense of his limits and that he approached them, but the priest still needed his help and he was determined to give it. The man was lucky in some ways. The surface of his robes had burned, but the layers underneath protected his torso, if only a little. Flames had singed the hair from one hand, the other one that had held the crucifix had deeper burns. The gold metal must have heated in the fire to a dangerous level. The lower part of his face had also blistered, and Jamie would do what he could there to preserve the man's appearance and ability to speak and eat.

But his worst injuries were invisible. His throat was scorched and kept swelling. Smoke and soot in his lungs made breathing nearly impossible. Jamie fought to keep the throat open as he worked to save at least one of his lungs. If he could not, the external burns would not matter. The man would not survive.

Healing those injuries agonized Jamie and robbed his own ability to breathe. He had to work slowly or he would pass out before he could save the man's life. But by working slowly, he fell behind as the man's body did what was natural much more quickly than Jamie could combat it.

The longer it took, the more ground he lost, and the more danger he was in. He knew he could not be present in his talent as the man died. He'd learned his lesson with Calder—it would be too easy to follow into oblivion. His men knew the risk he took. On his orders, they all watched closely for any sign that it was time to pull him away from his task.

He shook his head as another wave of agony washed down his throat into his chest. Not yet. He could do more. He must.

There! He'd cleared one lung, and Jamie felt some ease in his own chest, but the man's throat closed again. Jamie sucked in air and forced down the swelling, gratified to see the man's chest rise and fall. He couldn't stop yet. The body fought him still. Blackness filled his vision and he forced himself to breathe, then lift his hands away from the man's body.

"Drink," he rasped. Rabbie put a cup in his hand and guided it to his mouth. He drank greedily. Cider. The sweet drink would help replenish his strength. "More." He consumed three more cups, then dropped the cup and turned back to the priest.

The man's throat kept closing against the burned tissue. Jamie cleared the swelling and felt air enter the lung he'd saved. He turned his attention to the other lung and used his newfound energy to repair what he could and clear the fluid that threatened to fill it, coughing as he did so. He was finally gaining ground. The throat stayed open and the man breathed. Jamie stilled for a few heartbeats, waiting, but the man's chest continued to rise and fall. He could breathe on his own for now. Relieved, Jamie rubbed his own chest and took a deep breath. He wasn't finished.

The hand that had held the crucifix was next. The cloth he'd bundled around it as he carried it out of the burning kirk had prevented worse damage, but Jamie could see a bit of tendon or bone exposed in the midst of blackened tissue on two fingers. He would not repair them now. He would have to cut away the most severely burned flesh, and the man needed to take in as much water and cider as he could before Jamie could help his body build new tissue. "Bandage that loosely," he said, knowing Bhaltair would hear him and do what he needed. "His face, too." He checked the throat and found it remained open. "See if ye can get some of that cider into him. He needs it. And water. Keep trying, but dinna drown him."

As his men did as he asked, he collapsed onto his back on

the ground and closed his eyes, resting, breathing, and willing the pain away.

"Should we take him back to the keep?" That was Bhaltair.

"Nay, a chamber here will do. I will stay with him. One of ye, too, must watch over him while I rest."

"I'll go beg a chamber from the abbot," Rabbie said, and moved away.

"What can I do?" Aftyn's voice, close, comforting. Did he imagine her bending over him? Touching his face? Nay, he didn't imagine her. Her touch gave him a bit of pleasure in the midst of all the pain. He clung to that.

"See if the abbot has a place inside for the less injured," Fearchar answered for him. Jamie didn't have the strength.

She must have moved away. Jamie didn't hear her any more. Or anything else. The next he knew, he woke in a strange chamber on a pallet. The injured man lay on a similar one on the opposite wall. Rabbie sat on a bench between them, his gaze on the other man until Jamie moved.

"Ach, ye're back with us," Rabbie said. "I've food and drink aplenty for ye. And I've gotten a few drops down him a time or two."

"Good," Jamie told him as he forced himself up. "Keep trying."

Rabbie handed him a cup and set the platter beside him. Bread, butter, sliced venison, honey, cheese, apples, enough for both of them twice over. He made short work of two of the four pitchers of cider and water lined up under the bench. Once he finished, Rabbie ate from what he left, while Jamie drank another cup of cider.

"Ye did more than ye should," Rabbie said, censure plain in his tone.

"I did what I had to do," Jamie answered, his gaze on the injured man. "He's still breathing freely?"

"Aye. Ye saved his life. Nearly at the cost of yer own."

Jamie dismissed that. He'd survived, and so had the priest. "There is still much to do."

"And the abbot is most concerned. I doubt he slept all night, but with Lathan and Keith help, all the fires are out and cleanup has begun."

"Bhaltair and Fearchar?"

"Resting outside this door."

Jamie forced himself to his feet, every joint aching. But the pain of the man's injuries had faded. His throat no longer burned. He took a deep breath. His chest felt clear. "Did ye bring in my bag? I must work on his hand if he's to have the use of it."

Rabbie nodded toward the opposite corner of the room. Good, it was there.

"Aftyn and Neve?"

"With the other injured and some of the Keith men."

"Aftyn will come here, soon enough. I must finish what I can with him and cover the wound before she arrives."

"Ye dinna think ye can tell her? Show her what ye can do?"

"Nay, ye ken I canna. 'Tis too dangerous."

"She might understand..."

"It doesna matter if she does. Remember where we are. The kirk frowns on abilities such as mine. If she doesna accept it, my life could be forfeit. All our lives here. Perhaps even those in the Aerie. The risk is too great."

12

Aftyn tapped on the door, hoping not to disturb the injured man. But she had to know how Jamie was. She'd seen Bhaltair pick him up and carry him into the abbey's guest quarters while others carried the injured man.

Jamie was probably just exhausted, but in thinking back over the reactions she'd observed in him at the market, at Robena's, and with Braden, she wondered. She needed to see for herself that he was safe, and not suffering along with his patient's pain.

When no one answered, she rapped on the door and waited. The door was made of thickly hewn oak, but still, she thought she heard someone moving around inside.

"Jamie?" When no one answered or came to the door, she called out louder, "Rabbie? Are ye in there? How are they?"

Still no reply. Her frustration building, she pounded on the door. "Somebody answer me!"

Suddenly, the door opened, if only a crack. Rabbie's brown eye peered out at her, most of his face still hidden behind the door's oaken shield. "Go on with ye, Aftyn. They're sleeping."

"I heard someone moving around. I thought I heard voices."

That was an exaggeration. She'd heard no one speaking, but if someone had been talking, Rabbie wouldn't know she hadn't heard them.

"Ye're imagining things. Jamie is resting. The father is, too."

"How is Jamie? I want to help."

"Ye canna. Truly, lass. This is beyond yer skill."

Rabbie's words, though spoken in a kind tone, stung. She sniffed and stepped back a pace. "How is my skill ever to improve if I am no' given the chance to learn and to practice?"

"Some other time, Aftyn. I'm sorry, truly. I ken how important that is to ye. But ye canna." He closed the door.

He had no idea how important *Jamie* was to her. Aghast, Aftyn pounded on it again. Rabbie opened it quickly. "Aftyn... wheesht!" he hissed.

"Nay, ye canna shut me out this way. This is my home, nay yers. 'Tis my responsibility to aid them. I saw Jamie carried in. He's hurt."

"Nay, lass. He's exhausted. There is nought for ye to do," Rabbie repeated. "Now dinna bang on the door again or ye'll wake him. He must rest." With that, he closed the door again.

Aftyn fought the urge to kick it. She'd only break a toe, and accomplish nothing. Instead, she crossed her arms and fought back angry tears. Rabbie was right. She'd seen the exhaustion on Jamie's face.

She whirled and stalked back down the hall to the larger room where Neve remained, tending the other injured. Neve saw the expression on her face and held a finger up to her mouth, then dipped her chin and turned her head to regard the men sleeping on rough pallets. Her message was clear. No matter what had Aftyn raging, she was not to disturb the men they cared for.

Aftyn huffed out a breath and nodded, then canted her head for Neve to join her out in the hall. Neve nodded and stood. Only then did Aftyn note that she'd been sitting by the same acolyte Aftyn had seen her talking to by the burn.

Neve didn't waste any words once they were in the hall, but went right to the point. "What's got ye so fashed?"

Aftyn clenched her fists, then forced herself to open them. "Rabbie willna let me in the chamber where Jamie and the burned man rest. I want to do something to help them, but Rabbie said this was beyond my skill."

Neve gasped. "Ach, Aftyn. 'Twas unkind of him."

"If I could, I would break down the door," Aftyn complained. "But I cannae." She turned and put her back to the wall. "I feel so useless."

"Nay, ye are never that." Neve reached for her and wrapped her in a hug. "But ye ken fine that neither of us is ready to deal with that man's injuries. If Jamie can help him, then ye must let him."

Aftyn knew Jamie would take good care of the injured man. She only wanted—no, needed—to help Jamie. She patted Neve's back and stepped away. "I ken it. But I dinna like it."

Neve peered into the room. "Come with me and meet Hamish."

"The lad ye were talking to after the fire?"

"Aye. He hails from Crieff."

"He's here by himself?"

"Nay. He studies to be an ordained healer, something like us, not quite a priest. The kirk supports infirmaries in abbeys across Scotland. A trained healer is due in a few weeks, and Hamish came to help the abbey make ready for him."

Aftyn froze. Another healer, experienced, soon only a mile away from the keep? He could be exactly whom she needed to continue her training after Jamie left, or his presence could convince her father the clan no longer needed her. All her insecurities, her anxiety, flared anew in her belly. Stop being selfish, she chided to herself. The man could have helped here.

"Too bad he didn't arrive early. Yesterday would have been helpful. How much of healing does Hamish ken?"

"A fair amount, and says now that he's met me, he might change his mind about taking vows. He could help us."

"Neve! Nay. Ye canna make him stray from his path."

"I willna. 'Twill be his choice." She paused, then added, "Though he does have the deepest blue eyes. Like a loch, they are." She sighed and shrugged. "I canna stop thinking about him."

"Ye just met him. And he's to be a... some sort of priest!"

Neve's lips lifted in a sweet smile. "Mayhap."

Against her better judgement, Aftyn followed Neve to Hamish's bedside. His eye opened and Aftyn had to admit Neve was right. She'd never seen such a clear, deep blue. But his gaze never left Neve and his smile was all for her.

"Angel mine," he whispered. Someone, probably Neve, had tried to clean his face. Flecks of soot remaining around his nose and mouth explained the rasp in his voice.

The soot told Aftyn he must have helped clear the kirk of sacred objects before the roof came down.

"I am neither an angel, nor yers," Neve told him.

"But ye could be," he whispered and coughed, then, once he caught his breath, continued, "when I am better and free of this pallet."

"We'll talk about that when ye are better, then. For now, what do ye need? Water? Are ye hungry?"

"I only need to see ye, Angel mine."

Aftyn fought not to roll her eyes. "I'm Aftyn," she said, hoping to interrupt the longing gazes Hamish and Neve were sharing. "The Keith healer. With Neve. And ye do need water," she added, placing a hand on Neve's shoulder and squeezing. "'Tis good to meet ye, but now, we must check on the others.

Neve grimaced at Aftyn until she released her shoulder, then turned back to smile at Hamish. "Aye, we must." She indicated the cup beside his pallet. "Drink. I'll check on ye again soon."

"Ye dinna have to drag me," Neve told her softly as they moved away.

"After the way ye two were looking at each other, aye, I did."

"'Twas no worse than the way ye look at Jamie Lathan."

"What? I dinnae do any such thing."

Neve snorted. "Ye canna fool me, Aftyn. Ye wouldna be so angry if ye didna also fear for him. Ye care about him."

"That is the daftest thing ye have ever said."

"Perhaps, but mark my words. I ken that look."

Mark her words, indeed. Neve knew that look only because she and Hamish wore it. Aftyn huffed and bent over the next patient, determined to put Neve's words out of her mind. Still, Neve was not entirely wrong, not that Aftyn would admit such to her. Fearing for Jamie Lathan was appropriate, after seeing him carried into the abbey. Caring in the way Neve meant, for a man due to leave in a few days, would gain her nothing.

TWO DAYS LATER, Aftyn finally left the abbey. She worried that Jamie, remaining behind, would not be able to keep up with caring for the burned man and dealing with all the other, less serious injuries, but she'd left Neve behind, and Bhaltair and Fearchar remained with him. Rabbie joined the Keith warriors escorting her, charged with checking on Niall, then returning to the abbey to give Jamie a full report.

When she entered the Keith great hall, Niall sitting at one of the tables, a cane propped against the bench next to him, surprised her. She went to him first.

"How do ye fare? I'm pleased to see ye able to walk about without assistance."

"No' entirely." Niall indicated the cane. "I have been walking every day since ye saw me last. With a little help." He indicated the cane. "Jamie insists I will regain my strength faster this way."

"Aye, ye will. Ye must be eager to return home."

Niall nodded. "Will ye join me? I wish to hear about what happened at the abbey. Did the others return with ye?"

"Only Rabbie. He must be helping tend the horses." She took a seat across from him. "One priest was badly burned saving the abbey's gold crucifix just before the roof collapsed. Jamie has spent most of time since the fire with him. I heard the priest was able to sit up, drink, and take a little food, but I did not see him before I left. There were more injuries that Neve and I tended to, but the rest were minor."

"When does Jamie expect to return?"

Aftyn's heart sank. When he got back and saw how well Niall was, surely he and the rest of the Lathans would leave within another day or two. "He didna say."

Niall nodded, his expression grim. "Very well. Ye must be tired. Ye need no' sit with me. Rabbie will be in soon."

"I should examine your leg."

"Nay." Niall shook his head. "'Tis healing well. Go to yer rest, lass."

Why didn't he want her to see his leg? Aftyn had no reason to be suspicious of him. But something in his manner put her off. "I am tired," she admitted. Too tired to wrestle him to the ground and remove the wrapping from his leg. "But I must speak with the laird first." She stood. "Take care moving about, Niall. Ye dinna want to tear open yer wound."

"I will. Thank ye."

She nodded and headed for the laird's solar, where her father spent most of his time. He sat at his desk, reading, but looked up as she entered and set aside his papers.

"Aftyn." He addressed her in his usual disinterested tone. "How fares the abbey?"

There was no "How are ye, daughter" to be had from this man. She expected none. She took the seat he indicated and told him about the damage to the kirk's roof and the injured men. "None of ours."

He nodded and put a hand on the papers he'd been reading when she entered, as if ready to return to them. "I will ride over soon to speak to the abbot and offer our assistance in rebuilding."

"I'm sure he'll appreciate yer offer," Aftyn told him and stood, taking his comment for dismissal.

"Everyone is returned?"

"All but the Lathan healer and two of his men. Rabbie and our men returned with me. Neve will follow soon." She didn't want to tell him that Neve remained behind because of Hamish.

The laird leaned his elbows on the desk and steepled his hands. "And what did the Lathan healer do there?"

So that was what he truly wanted to know. What Jamie had done. Not how she and Neve had helped. "Mostly he tended a priest who was badly burned as the kirk's roof collapsed. Neve and I cared for the rest."

"So the man he tended still lives despite his injuries?" The gleam in his eye betrayed the first true interest he'd shown.

"And is improving. The abbot calls it a miracle he survives, and that no others took worse hurts." The minute the words left her mouth, she wished she could pull them back. She'd just made her father even more interested in the Lathan healer. Clearly, he had no interest in anything she and Neve had contributed, how many wounded they'd tended, or what else might have happened while they were there. She'd hoped when she told him they'd tended the rest, he might ask what they'd been called upon to do. If he'd showed any interest at all, she would have been proud to tell him how much they'd learned, and used that knowledge in caring for the abbey's brothers.

"Indeed. Perhaps I'll make that visit sooner than I planned. Very well. Go to yer rest."

Aftyn escaped her father's presence before he could comment that even with the little he'd asked her to describe, if the abbey no longer needed her services, they must not be worth much.

JAMIE LOOKED up as Fearchar entered the chamber he'd shared with the burned priest for the past two days.

Fearchar closed the door behind him. "How is he?"

Jamie shrugged. "I've kept him in a light healing sleep, both for the pain and deep enough to encourage the repair his body needs, but not so deep that he canna drink as much as we can give him. I got him to sit up and eat a little."

"That's amazing. The blisters on his face are nearly gone, too."

"If I took them away completely, that wouldha been noticed. They'll last only another few days, and they willna pain him. Once he is well enough to leave his care to others, I will remove the healing sleep. The man will remember nought of these days since the fire."

"Surely that will be counted as a blessing by all who care about him."

"Have ye seen aught of the abbot yet today?" The greatest danger Jamie faced came from the well-intentioned abbot, who insisted on seeing his man every day. Jamie could not deny him, but Bhaltair and Fearchar stood sentinel at the door and were masterful at delaying the cleric until Jamie covered the burned man's injuries and opened the door. The abbot seemed satisfied that his priest continued to breathe well and sleep, claiming healing rest was God's blessing. Jamie didn't argue. He might be right, though he couldn't know the kind of healing rest his priest benefitted from. The talent that ran in Jamie's family came from somewhere. His mother had never speculated, simply accepting that her ability came from her mother and grandmother and on through the generations. The abbot's explanation was as good as any.

"He was having his midday meal when I left the hall. He'll be here soon, I think."

"I'll be ready." Jamie lifted the covering and showed Fearchar the man's hand. Muscle tissue now plumped the flesh that just days ago had been exposed tendon and bone, and shiny pink skin edged in red, extended from his palm onto each finger.

"I didna think ye could do that," Fearchar told him, eyes wide. "He canna ken the debt he owes ye."

"Nay, he canna ken." Jamie shook his head and dropped the cover over the hand. "Never. He owes me nought. He took honorable—but foolish—action to save a relic of great value to the abbey. He might have died there."

"He's damn lucky ye were nearby."

The door opened and Bhaltair leaned his head in. "The abbot is on his way."

Jamie nodded. "Send him in."

When the abbot asked, Jamie gave him an edited version of the state of the man's injuries, continuing to make light of the burns he'd treated. Then he reminded him that his priest needed rest. Jamie was loath to reveal the hand that had held the crucifix quite yet. In another day, he'd awaken the man and work with him to ensure the new flesh he'd given him would let him regain the use of it.

Without Jamie's healing touch, his ruined hand would not have mattered. He would have died, but that truth could not be shared, no matter how devoutly the abbot believed in miracles. He might also believe in witches.

The abbot prayed over them as he usually did and thanked Jamie for his devotion. He turned to leave the chamber when an acolyte reached the doorway. "The Keith laird is here to speak with ye, Abbot. I placed him in yer study."

"Thank ye. I'll be there in a moment. See that ye offer him our best wine."

"Aye." The lad left.

The abbot turned to Jamie. "Come with me, lad."

To meet with the Keith? Nay. He did not want a repeat of his earlier interview with him. "I should remain with my patient."

"Ye have taken such care of him that he willna miss ye for a few moments."

Jamie knew when he was outranked. "Verra well." He gestured toward the door and followed the abbot out, stopping long enough to ask Fearchar to remain within the chamber and fetch him if his patient needed him.

Laird Keith rose when they entered the abbot's study and bowed over the cleric's hand. "I am here to see how else my clan may aid ye," the laird said.

"Yer men, and yer healers have already done so much. The injured are getting well, and yer men assist my young men with rebuilding the kirk's roof. I canna think of anything else ye might offer us. Ye have been generous."

"I will give ye any aid ye need," the laird repeated.

"I ask only the boon of this healer for a few more days," he said and smiled at Jamie. "He's been a godsend for my most grievously injured man."

Laird Keith glanced at Jamie, a speculative gleam in his eye that immediately put Jamie on his guard. The abbot's praise had only served to increase the Keith's interest in him.

"I will leave that up to ye, healer Lathan. I'm aware yer man Niall is doing well enough without ye. But we look forward to welcoming ye back to the Keith keep when ye feel yer job here is done. Those of my people ye treated still require yer care."

"I understand the healer Aftyn returned to ye recently," the abbot interjected.

"Aye, but she hasna the skill this man possesses, and we have our own grievous injured and ill who need his care."

"I feel I owe ye a boon for putting our needs ahead of yer own," the abbot began.

"Not I," the Keith answered, "but perhaps the healers and my clansmen who still aid ye."

That comment surprised Jamie. It sounded very unlike the laird Jamie had met, but perhaps the abbot's benevolent presence had inspired the Keith's generosity.

"Indeed. I will offer the highest honor I am able, and hear their confessions personally," the abbot said.

Surprised, Jamie frowned. He'd never heard of a senior cleric hearing confession of anyone other than junior clerics. Certainly not members of the flock tended by those junior clerics. But it didn't matter. Jamie had no plans to take him up on the honor he offered. If all went well, he and his men would be on the way back to the Aerie in two days. Three at the most. Leaving Aftyn behind, if she still refused to come with him. That thought didn't set well.

13

I n the great hall, Aftyn sat with Braden for the midday meal. Jamie was at the abbey, and so was the laird. Since the Lathans had arrived, she'd had little chance to share a meal with Braden in the hall, and though she ached to spend time with Jamie, their father's absence lightened both their moods.

"The horses Da traded for in Crieff have arrived," Braden told her, pleasure shining in his gaze. "Ye ken the age of most of our stable. Younger, stronger mounts will give us an advantage for years to come."

"So ye are already planning how ye'll run the clan and the keep, aye?" Aftyn teased. "Right down to the horses in our stable."

"They're important!" Braden insisted. "If cats and kittens were important, I'd plan for them, too."

"Dinna let Cook hear ye say that. Or the stable master. Those cats and kittens keep rodents out of Cook's stores and the horses' feed."

"Aye, I suppose ye are right. But cats do what they will and keep having kittens, no matter what. I dinna think I can plan on them for more than that."

"Wise words, brother mine. Wise indeed. And if ye think on it, people are very much like those cats. Some things ye willna be able to control, but ye can encourage, or discourage, as the need arises." She had no doubt Braden would be a better, more fair laird than their father had been up to now. "Or think of it another way. Yer mount responds best to a light hand on the reins, aye?"

"Aye, save for in battle, when I must be in control at risk of my life, and my mount's."

"Exactly. But ye are no' in battle every day. And I'd wager there are times in battle when yer mount sees a threat ye dinna, and takes control to save ye both."

"Aye."

"Or ye have to ride another, even take the mount of an enemy."

"I havena, but I've seen it happen. I think I see what ye mean, Aftyn. Da has never given ye the respect ye deserve, nor the chance to improve yerself. No' even the chance he plans to give these new mounts. The training."

"Aye. And experience. Jamie Lathan has helped, but 'twould be best for me to be able to go elsewhere. For the clan, as well. I could foster with another healer, or bring one here for a time."

"He willna."

"I ken it. But If ye talk to him..."

"I can try, but ye ken his stubbornness."

"Aye, more than most."

Braden gave her a sympathetic nod.

Aftyn glanced away, suddenly sorry she'd started the conversation, and noticed Niall making his way down the stairs. "He's much better," she said, though he still leaned on a cane and took each step favoring his injured leg. She stood and beckoned him to their table.

Braden watched Niall's halting progress with a frown. "Did

ye ken he's one of their best horsemen? Rabbie told me. I hope
he is soon well."

"Good day," Niall greeted them.

Braden gestured to the seat next to him. "Are ye hungry?"

"Aye. That's what drove me down the stairs."

Aftyn took that as a very good sign. If his appetite had
returned enough for him to come to the hall instead of waiting
for a tray to be brought to him, he must be getting stronger. She
hailed a passing serving lass and requested a trencher and ale
for their guest. Then she turned back to watch Niall and
Braden talk horses, reminded that Niall's recovery meant the
Lathans' departure was approaching.

Her belly hollowed at the thought. When Jamie left, would
she ever see him again? Or would he forget her the moment he
rode through the gate, headed home? After the way he'd kissed
her in the wood, she hoped he cared for her as much as she had
come to care for him. Her body still burned any time she
thought about his kisses, on her lips, her face, her throat.

She tried to convince herself she wouldn't miss him, but she
was wrong. She'd miss catching him looking at her with heat in
his gaze meant only for her. Though they'd barely touched, and
had done nothing that she would need to worry over, the
thought of her hand in his, or his firm, full lips on hers, and his
muscled arms wrapping her in a heated embrace made her
realize he'd come to mean more to her than she'd ever imagined he could.

She needed to stop pining for a man she'd never have, a
man who had said nothing to her about a future together. He'd
only offered to take her with him to find a place where she
could be safe. Should she go with him? To the Aerie? Perhaps.
But if he meant to leave her at another clan, in the midst of
strangers, away from everything and everyone she knew, then
nay. As much as she wanted to fulfill her mother's wishes and
become a healer her clan could depend upon, that is not how

she wished to make it happen. She lost herself in the fantasy of leaving with Jamie to return to his home, to be near him. Knowing it would never happen made her sad.

If this is how it would be once he went home, she would be brokenhearted to see him go. Despite what he'd thought about her when he arrived, she appreciated that he hadn't ignored her. Instead, he'd helped her, given her confidence, even his affection.

What was she going to do without him?

She forced herself to pay attention to the activity going on around her. Braden and Niall were still deep in conversation. The rest of the people who had been in the hall before her longings took her mind away were still there, too. She hadn't been dreaming for long. She hoped no one had seen her thoughts reflected on her face.

After he finished eating, Braden offered to take Niall to see the new stock, but Niall begged off, saying his leg pained him and he'd best go rest it. Aftyn could see the disappointment on Braden's face, but Braden nodded and promised they'd do it another day.

Later, Aftyn happened to walk by the door to Niall's chamber as Fearchar opened it, then turned back to say something else to Niall, who was pacing without a cane across the chamber. Over Fearchar's shoulder, she glimpsed him turn and walk back again. As she ducked away, it took her a moment to realize he wasn't limping. So his leg pained him, did it? What magic had Jamie Lathan done for his clansman? She'd give quite a lot to see under that wrapping on Niall's lower leg, and to find out why they were lying about it.

LATER THAT AFTERNOON, Aftyn rode back to the abbey. Neve had sent for her, though her message said the need was not urgent, but Aftyn worried if she left her there much longer, the lass would convince Hamish to leave the kirk for her. She didn't want Neve to have such a stain on her soul.

She found Neve in the abbey's hall, sitting with Hamish and two others Aftyn recognized as having been injured in the fire, though only slightly. The men stood when they saw her approaching.

"Aftyn!" Neve smiled and patted the bench beside her. "Conal just told us about his home up near Aberdeen. Truly, the brothers in this abbey come from all over Scotland."

"And at least one from Ireland," Conal said and nodded toward a pale redhead eating with two other acolytes.

"How interesting," Aftyn said as she took the seat Neve indicated. "How are ye all?"

"Ach, they're well," Neve answered. "And ready to return to their duties for the abbey."

All the men nodded agreement, except Hamish, whose gaze remained fixed on Neve. Aftyn wondered if she should have stayed here and sent Neve back to Keith instead of indulging Neve's wish to remain near Hamish.

"I'm glad of it. Neve, that means ye can return home with me."

Out of the corner of her eye, she saw Hamish's gaze flick to her, then back to Neve, and his face fell.

"Must ye?" He lifted a hand, then put it back on the tabletop.

Aftyn believed he'd been about to reach for Neve's hand and thought better of it.

"Aye," Neve said, and glanced aside at Aftyn. "Soon. But Aftyn, I havena told ye the reason I asked ye to come. 'Tis quite an honor. The abbot has offered to hear your confession. The abbot! In thanks for the work we did caring for his people."

Aftyn frowned, though she recognized the truth of Neve's words. It was an honor. One she'd never heard bestowed to anyone lower than a senior priest. She and Neve were nothing to the kirk except souls to save. And hers, after the Lathans' arrival and Jamie's kisses, was in sore need of tending.

"How are we to make ourselves known to the abbot?"

"I'll take ye," Conal offered, standing. The others stood, too, and left them, crossing the hall toward a priest who'd just entered. Conal held up a hand for them to wait, then joined the others by the priest.

"Now?" Suddenly, Aftyn's confidence deserted her. How much dared she reveal to another person—the abbot!—about her feelings toward Jamie Lathan? Or her suspicions?

"Dinna fash," Neve said and smiled. "He is a gentle soul. I was honored by the kind things he said." She colored and added, "He waved any penance, even when I admitted to having feelings for Hamish."

Aftyn looked away to avoid reacting, and noticed Conal speaking to the priest and gesturing toward her and Neve, but he made no move to join them. The abbot's generosity was shocking, but if he didn't take offense at Neve's admission, perhaps she could get her envy of Jamie off of her conscience. He would be gone soon, and she would like the weight of her feelings for him—and her earlier ones against him—off her shoulders. "I should take the abbot up on his kind offer, then," she told Neve and stood. Across the hall, Conal nodded to the priest and left the group to walk back to Aftyn.

"Ready?" He gestured to the side of the hall.

"Thank ye for guiding me." She turned to Neve. "Wait here for me?" When Neve nodded, she turned back to Conal. "I hope I am not causing a problem for ye."

"No' at all," Conal told her as they walked. "Father Dexter needs some weeds pulled. Ye are saving me from that, at least for a few minutes."

Aftyn nearly laughed, but held her mirth in check. The abbey's hall didn't seem the place for it. Still, the idea of Neve's

Hamish weeding a garden somehow pleased her. She should add that unkind impulse to her confession.

An hour later, Aftyn found herself wishing she hadn't agreed to confess to the abbot. Her sins seemed too petty to devote his time to. Didn't all daughters complain about their parents? Yet the abbot had spoken quietly about family, and that love was not always demonstrated in a way one expected. Or that one wanted. She supposed he meant that her father ignored her out of some subtle attempt to make her a stronger person. But she didn't believe it. She confessed to being jealous of the Lathan healer's expertise and admitted her suspicions that Jamie had some special empathy that let him feel what others did, and that helped him treat their illness or malady much faster than anything she'd ever seen before. The abbot chided her that such would seem more a burden than a gift. When she mentioned wrestling with the idea of going with Jamie when he left, the abbot spoke of duty. None of that made her feel better. She consoled herself that the abbot could not repeat what she told him, so she should not worry. He'd absolved her of her sins and excused her from penance for her service to the abbey, just as he had done for Neve. And she'd forgotten to mention picturing Hamish pulling weeds.

As she and Neve rode home, she reflected on her confession and she realized she'd left out something important. Despite how mixed her feelings were about the Lathan healer, it saddened her to imagine living her life without him. But perhaps it was for the best.

JAMIE, feeling rested after returning to Keith and sleeping undisturbed for several hours, made his way to the herbal, trying to make more sense of Aftyn's mother's journal. Aftyn had gone to the abbey, so he had some time alone to puzzle out another page. If he intended to leave with his men, he didn't have much more time to devote to it. But he would go only if he could be sure that Aftyn was safe.

He'd written out many of the preparations, but some were obviously scrawled in haste or when the woman was tired or ill, and were all but illegible. After several hours, he concluded he might never uncover what she intended, and it would be dangerous to guess, when his interpretation would be prepared by others and used on people whose lives might be at stake.

Frustrated, he tossed aside the journal with an oath, rose and stretched. A noise near the door made him turn, prepared for battle as he'd been trained, but Aftyn, back from the abbey, stared at him from the doorway.

The look on her face could have been a dagger to his chest. Hurt and anger filled her eyes. He glanced aside at the journal and back to her. "'Tis no' what ye think," he said, though truly, he didn't know what she was thinking. Only that she appeared upset.

"'Tis all I have left of her, and ye toss it aside as though it means nought." She approached the table and picked up the journal, then hugged it to her chest. "Though to ye, I suppose it does mean nought, save an interesting problem to solve. Something to while away the time until Niall is ready to travel and ye can leave here and return home."

"I'm sorry, lass." He was. He knew her well enough by now to understand how conflicted she was about her mother—missing her, and yet hurt at being left and angry at being left unprepared to live a full and useful life. He'd hurt her again. Not with his words this time, like the ones she'd overheard the night he arrived, but with his actions. "I didna mean to give ye that impression. I'm frustrated that I canna make more sense of it for ye."

"Ye are frustrated? Ye? How long do ye think I've tried to

tease out its secrets? Ye dinna ken what it means to be frustrated."

Jamie nodded, then gave into his urge and pulled her into his arms. "I'm sorry. I ken ye miss her, and that ye wish ye could speak to her." He felt her tense, but didn't release her. He would hold her until she made it clear she wanted him to let her go. She wasn't the only one grieving and angry and needing comfort, though it had taken him until now to recognize it. He still grieved for the friend he'd been unable to save.

"Aye," Aftyn whispered. "I'd tell her how angry I am that she left me in this impossible situation," she grated out, and pounded on his chest with the heel of her hand. It took a moment for her words to make sense.

She couldn't hurt him. Not physically, not when he was caught up in how good Aftyn felt in his arms. She fit. She made his blood sing, and his body responded, tightening. But she needed his support and comfort, reminding him this was not the time to give in to his body's reaction.

"Impossible situation? What do ye mean?" He felt her pull back, and reluctantly let her slip out of his embrace, leaving him empty and longing to hold her again. But her cheeks were pink and she kept her gaze downcast. At the market day, he'd felt she hid a secret. Now he suspected he was one step closer to finding out what burden she carried alone.

"I... nay, I canna say."

"Canna? Or willna? What is so terrible that ye canna speak of it?"

Though tears glimmered in her eyes, she pulled herself upright and squared her shoulders. "Willna. Ye will leave in a few days. What happens to me once ye are gone will be none of yer concern. Ye will forget me and Neve and go on with yer life as though ye never met us."

Jamie shook his head. "Nay, that isna true." Aftyn Keith would fill his heart and his fantasies for the rest of his life. He wanted nothing more than to find a way to keep her with him. "I promised to protect ye. I want ye to come with us. To the Aerie. To be trained." If she discovered and didn't accept his and his mother's talent, it would be dangerous, but he was beginning to think she could understand. "Or I will take ye to any healer ye prefer. But ye ken ye are no' safe here."

"Perhaps. I ken ye want to keep me safe, but yer life isna here. Ye canna stay forever." She wrapped her arms around her and turned her gaze to the tabletop. "Since ye are ready to give up on the journal, I will thank ye for what ye have done. It will help. I just dinna ken if it will be enough."

"Enough for what?"

"Enough for me to remain with the clan as its healer."

"And if it isn't?"

"Then I dinna ken what will become of me, but ye need no' fash yerself. I will think of something."

Jamie didn't understand what she was trying to tell him. "What about Neve. Is she also at the same risk?"

"I dinna ken that either. Does it matter? She isna illegit..." Aftyn choked to a stop and her face flamed.

"Illegitimate? Is that what ye are trying to tell me. Ye are illegitimate and being the healer, succeeding yer mother, is the only place for ye in the clan? Who save the laird has the authority to banish ye?" Jamie paused then, as the realization washed over him. He recalled the laird's contempt for Aftyn's efforts. "He is yer da? The Keith is yer father and Braden is yer brother?"

Aftyn didn't speak, but the angry color drained from her face. That was answer enough. "Aye," she finally said. "He doesna acknowledge me. My mother remained his leman until her death. Braden's mother always resented her—and hated me. I reminded her of her husband's infidelity. She divorced him years ago, and took Braden back to her clan to foster until he was fourteen. The healer there treated his breathing problems and sent her treatment to my mother when he returned to Keith."

"What happened to her?"

"She remarried. Braden writes to her occasionally. I think her disdain for me affected Da, and he tolerates my presence only because I learned enough from my mother before she died to save Braden when he couldna breathe. The last time was over a year ago. Da's gratitude is wearing thin."

"Gratitude? If he felt gratitude, he would acknowledge ye and give ye yer rightful place in the clan."

"I dinna hope for that." The despair on her face made him furious. But it finally made sense. He felt sorry for what she'd been through, but he had to respect her strength of purpose and the fight she still fought to be accepted. "All the more reason," Jamie said, "to go with us, where ye could be trained, and not waste yer time guessing what yer mother meant. Ye could return the kind of healer yer mother was, that ye want to be, or better. One that yer da would respect." And she would be with him. He took her hand, marveling at its softness and how it fit within his. How touching her sent pleasure spiraling through his body to settle in his chest. His heart. Yet he felt her anguish there, too.

She shook her head. "He never will. He never has."

Jamie's gut twisted at the pain in her voice. The Keith laird was no better than Mhairi's husband. No wonder Aftyn felt so much compassion for that woman. "Then make him," he challenged. Though it was clear she would never change her father's mind if he refused even to see her efforts for the clan. Jamie's determination to take Aftyn away grew.

"Do ye think I havena tried? I saved his heir from suffocating to death. But that was a long time ago, and my da's memory grows shorter and shorter with time. What do ye think would have happened to me if Niall had died?" She waved a hand. "He would have banished me or turned me over to yer laird, fearing yer clan's retribution."

No wonder she seemed afraid of every unfamiliar aspect of being a healer. Her future—even her life—depended on being good at it, but she had never been given the chance. "Ye wouldna be harmed by the Lathan laird."

"How would I ken that?"

Jamie huffed out a breath. "Ye wouldna, of course."

"My half-brother, his heir, is my ally, but he is powerless against our father."

"Does he still need ye to care for him, for his breathing?"

"Nay, thank the saints. The last attack wasna long after my mother died. He nearly died, too, but I still had the medicine she gave him, and was able to make more."

Jamie didn't know what to do for Aftyn if she would not leave. Despite his promise to stay as long as it took to make certain she was safe, he could not stay forever. They were pulled in different directions, and he couldn't see a solution to her problems if she remained here.

"I'm no' leaving yet. Perhaps something will yet occur that will be the answer ye need."

She shook her head. "Long after ye are gone, I will still be here, doing what I can. Ye have helped me more than ye ken, and I appreciate it." She gestured at the journal, then at the neat pile of parchment where he'd written out her mother's preparations. "That will have to be enough."

14

After spending the day trying to think of a way to help Aftyn that she would accept, and checking on his patients scattered around the village, the glen, and the abbey, Jamie got back to Keith in time for the evening meal. Later, he gathered his men in Niall's chamber, where he told them about the Keith laird's visit to the abbey, and being included in the abbot's interview with the laird. "The Keith has me much on his mind, that is clear." Jamie grimaced. "In one or two more days with the priest, I will feel confident giving him over to another's care. But it might be best for the rest of ye to leave in the morning."

"Ye think the Keith will use us against ye? He canna force ye to stay, or to become his clan's healer," Fearchar said.

"He'd be a fool to think any healer would do as he wishes under duress," Niall added as Jamie removed the wrapping on his leg and examined the new, pink and healthy flesh in the wound track.

"I'm sorry being at the abbey has kept me from doing as much for yer leg as I meant to by now."

"Dinna fash," Niall said. "'Tis healed enough to get me home. Ye can do the rest there." He flexed his foot, stretching the calf, and grimaced. "I can ride."

"Good," Jamie told him.

"As I was saying," Niall continued, "Why would the laird risk ye doing more harm than good?"

"Nay risk," Bhaltair argued. "No' if he threatened Aftyn or Neve, or even one of us. Jamie would have to do as he wished."

"Which is why I want Aftyn to go with us." Jamie crossed his arms. "Neve knows enough to clean cuts and bind wounds, chill a fever, and make simple cures. But Aftyn is his daughter. While I'd say no man would harm his own flesh and blood, he holds her in little regard."

All three of the other Lathans frowned in surprise, but Fearchar spoke up. "Why? What did she do?"

"She was born on the wrong side of the blanket," Jamie told him. "And she's been too ashamed to tell us. But it explains a lot about her life here. He hasn't acknowledged her and won't support her."

"Bastard," Bhaltair muttered. "What can we do?"

"'Twould be dangerous for ye and yer ma for her to be trained at the Aerie," Fearchar added. "But perhaps another clan..."

Jamie rubbed his chest. The twinge he felt had nothing to do with what he'd done today for Aftyn's patients around the village. Fearchar's words reminded Jamie that what he had begun to hope for with Aftyn seemed impossible. Yet he still wanted to take her home—to the Aerie. "I've suggested such, but she willna leave."

"Ye could kidnap her," Niall said with a grin.

"And have to wed her? Are ye daft?" That from Fearchar.

Jamie frowned. He hadn't considered anything so drastic. He had come to want her, to respect her, and to care for her. He wanted to help her. But marry her? His thoughts strayed to Aftyn insisting she would never marry, then to their tryst in the woods. She was unlike any lass he'd ever held, ever kissed, and more. What he'd felt there with her sparked something like his talent, but with pleasure, not pain. With longing. With need. He admired so much about her. Her beauty, aye. No man would regret waking to her smile each morn. But the beauty of her spirit on the inside was even more important. As best she could, she fought to protect those who needed her. Had her mother lived to train her properly, she would have already become a fierce and determined healer. The more he thought about it, the more the idea gained in appeal. If only he could convince her that marrying him was in her best interests. As cold as that sounded, Jamie worried she would come to harm if she stayed. He wanted her. She wanted him. Many marriages had started with far less.

"'Tis no' in my plans for her," Jamie finally said, as the others waited for his reaction. It was too soon to make his feelings for Aftyn known. "But I will continue my attempts to convince her to leave with us. Without help, she has little future here."

"To stay out of the Keith's clutches, perhaps 'tis best ye remain at the abbey," Bhaltair said.

That brought the discussion back to where Jamie wanted it —on what they were going to do, not on him and Aftyn in some future that, if he could not change her mind, would not happen. Jamie shook his head. "I can ride back and forth each day. I dinna want to appear worried by avoiding this keep. The Keith kenned I saw how he was thinking. He didna make a threat of his comment."

"Perhaps he dared no' say more in front of the abbot."

Bhaltair was an excellent tactician. Jamie knew he'd be wise to heed his advice. "Rabbie, I want ye to take Niall, dressed as Fearchar, back to the Aerie. Leave in the morning. Then the state of Niall's leg willna be a threat. Ye dinna need haste, but tell them how things are here."

"Why the deception?"

"If they ken Niall is gone, then none of us would have a reason to stay. Fearchar will stay out of sight and Bhaltair can tend to him as he has Niall." And Jamie would have a little more time to convince Aftyn to come with him, if only for her own safety. "With two of ye gone, there are fewer here for the Keith to use, if he has a mind to, and he'll ken the Lathan will be told all there is to tell."

"Aye, but he'll prepare against it," Bhaltair added.

"Perhaps." Jamie nodded. "I'll bed down in here. Bhaltair and Fearchar, ye take Rabbie's chamber and bar the door. That window gives out onto the roof of the laundry, so ye can get out that way if ye must. But if ye must, dinna come for me. I'll no' be harmed. Rabbie and Niall, sleep in the stable, out of sight, then go as soon as the gate opens at first light to let in the workers from the village. Try no' to be seen making yer way there."

Rabbie nodded agreement, then said, "If we're discovered taking these precautions, do ye still think ye'll be able to go to the abbey? Perhaps we all should leave."

"The Keith willnae refuse the abbot. I'll take Aftyn with me in case we can leave from there."

"Braden, the heir, is keen to try the new mounts that arrived today," Rabbie added. "If he goes with ye..."

"Nay. We'd have to go with a Keith escort."

Fearchar crossed his arms. "Is that good or bad?"

"Both," Bhaltair said. "It gets a few of them out of the keep and out of our way, but means there's a guard to control Jamie's movements."

"I dinna think it will come to that," Jamie said. "But if it does, ye all ken what ye are to do."

J AMIE ROSE before dawn to ensure Rabbie and Niall, dressed as Fearchar, were able to leave the Keith stronghold at first light. He had not been disturbed during the night. Nor, Bhaltair told him when they met in the great hall, had he and Fearchar.

Jamie and Bhaltair kept their distance and watched as Rabbie and Niall headed out as soon as the gate opened. Workers streamed into the keep around their mounts. When the guards made no move to delay or stop them, Jamie breathed a sigh of relief and traded a look with Bhaltair that acknowledged the risk of losing two men. But Jamie felt it wise to have his men carry home news of their whereabouts and Jamie's concerns. If necessary, the threat of Lathan reprisals would keep the Keith laird from doing anything foolhardy. And remove the risk Niall's mostly healed leg posed to Jamie.

He hoped he was right. But the prickling at the nape of his neck told him this was no time to let down their guard.

He and Bhaltair went back into the hall to break their fast. As they'd planned, Fearchar remained in their shared chamber, waiting for them to bring food back up to him. As long as they didn't have to say who remained and who left, he hoped Niall would not be missed. He had a moment of regret that Niall had made his way down to the great hall more than once. It would be simpler now if he had remained above stairs. Still, their hosts could assume whatever they wished about him no longer venturing out of his chamber.

In the meantime, there was no sense all being together, making it easier for the Keith to do whatever he planned to do. And Jamie had no doubt he planned something.

Everything seemed normal. He didn't notice any tension among the Keiths who passed through the great hall, nor among those who sat at nearby tables to start their day. They weren't being surrounded. Nor was the path blocked to the keep's door or the stairs to the level where Fearchar awaited them.

Jamie finished eating and sat back, keeping Bhaltair company while he ate, and keeping an eye on their surroundings. Neve had returned, he noted, as she crossed near them and gave them a friendly wave before disappearing into the hallway that led to the keep's kitchen.

Finally, Bhaltair finished. He caught a serving lass's attention and ordered food for Fearchar.

Jamie stood. "Ye take that up. I'm going to the stable."

Even if he didn't ride on a given day, he liked to stop by the stable to make sure the Lathan mounts were being well taken care of. But today, he needed to find out if the stable master had expressed any concerns about two missing Lathan mounts. Better he tell Jamie, who could reassure him, than go to the laird.

When he entered, he heard a voice, but not the stable master's deep tones. Once his eyes adjusted to the interior gloom, he saw Braden and Aftyn standing outside a stall door, a new horse nosing at their shoulders. He'd heard Braden, then. Aftyn nodded at something he said to her, and reached up to stroke the horse's muzzle.

"Am I interrupting ye? I can come back later." He gestured toward the doorway, as though asking if he should leave. He thought they would probably like to give him a resounding *aye* and see the back of him, but instead, Aftyn shook her head.

"Nay, Jamie. Join us. Braden was telling me about the new horses that just arrived from Crieff."

"Indeed?" He'd bet his left arm they hadn't been discussing those horses. He could read Aftyn, and she wasn't telling the truth. Had they noticed two missing Lathan mounts? Or had they not been missed with new mounts replacing them this morning?

"Aye," Braden agreed, then cleared his throat and gestured

at the stalls on either side of the one where they were standing. "Look at these beauties. They will do much to improve our stock."

"They should," Jamie replied. He kept his expression noncommittal, curious to see how far they would take this tale.

"I understand Niall is one of yer best horsemen," Braden added. "I'd enjoy seeing him ride."

That took the conversation in an uncomfortable new direction. Niall was gone, but Braden couldn't know that yet.

A serving lass stuck her head in the doorway. "Aftyn, I found ye! Can ye come? Janet sliced her thumb in the kitchen, and I went first up to yer herbal. Someone told me they'd seen ye coming out here."

Aftyn headed toward the door. She paused and turned back to Braden for a moment. "I'll be back soon. This willna take long." Then she followed the lass.

Jamie might never get another chance to be alone with Braden. He wanted to do something for the lad before he left. He opened the stall door and entered, Braden on his heels. "These look to have Spanish lines."

Braden settled on a nearby bale of hay. "I see that."

"Do ye ken who yer Da got them from?" As he spoke, he moved around the horse, running a hand over its withers and along its back, a path that took him in arm's length of Braden.

Jamie reached out and quickly laid a healing sleep on the lad, caught him as he slumped and leaned him back against the wall behind him.

Aftyn had saved him from his last breathing problem more than a year ago, but she worried constantly that he would have another episode. Jamie ran a hand from Braden's chest up his throat to his face, extending his talent and probing for anything that seemed out of place. Jamie had seen something similar to the slight swelling in his airway in a young lass at the Aerie. Every time the weather got cold and dry, her body reacted and she choked, unable to breathe. Mint leaves in steam had helped her, but Jamie found the problem and fixed it. Braden's condition was minor compared to hers, but he was older, and Aileanna had mentioned that some children in the village where she grew up who had this affliction grew out of it.

Braden might be well on the way to achieving that, but Jamie eased the swelling and did everything he could to ensure Braden—and his sister—no longer had to be concerned.

Braden's breathing affliction had kept him from being as strong as he should be. Now he'd have a chance to grow into the leader and develop the strength and skills of a warrior that a laird needed to have.

Satisfied he'd done all he could, he woke Braden, stepped away and continued around the horse he'd been inspecting.

When he glanced around, Braden was awake, but bleary. Jamie kept talking, giving him time to recover. Braden would assume he'd dozed off for a second in the middle of whatever Jamie was saying.

"Ah, aye, of course," he said when Jamie paused.

Jamie hid a grin behind the horse's mane. "Very good, then. Let's look at the other two," he told Braden, and quit the stall. They had time to admire them before Aftyn returned.

"Janet shouldna be allowed near a blade," she groused as she walked up the center aisle to them. "I have to wrap a finger of hers at least once a sennight. One day, she'll chop one off, and then what will she do?"

"Ye will sew it back on," Braden told her, smiling.

Aftyn rolled her eyes and crossed her arms.

Jamie knew she thought it impossible, but he wondered. With his talent, could he do it? He'd treated frightful battle injuries but never tried to reattach a completely severed limb.

"What weighty matters did ye two discuss while I was gone?"

"Horses," Braden said, Jamie echoing the same word at almost the same time.

"So, lasses, then." She grinned. "Ye dinna need to lie. I've heard the lads when they didna ken a lass was near."

Braden gave Jamie a look that said *whatever is she going on about*, and shrugged. Jamie returned the shrug and turned back to Aftyn, just as Neve ran into the stable.

"Ach, there ye are. Aftyn, I looked everywhere for ye. I have bad news." She put a hand on Aftyn's shoulder. "Robena died in her sleep, sometime during the night."

Jamie collapsed onto a nearby bale of hay. He'd failed her. He thought he'd given her more time, but he hadn't.

Aftyn burst into tears, and clung to Neve and Braden, who told her, "I ken ye tried to help her. It was no' to be, lass. Ye did yer best."

"She fought for so long," Aftyn cried, then her watery gaze found Jamie. "She was better."

He pushed to his feet and went to her, taking her hand and bracing against the pain in her heart, so much like the pain already in his own chest. "Sometimes that happens," he told her, wishing he had better words to console her. "Someone seems better before they pass on. 'Tis a gift, I think."

"A cruel one," Neve replied, frowning, "to give someone hope, then snatch it away."

Was that what he'd done? Given Colin—and Aftyn—and even Agatha hope, only to have Robena snatched away? He blamed himself for not being able to help her. He thought he'd have more time. Being delayed at the abbey by the fire was no excuse. Being too hot-headed and close-minded to accept his mother's teachings, aye. Perhaps if he'd learned as she wished him to, Robena would still be alive. Now he'd never know.

∾

LATER THAT MORNING, Braden found Aftyn in her herbal, sitting before a mound of greenery, staring at nothing. She couldn't think. Couldn't focus. Robena's sudden death held her in shock.

Braden touched her shoulder, then held up a finger, glanced around, making no secret of checking to see if they were alone, then closed the door. Aftyn frowned and pivoted away from the table where she had intended to chop herbs for a poultice, but had done nothing. "What's amiss?" Braden never sneaked around. This behavior was very unusual.

"I just came from the strangest conversation with Da about the abbot."

"The abbot? What is he doing here?"

"He isnae here. He sent a missive that has Da scheming."

"What missive?"

"Thanking the laird for Keith help, o'course. And relating interesting observations about our visiting healer."

Aftyn's heart froze in her chest. "What kind of observations?"

Someone knocked on the herbal's door. "Aftyn?" The voice belonged to one of the downstairs serving lasses. "Yer da is asking for ye. I think ye'd best hurry to him. He seems fashed."

Aftyn exchanged a look with her brother.

"Aftyn? Are ye in there?"

"Ye could head back to the abbey to check on the injured," Braden said in a low voice.

"I'd be seen. Da will be furious if I ignore his summons. Nay, I may as well get this over with."

"Do ye want me to come with ye?"

Aye, she did, but she didn't want their father to take out on Braden whatever had upset him. "Nay. Whatever this is, 'tis best ye keep clear of it. If I need yer help after I talk to Da, I'll find ye."

"Or send someone to find me. I'll do whatever I can, ye ken that."

"I do." Aftyn gave him a quick hug. "Ye are the best brother a lass could ask for."

"Ye saved my life, so there canna be a better sister."

"'Tis the best thing I've ever done. Now, let me go. Ye wait a wee before ye leave here. No sense having someone tell Da ye were in here, warning me of trouble."

"I'll do as ye ask."

Aftyn went to the door and opened it. The serving girl had gone, so Aftyn hurried to the stairs and down them to the laird's solar where she could always find her father.

"Da? Ye sent for me?"

Even at this early hour, the laird sat at his table, reading something. Aftyn feared it was the abbot's letter, the thing Braden thought had brought about his summons.

He lifted the missive but didn't bother to meet her gaze. "The abbot has some interesting things to say about our visitor. And some of the most interesting, he claims to have learned from ye."

Under the seal of confession! Aftyn's blood turned to ice. So much for the 'honor' of the abbot hearing her confession. Not if he shared what she'd said with her father.

"I dinna understand," she said, fighting not to stammer, keeping her back straight and her head erect. She dared not flinch. He would take that as an admission of some sort of guilt.

"He says the Lathan healer has unheard of skill and the ability to heal grievous wounds unnaturally quickly." He put down the missive and lifted his gaze to hers. "What do ye ken about this?"

Aftyn fought not to react. She hadn't challenged Jamie after seeing Niall walking normally in his chamber. For Niall to be able to move about freely this soon, Jamie had done something miraculous. She just didn't know how.

"Only what I observed," she replied, keeping her expression

indifferent. "Mostly after the fire. While Neve and I cared for the less injured, the Lathan healer cared for the one hurt the worst. I canna say whether anything he does is more or less than any other healer can do. He brought many of his own medicines. They may simply be better than ours."

That seemed to satisfy her father, and Aftyn let herself take a breath. She thought she'd diverted him and laid Jamie's success to the potions he'd brought with him, which could very well be true, both for Niall and for the burned priest. She could have made too much of what she thought she saw at the market. She'd needed someone to talk to and thought a confession would be safe. Sacrosanct. Thank God she hadn't seen Niall walking around his chamber before she confessed. She racked her memory for exactly what she'd told the abbot.

Then her father pounced.

"Why then do ye think the abbot believes these things?"

"I dinna ken. Perhaps others at the abbey said something."

"He says he learned them from his own observation—and from ye. Do ye accuse the abbot of lying?"

"Nay, Da. Never. But perhaps he misunderstood…"

"He seems possessed of an astute mind. And he says he canna determine whether the healer is a devil's spawn or a God-given gift."

Aftyn didn't know what to say to that, so she didn't say anything. But her knees were quaking with the urge to find Jamie and warn him to leave.

"Verra well, go on with ye. I can see ye'll shed nay more light on this. I'll have to discuss this with the healer himself."

"Ach, Da, would ye accuse him after all the good he's done for us and for the abbey?"

"Accuse? Nay. But I will ken what secrets he keeps. Perhaps then he can be convinced to remain here."

Aftyn blanched. Just as she'd feared when she heard what

the abbot told him, her father saw Jamie as too valuable to lose. If he could not entice him to stay, he'd use other means. She didn't know what those would be, but her father was ruthless when he wanted something. And he wanted Jamie Lathan.

So did she, but not at the risk of making him her father's prisoner.

15

The herbal's door was closed when Jamie arrived. He knocked once to be polite, then listened.

"Come," Aftyn called.

He opened the door, not surprised to find Aftyn inside, but so was Braden. "I ken I've asked ye once today, but am I interrupting?" he greeted them as he entered.

Aftyn spun about to face him, surprise lighting her face. And something else. "I thought ye had gone to the abbey."

Jamie didn't have time to consider what he saw there before Braden stood and moved toward the door.

"I'll leave ye two to continue yer work. Thank ye, healer. And good day to ye, healer Lathan."

"I didna mean to interrupt," Jamie said.

Braden shook his head. "Ye didna. I was just leaving."

Jamie nodded and turned to Aftyn as Braden left the herbal. "What are ye working on?"

Aftyn colored and turned away, gesturing at the worktable. "I was about to prepare some willowbark for tea. Treating Niall depleted my store to fight fevers."

Nothing about that simple task should cause her distress,

yet her color was still higher than normal. Why had Braden been here and what had they been talking about? Braden seemed in a hurry to leave.

"I'll try again with the journal, then," Jamie told her, and moved to the side table, where he kept it with his notes for Aftyn. "What did Braden want? Does his arm still bother him?"

"Only a wee bit. He moves it well and says it doesna hurt, only aches a bit if he uses it too much."

He didn't believe that was the only reason for Braden's visit, but Aftyn had turned back to her work. Jamie said, "That's good, then," and opened the journal to continue, hoping a new day would give him insights into the notes that had frustrated him the last time he attempted it. He'd spend an hour here, giving him time to win Aftyn's confidence and find out what he could, then go to the abbey as he'd planned.

A few minutes later, Braden returned. "I apologize for disturbing ye," he said, his gaze on Jamie rather than Aftyn, who stood up. "My father wishes to speak with ye in his solar."

Jamie nodded. He'd been expecting this summons. "I'll be down in a moment. Thank ye."

Braden nodded and left. Jamie turned his attention to Aftyn. Her gaze was still on the doorway where Braden had been. Her fists were clenched and her face had whitened. "Are ye well, Aftyn? Ye are pale."

She shifted and turned back to her table. "Nay, I'm fine. I've been standing too long in one place." With that, she sat on the stool she'd been on since Jamie entered.

He let the lie slide by and stood. "Best I go see what yer laird wants. I'll come back to work on the journal if I have time, but I plan to pay a visit to the abbey today."

"Is the priest better?"

"Aye. He's fortunate his robes protected him as well as they did."

Aftyn nodded but kept her face angled away from him. "Very well."

Something bothered her. Jamie wanted to stay and convince her to open up to him, but he was out of time. He left the herbal and went down the stairs to the laird's solar.

THE KEITH WAS at his worktable, sunlight streaming through a window onto the surface and a missive that held his attention. He picked it up as Jamie entered and tilted it more to the light, a slight frown drawing a shallow line between his brows. Then he glanced up. "Lathan," he said and gestured to a chair by the hearth. Jamie went there and waited until the Keith joined him, sitting in the opposite chair. So this was to be a friendly meeting. At least to start.

"What can I do for ye?" Jamie took the Keith's cue, but speaking first put him on a more equal footing than waiting for the laird to take charge and open the conversation. Jamie wanted some control, but needed to appear cooperative for as long as he could.

"'Tis what ye can do for my clan, and for all the people in Keith territory."

Jamie braced himself without moving a muscle, intent on appearing to listen calmly.

"The abbot speaks highly of yer skill." He waved the missive in his hand, but did not proffer it, leaving Jamie to wonder what it said. "I am prepared to offer ye much to become the Keith healer."

"What do ye mean?" The more the Keith talked, the more Jamie would find out without agreeing to anything. Had Aftyn known her father would summon him? Was that the subject of her conversation with Braden and the reason for the disquiet on her face? If so, perhaps he had good reason to fear he was running out of time to leave before his companions lives were threatened. How could the Keith expect him to foreswear his loyalty to his own laird and clan? And why would he trust him if he did? Nay, when he left here, he intended to go back to being a Lathan warrior, not a healer, except by necessity.

"I mean to convey to ye great honor as the clan's healer, control of the herbal, a larger, more comfortable chamber than the one ye have now, and coin in an amount we can discuss. For that, ye will swear fealty to me and remain here. Ye will train other healers."

That was impossible, yet he knew what the Keith meant. He expected a different clan to have different potions and methods of healing. And since his had been shown to be more effective than anything Aftyn had been able to do, his would be valuable, indeed. He wanted to ask why the Keith had not offered to see his daughter trained, but decided to wait before challenging the man.

"Many of my cures are kept within my family and I am no' free to share them."

"But ye are free to use them, and ye have done so here, if the reports that have reached me are true. Yer methods are more effective than anything we have. Even the abbot canna decide if yer ways are a gift from God or... well, we willna speak of the other."

Jamie kept his expression placid. Clearly, the Keith had expected a reaction to that statement. Fear, perhaps, at his veiled threat of witchcraft?

But for the moment, the Keith seemed focused on enticements.

"All that is worth much, as I'm sure ye ken. And Keith will become yer family, so ye may be assured of any cooperation ye require to find what ye need to compound yer potions."

"Yer offer is generous," Jamie said, and paused. He could not agree or disagree too quickly. And of course, he could not agree at all. "I am promised to the abbey this afternoon. Perhaps when I return, we can discuss terms." Jamie counted on the Keith's wish to stay on good terms with the abbot.

"I ken ye and Aftyn have become close. I'll give her to ye, if ye agree."

Anger starting to heat Jamie's blood. "What do ye mean, give her to me?"

"Anything ye wish. Make her yer mistress. Marry her. She means little to me as she is. Under ye..." He paused and snorted at his own double entendre, then continued, "her skills will improve. Perhaps in more than one area, aye?" He laughed.

Jamie did not. "I willna use her like that."

"As ye wish. Then let me offer another enticement. If ye agree, yer companions are free to return to Lathan."

"And if I dinna agree?" Jamie's belly suddenly hollowed out. Had Rabbie and Niall been caught? That could explain the Keith's veiled hints of witchcraft.

"Two of yer companions have already been taken to the dungeon. Two are missing and I'm told they left the keep at first light."

Jamie went weak with relief that Niall had not been discovered. Then anger rose, and his strength with it, that Bhaltair and Fearchar were in the dungeon.

"I've sent riders to bring them back. Until ye swear to me— before the abbot, mind ye—yer men will remain in the dungeon without food." So the Keith counted on intercepting Jamie's men, to keep word from reaching Lathan.

Jamie surged to his feet. "Ye canna starve my men." And he could not swear before the abbot to follow this man. In order to save innocent lives, he'd come to terms with breaking the vow he'd made in anger eighteen months ago. But this? Even made under coercion, this would be a vow he could never break, lest he risk whatever remained of his immortal soul.

"They will have water. They can live much longer without food, so ye will have time to change yer mind."

Jamie hoped Rabbie and Niall had disregarded his comment that urgency was not required, and ridden like the wind toward the Aerie. "This is how ye entice someone to aid ye? By threatening my men?"

"Yers nay longer. Ye are a Keith now."

"I am a Lathan. I only agreed to help your healers for..."

"And ye shall continue to do so, though for longer than ye expected."

Jamie, on his feet, loomed over the seated laird. But the Keith appeared unworried. A slight sound by the doorway behind him told Jamie the Keith had prepared for his arrival and guards stood by to prevent Jamie from doing what he longed to do—wrap his hands around this arrogant man's neck and squeeze the life from him. Then free his men, take Aftyn, and leave this place.

But he could do none of that, certainly not at this moment, perhaps never unless he wanted a war with Keith and its allies. If Rabbie and Niall had reached the Aerie, Keith might get one, very soon.

He fought not to cross his arms over his chest. "Ye have me at a disadvantage."

"Only a temporary one. If ye swear to me, all will be well, and ye will be well rewarded. Ye have only to decide."

"I must see to the priest who was burned." Jamie hoped to divert him from thinking about the other Lathans. He couldn't do anything from the abbey except finish with the priest. Even if he took Aftyn with him, he could not return to Lathan without Bhaltair and Fearchar. He would not leave them in the Keith dungeon.

"Ye may go, but with a Keith escort to ensure yer safety."

"My safety hasna been at issue before now."

"Until ye swear to me, that has changed. For ye, and for yer men."

Jamie kept his hands at his side and did not allow himself to clench them into fists. The Keith knew him as a healer. Best he continued to regard him as such and underestimate him.

As soon as Jamie saw a chance, the laird would meet the warrior.

By the time Aftyn went down to the great hall for the midday meal, the keep was abuzz with the news that Jamie Lathan had gone to the abbey with an escort, and that two of his companions were currently in the dungeon. No one mentioned the other two, or any names. His companions—even Niall?—in the dungeon! Wait, only two of his companions were there. Where were the other two?

She immediately forgot any thought of food. Her stomach clenched and ice formed in her veins. Her confession had caused all of this. Jamie under guard made no sense, but he still did his best to help. Aftyn hoped the burned priest knew what a sacrifice Jamie was making for his sake. Surely Jamie had to be worried about his men. And wondering what her father would do next.

She left the great hall through the main door, desperate for fresh air before she passed out or burst into tears. She wasn't sure which was most likely, but she was ready for either. This was her fault.

She had to get to the dungeon! Niall should not be there. His wound would get infected. He'd sicken again. Dear God, he could die! What was her father doing? Had he lost his mind?

She paced, thankful most of the clan was in the great hall eating, leaving her alone out here, save for the guards on the wall walk whose attention should be directed outside the keep, not into the bailey.

What would happen to Jamie when he returned from the abbey? Would her father put him in the dungeon, too?

She had to think of something. Jamie had done so much for the clan, the abbey, and for her. He'd made his interest in her clear through his care and concern, his kisses and caresses, and his offers to take her back to the Aerie with him. He'd said he'd take her wherever she wanted to go for training, but she hoped he meant something more, for what had blossomed between them.

The abbot had given her father just enough information to make Jamie a prize worth threatening. Even worth risking trouble with his clan. She suspected her father had offered Jamie a place as healer and Jamie had turned him down.

He was a good man. She hadn't wanted to admit her feelings, even to herself, knowing that he would be leaving soon. But then he'd offered to stay, to protect her, and her attraction to him had deepened over time into something more real, more important, and now?

Now she would be forced to help him leave her. To defy her father and do whatever she could to keep him and his men safe, and to find a way for them to escape—and leave her behind.

16

J amie rode back to the Keith keep with his escort. Or rather, under guard. He understood what the Keith was up to. He allowed the escort because Bhaltair and Fearchar were his prisoners. Otherwise, Jamie would have disposed of the guards, collected his men and Aftyn, and headed back to the Aerie.

The injured priest no longer needed him. He was well enough that once he woke from the healing sleep Jamie laid on him before he left the abbey, he would be able to resume light duties for a few days, until he felt stronger and resumed his normal responsibilities.

Leaving the man in good condition satisfied Jamie in a new way. This had not been the same as saving a man's life in the heat of battle, then moving on to the next and the next. He'd spent hours with the priest over a period of days, and had become invested in returning the man to health. His talent, which he'd spurned for many years, had allowed him to give back the life the man had worked to achieve. The time Jamie spent with Niall doing much the same thing—ensuring he lived and could return to his duties as a Lathan warrior—had allowed Jamie to think a great deal about the legacy he inherited from his mother. Seeing Aftyn suffer the lack of training, of competency, that her mother should have prepared her with brought the lesson home even more clearly. The abbot thought his healing ability was a gift from God, and while he would never cease fighting for Lathan and his father's causes, and one day his brother's, he had a valuable skill few possessed, one that saved lives and changed lives that would have been ruined by disease or injury.

He owed Aftyn a debt of gratitude for helping him see for himself what his mother had tried to teach him. What he'd been too young and stubborn to hear and accept. What his fury at his foster father over his friend's death had led him to reject —at least until innocent lives were at stake. He was older and wiser now, and the dedication and heart Aftyn put into caring the best she was able for others shamed him. He could do so much more than she, and he'd wanted to throw it away. He'd ignored his ability and refused to accept his heritage. No longer. He would fight when he must and heal when he could. And give Aftyn her due.

The attraction and affection he felt for her had grown into something more. He wasn't sure what he felt, or whether he could offer her more than she needed to become the healer she wanted to be. But the thought of spending time away from her grated on Jamie. He'd solve that problem when he solved the others and brought them all away from here.

Once Jamie and the Keiths entered the keep and left their mounts with the stable master, they escorted him into the great hall and left him. Apparently he still had the freedom to roam within the walls.

Braden surprised him by approaching him, his expression pensive.

"Welcome back," Braden said.

Jamie could have responded in many ways, but chose not to

take his ire out on the young man. "Thank ye." He glanced at the stairs, wondering if Aftyn could tell him about his men, and opened his mouth to ask where she was, but Braden saved him the trouble.

"Yer men are well. I ken yer were going to ask that, aye?"

"Indeed. I want to see them."

Braden glanced around as he took a step closer. Apparently satisfied that no one could hear him, he said, "Aftyn has taken food and drink to them."

Jamie's heart swelled at the thought of her care for his men. And for the risk she took to defy her father. If he found out, the laird would not be pleased. But it was pure Aftyn. He should not have been surprised that she would do such a thing. She had a caring heart. Jamie nodded his acknowledgment. "She is kind to do so."

Then a little louder, Braden added, "My father has instructed me to show ye yer new chamber before ye venture anywhere else."

Jamie shook his head, anger building in his chest. Not at this lad, but at his father. "The only enticement I wish at the moment is to see my men."

"If ye would come with me," Braden said, making it sound like an invitation. "I can tell ye more." His voice dropped even lower on the last statement.

Jamie nodded at that. "Very well. Lead the way." It occurred to him that Braden had staged their encounter carefully to appear to be following his father's orders. But was he? He could be leading him into some sort of trap that would have him sharing accommodation with his men. But nay, the Keith wanted his cooperation. Tossing him in the dungeon, and using Braden to do it, made no sense. When Braden headed for the stairs to the upper floors, Jamie relaxed slightly and followed.

Braden led him to a sumptuously appointed chamber with a large hearth, a window looking toward the hills in the distance, draped in thick, rich fabrics, and with a solid shutter against the cold. A grand bed, large enough for two to sleep in comfort or engage in whatever bed sport pleased them, filled most of the side of chamber opposite the window. For a moment, Jamie pictured Aftyn there with him, but he pushed the image aside when Braden stopped.

"This is yers for the rest of yer stay," Braden told him. "My father means to keep ye, but prefers ye make up yer mind to stay."

"And that is why he holds my men in the Keith dungeon."

Braden pursed his lips and looked away. "My father also believes in hedging his bets."

"And what do ye think? Ye will be laird someday. Do ye agree with what yer da has done?"

"The clan needs ye," Braden answered and crossed his arms, then lifted a hand. "I dinna approve of all of my father's methods, but our need is real. Aftyn's need, Neve's need, is real. Ye could do much good here. Ye have already done much good. Ye dinna deserve to have yer men held against ye."

"Thank ye for that," Jamie told him. Braden would make a fine laird someday, if his father didn't corrupt him before that time came. He had a good heart and a sense of right and wrong. Or perhaps his father had a greater sense of expediency. Jamie pressed his lips together. In the Keith laird's position, what would he do? He could not think of that now.

"Are ye to deliver my answer to yer da?"

"Only if ye have one to give him."

"I would see to my men first."

Braden nodded. "I can take ye."

In the dungeon passageway, Braden greeted the guard and proceeded without stopping. Jamie ignored the man and kept pace with Braden. The cell Bhaltair and Fearchar occupied was not the worst Jamie had ever seen. And a large tray covered with the remains of a hearty meal sat atop one of the pallets. But still, it rankled to see his men behind bars.

"How are ye?"

Fearchar grinned. "We've been worse. We've been better. Have ye come to get us out of here?"

Jamie glanced at Braden, who shrugged and stepped back.

"It seems ye will enjoy the Keith's lesser accommodation for a while longer," Jamie told them. "But I will get ye out as soon as I can."

"We dinna doubt that," Bhaltair said.

"What do ye need in the meantime?"

"More blankets wouldna go amiss," Fearchar told him. "And candles and a means to light them."

Jamie glanced at Braden, who nodded.

"I'll see to it," the lad said. "And if there's anything else ye need, send for me. The guard is loyal to me. I'll speak to him on the way out."

"Thank ye," Jamie told him, then made his farewells to his men. "Now, if ye ken, where is Aftyn? I will speak to her next."

Braden led him from the passageway. True to his word, he instructed the guard to fetch him immediately if their guests asked for him.

Jamie had no reason to believe the guard would do as Braden asked, but he didn't argue. He doubted the guard saw his men as guests, and would likely not risk the laird's displeasure beyond allowing Aftyn to bring them food. They continued up to the herbal, and Braden left him in Aftyn's company.

Once Braden left, she ran to his arms and held him. "Ach, Jamie, I'm so ashamed. None of this should be happening."

"Thank ye for taking care of my men," he told her. She looked frustrated. Ah, she'd been puzzling over her mother's journal. Hoping to distract her, he added, "Braden told me what ye did, bringing them food and drink."

"I couldna let them be harmed. 'Tis shameful to use them against ye that way."

"Then will ye help me free them? And come with us when we do?"

"My da will hunt ye down and bring ye back. Or lay siege to yer keep to get ye back."

Jamie laughed. "That's been tried before. He canna do it."

Looking up, she met his gaze. "What can I do?"

"I have some ideas," Jamie told her, then brushed her lips with his. "But none will work without ye."

THEY SPENT the rest of the time before the evening meal planning how to release Bhaltair and Fearchar.

Aftyn argued against including Braden in their plans. He had to remain ignorant or his father might punish him, or worse, disinherit and banish him. Jamie agreed, but privately thought another insider's help might make all the difference.

The next morning, Jamie made his way to the dungeon and told the guard he recognized as Braden's man that he'd been sent to see to his men's welfare. The guard argued. Jamie suspected he wasn't as loyal to Braden as Braden thought. While the man was distracted by his incredulity that the heir would send Jamie alone to see to his imprisoned men, Jamie knocked him out. It was too easy. Jamie relieved him of his weapons and keys, then freed his men.

The most difficult part of the plan was to get to the stables without being seen or stopped. The entrance to the dungeon was a few feet down the bailey past the guard tower stairs that led up to the wall walk. Hooded cloaks and a foggy, cold morning made that trip somewhat simpler. There were few people about, and none paid attention to the stooped, cloaked figures making their way deeper into the bailey toward the stables.

When they reached their objective, Jamie expected to see two horses readied for Aftyn and Neve to go riding, as they'd planned. Jamie's men would take them, and Jamie would quickly ready his own mount, which Aftyn would share with him.

The horses weren't ready. Worse, Aftyn wasn't there.

Frustration and fear filled Jamie. Where was she? Had she betrayed them? If so, guards would fill the stables in moments, and he'd join his men in the dungeon. He tensed, signaling for Bhaltair to watch the entrance while he checked the stalls. He found nothing but the horses that belonged there. Nothing happened.

Confused and concerned, Jamie debated going with his men or staying to find out what happened to Aftyn. If her father found out what they'd planned, she could be in danger. Jamie didn't want to imagine what he could do to punish her.

"Saddle yer mounts, ride out and wait in the woods," Jamie decided and told them. If I dinna join ye by moonrise tonight, ride to the Aerie and tell my father what has happened here. Rabbie and Niall should have made it home by now. Ye may meet Lathans on their way here. If ye dinna, find out whether those two made it."

"Ye must come with us. Ye canna stay or ye'll wind up in the dungeon."

Jamie shook his head at Bhaltair. "The laird willna harm me. I have to find out why Aftyn didna do as we agreed. Something is wrong."

"We'll wait for ye," Fearchar said. "Come on, Bhaltair. We havena much time."

∼

JAMIE'S MEN would have no problem riding out through the open gate and disappearing into the woods. There were blankets aplenty in the stable for them to take against the cold. He'd thought they'd have to do without the food and drink Aftyn had promised to have waiting with the horses, but he found the stable master's stash of bread, cheese, and a jug of cider, and gave that to them while they readied their mounts, then left them to do as he'd instructed and went in search of Aftyn.

He headed up to the herbal first, but it was empty. Neve, he recalled, still spent most of her time at the abbey, being courted by Hamish, so Aftyn wouldn't be closeted somewhere with her.

Aftyn's chamber was also empty. She wasn't in the great hall or the kitchen. If nothing else, he thought enough people had seen him in the keep by now to take no notice of two missing prisoners.

He searched everywhere in the keep proper that Aftyn might be, and headed out to the laundry, blacksmith, and buttery, thinking that his men had time enough to leave, so there would be no issue if he was seen in the bailey. Braden found him leaving the keep.

"I've been searching for ye," Braden said, out of breath.

"Have ye seen Aftyn anywhere? I canna find her."

"'Tis for her I sought ye. She's been hurt. She needs ye."

17

B raden on his heels, Jamie headed for the village, but slowed when he heard Braden struggling for breath. "Where is she, lad?" He stopped once they exited the keep's gate and turned to Braden, who bent over and gasped for air. "Take yer time. Breathe," Jamie told him as he placed a hand on Braden's bare nape. His lungs and throat were slightly constricted, from fear and exertion, not from his affliction. Jamie gently eased them open, gratified when he heard Braden's breathing even out.

"I'm alright," Braden told him. "She's with Mhairi."

"Take yer time getting there," Jamie told him. "I'll go ahead and see how she is."

"'Tis bad," Braden said. "I'm sorry to slow ye down. Sorry I didna find ye sooner."

Jamie clapped him on the back, then ran for Mhairi's cottage, grateful that most of the villagers were in the foggy fields or within their homes.

He didn't bother to knock. He flung open the door and rushed in. "Where's Aftyn," he demanded, blinking rapidly, peering into the relative darkness of the interior. Finally, he saw

Mhairi, who bent over a still form on the wee couch Jamie had assumed her son used.

"Here, healer. She needs ye."

He glanced around. "Braden is coming. Please go meet him and tell him to wait outside. Ye, too, if ye will. I'll call for ye if I need anything."

Mhairi hesitated. "I should stay to help ye."

Jamie needed her outside. "Braden was having trouble breathing," he said, hoping he lied, and that Braden still breathed easily after he helped him. "Could ye check on him, please?"

That got her moving. Alone with Aftyn, he dropped to his knees beside her. Blood and dirt covered her. Her hair tangled around her head and over the tear streaks through the dirt on her cheeks. Curled up in a ball of agony, she looked as if she'd been dragged by a horse or survived a pitched battle. Perhaps she had. Dismay filled him even before he touched her.

He bent closer, his chest tight with fear for her, and murmured, "Dear God, Aftyn, what happened to ye, lass?"

"Agatha's husband, and Mhairi's," she answered, rocking a little. "At the stable."

She surprised him. Even though her voice was weak and strained, relief that she was awake let his chest expand. He took a breath.

"They said healers... useless. I screamed. Cried. No one to help me."

Her whimper broke his heart.

"So they hit me." A tear leaked from one very swollen eye. "Knocked me down. Kicked me." She took another ragged breath. "Dragged me by my hair. Did it again... and again." She shuddered. "I fought. Nay good."

Fury filled Jamie, deeper and redder than any fury his temper had endowed him with in his life. Two men beating a lass? "I'll get them for this. There's nowhere they can hide." He ran a hand gently along Aftyn's curled form, touching skin through her torn clothes. He winced as he assessed what the men had done to her. What he found shocked him. How was she still alive? "Did they..."

"Nay. Enough... to beat me... I guess. Carried me past... gate... guards in... blanket and dumped me behind Mhairi's... where ye left Rory. Message... ye're next."

Jamie shook his head. "The two o' them canna take me. They'd best bring more men."

Aftyn frowned at his boast. "She... must have heard. Got me inside... when men left. Sent Alastair... for ye."

"Braden found me. I havena seen her lad."

"I hope... men dinna have him."

"Once I see to ye, I'll find out."

"Everything hurts."

Jamie took a breath to steel himself. Aftyn needed the best he could give her, but he didn't know if he could do what she needed without killing himself in the process. There was no one here to pull him from her if she slipped away. He clenched a fist. This was Aftyn. He would not let her slip away.

Even putting her into a healing sleep seemed too great a risk. If ever he was going to trust her, now was the time. "I have a confession to make," he started, but stopped when she groaned.

"I, too. My fault da locked... yer men... dungeon."

A chill ran up his spine. What did she mean, her fault? He didn't know what to process first—her fault or her father. "Ye can tell me later. I must make ye better."

"Ye canna. 'Tis too much..."

"Nay, lass. I owe it to ye to show ye how I heal."

Jamie pulled aside her torn dress and placed his hands on her belly where the men's boots had done the most damage. Agony assailed him. She bled inside. It took some time, but Aftyn finally uncurled a little and took a breath.

Jamie fought to control his own reaction to the pain and pressure he'd taken from her. It now encircled his torso like a vise, crushing him. He lifted his hands from her and straightened, then wrapped his arms around his middle. A groan slipped out.

Aftyn went still and for a moment Jamie feared she'd passed out, but then her eyes opened and her gaze fastened on his. "I was right."

"I dinna ken what ye thought," he ground out, "but... let me show ye." He took a breath to steady himself. The pain was ebbing. But he wasn't done. He touched her neck, his senses reaching into her, clearing the bruising from her muscles and her kidneys, soothing her pain, and taking it into himself. His body went cold and he started shaking. How had she stood the agony? He willed himself to concentrate, cursing under his breath.

"Ach, what have ye done? Did ye take... into yerself? Ye mustna!"

She pushed his hand away, breaking the contact before he was ready. Fire flashed along his veins and spread throughout his body. He couldn't breathe.

For a moment, he thought this must be what it feels like to be struck by lightning. A groan escaped him, and his chest expanded. He breathed through the pain and took her hand, noting the skinned knuckles, but leaving them for later. He moved to the swelling around her left eye next. He didn't want her to lose her sight. With his other hand, he lightly skimmed the area around her eye, nodding as the swelling went down, feeling the pressure and pain inhabit him. At least they hadn't managed to break the bones around the eye, or her jaw, but she was bruised and swollen there, too.

He stroked the side of her face to soothe her, but also to repair the damage the men had wrought. Aftyn whimpered and drew back, but he still held her hand and didn't let her pull away from him. They'd hurt his woman. They'd suffer the same, and more.

"Dinna fear me, Aftyn. Dinna fear what I can do. I am helping ye."

"Dinna fear ye. Fear *for* ye. Why must ye suffer?"

Jamie managed a chuckle around the tightness that still coiled around his middle, his back and belly burning, his lungs on fire. "That is a question... I've never gotten an answer to. 'Tis the way this works."

"'Tis unfair," Aftyn said, and laid her free hand on the side of his face.

She breathed more easily. If he squinted, he could tell her color had improved.

"I'm so sorry," she told him. "And thankful ye are willing to bear this for me."

"I would bear... anything for ye, Aftyn. Anything... to make ye better. To save ye. Ye must ken that."

She shook her head. "I didna. But I do now. Who else would take my pain into himself, save ye?"

Jamie forced a smile, then looked away. "I dinna think there's another who can, lass."

"Then I'm lucky ye are here." She pushed herself to sitting, wincing as she braced herself on one arm.

"Yer shoulder?"

"Aye, but it can wait."

"I'd be grateful for that," he said, attempting a jest but meaning it. He needed to rest. To let the pain subside. "Do ye ken where Mhairi keeps her mead? Or ale? Or even water? We could both do with something."

"There's a pitcher on the table. I dinna ken what's in it."

Jamie pushed to his feet and stumbled to the table, hugging his middle as he moved. When he reached it, he placed both hands on it and rested there, breathing hard. Once he could, he poured a cup and sniffed. "Perfect. 'Tis cider." He swallowed it down, then poured another and took it to Aftyn, along with the pitcher. He watched her drink, then joined her on the pallet and poured another. "Drink. Then I will. Then ye'll have another until we are ready to continue."

"What if Mhairi comes back in?"

"Ye will say ye lost yer breath from the beating, but ye are better now. Sore. Move carefully, as though ye are still in pain."

"I *am* still in pain."

"I ken it, lass. But ye willna die..."

"Die!"

"Ye were bleeding. Inside. They wouldha killed ye, Aftyn, had Braden no' found me when he did. 'Tis why it hurt so much."

"And now ye are bleeding inside!"

"Nay. I was never in danger." The lie came easily. Aftyn needed to hear it. If she stayed with him, she would learn the truth eventually.

He leaned his head against the wall behind them. "I shoulda killed Rory for what he did to Mhairi. Then he wouldna have been able to hurt ye, too."

"Nay, Jamie. Ye wouldha been outlawed."

"'Twould have been worth it to save ye this pain."

AFTYN COULD NOT BELIEVE what Jamie had revealed to her. He put his life in her hands, not knowing she'd already betrayed him and his men. He'd saved her life. And took her pain into himself.

She wanted to curl back into a ball and cry until the shock and shame of it left her. If they ever did.

She'd been at least partly right when she thought Jamie felt pain when people jostled him in the market. And when he turned to follow the old woman with his gaze, she now knew he'd wanted to help her, but dared not. Not only would he harm himself, her sudden improvement would cause questions to be asked that Jamie dared not answer. Braden! "Was Braden's elbow broken?"

"Aye."

"And ye fixed it."

"Aye. And his breathing. He's not as hale as he wants to appear to be. But I helped him. He'll get stronger."

What had she done? She dropped her head onto his shoulder and squeezed her eyes closed, now that she could. Tears leaked from their corners, and she let them run down her face, covering her mouth with one hand, lest a cry of anguish escape when Jamie wrapped her in his arms. "I'm so sorry, Jamie. I confessed to the abbot that I was jealous of yer skill, and thought ye had something... I didn't imagine anything like this, but some empathy. I told him, and he told my father. And he locked up yer men to keep ye here." She shook her head, rocking it on Jamie's broad, strong shoulder.

"Ye ken ye are no' safe here. Ye will come with me, back to the Aerie. There ye may learn as much as ye have dreamed of, and we will be together... if that is what ye wish."

She lifted her head and met his gaze, thinking about their brief time in the wood. "I would like that." Was it possible? She was still torn over leaving Braden, and leaving Neve to carry the burden of the clan's welfare. "But ye canna teach me what ye do. What ye just did, can ye?"

Jamie shook his head. "I'm sorry, nay. 'Tis something I inherited. I dinna ken how it works, or why. Only that it does." At her crestfallen expression, he pulled her onto his lap. "But ye can become the best healer the Highlands have ever seen, and learn every cure a wise woman must ken."

"I'll never be best. Ye are."

"Nay, lass. I fought using this ability for years. I was trained as a warrior and I'm a good one. Even a great one. I thought healing was something for a lass to do, no' a man. But ye have taught me the value of it. The value of what I can do. I'll never disparage it again."

"I'm glad of that. And that ye care so much for me."

"I love ye, Aftyn. I would give my life for ye."

She tucked her head back into the crook of his neck and sighed. "I love ye, too. And I wish we could stay here, like this, forever."

Jamie's heart soared at her admission. No matter what stood in their way, they would be together. He would make sure of it. "No' quite like this," he said and dropped a kiss on the top of her head. "Ye still have pain."

"I didna notice it, now that ye are holding me." She looked up, her gaze on his mouth. "Perhaps a kiss would cure the rest..."

JAMIE DIDN'T NEED to be asked twice. He dipped his head and met her lips, softly at first, then with more fervor as she answered his kiss with her own, sweet mewling sounds accompanying each brush of his lips on hers. He extended his talent each time his lips touched hers, and found that his healing strength grew even greater than he was accustomed to. Could affection, caring, even love, amplify his ability? If he noticed this much from simple kisses, what would more intimacy reveal? And why hadn't he noticed the same effect kissing her in the wood? Because no one was hurt?

Before he could deepen the kiss and find out, the door swung open and Mhairi entered.

Jamie released Aftyn, thankful for the few moments it took anyone's eyes to adjust to the dim interior from the daylight outside. Aftyn leaned against the wall, while Jamie stood to meet Mhairi. "She's better," he told her. "No' well, but better."

Mhairi knelt by Aftyn and winced. "Ach, Aftyn. I'm so sorry Rory did this to ye. I'm so ashamed."

"Nay, Mhairi," Aftyn said, her voice weak. "'Tis no' yer fault. And he had help."

"Aye, Agatha's man. I heard. She should be ashamed, too." She cupped the side of Aftyn's face and tried to wipe away the dirt and dried blood on it. "How could they do this to ye?"

"Do ye ken where Alastair is?" Jamie didn't want to worry her, but he did want to know if the lad was safe.

"I do. He's with a friend. She'll keep him out of sight until all this is settled."

"Good. Is Braden with ye, outside?"

"I'm here," Braden's voice preceded his silhouette in the doorway, then he stepped into the cottage. "Are ye well, Aftyn?" He moved toward her and dropped to the floor, kneeling before her and taking her hand, his mouth turning down as he studied her.

"I've been better, but Jamie has seen to me, and I will be well soon enough."

"Damn it, Sister, if our father treated ye as he ought, those men would never have dared to touch ye."

"Perhaps," she answered, and shrugged, then winced.

"I'll wager they never do the like again," Mhairi said with a glance at Jamie.

"I'd like to kill both of them for what they did to Aftyn." But he knew better than to start a clan war. He turned to Braden. "As much as I want to, 'twill be better for the clan if the laird metes out their punishment."

"I'll see to that," Braden announced. "He tolerated Rory's treatment of Mhairi. If he willna act for Aftyn's sake after this, then other measures will be needed, and I will see to them."

"Walk carefully, lad. He is still the laird."

"Aye, he is. And he's looking for ye."

"I dinna want to move Aftyn yet, and I must stay by her for a time. Will ye spread the word that she has gone back to the keep, but ye dinna ken where? Only that she wished to be alone?"

"Aye. That will have them searching the entire keep for both of ye." Braden grinned. "I will enjoy seeing that."

"And Mhairi, if ye will go on about yer day as if nought occurred and no one is here with ye," Jamie said, "that will confuse them, too."

"Gladly. I've work to do outside, but will be in and out."

"That will serve."

"What do ye need, healer?" Braden glanced around. "I ken yer men always brought ye food and drink. I can..."

"Nay, lad," Mhairi interrupted. "I will provide. If ye come back here, ye will lead men to my door."

"Very well. Whatever ye use, I will replace from the keep's stores and be generous about it," Braden promised. "I've heard how Alastair can eat," he added with a grin. "He's a good lad."

Once again, Jamie saw what a good laird this lad would someday be if he was given the chance.

"I will go back to the keep and do what I can to confuse the searchers," Braden continued. "I'm sure I can recruit some of the lasses to help. We can spread conflicting stories that will keep them occupied for a while."

Jamie nodded. "I need a few hours. Do the best ye can, lad. And thank ye."

"Aye, Brother. Thank ye," Aftyn said, then lay down with a sigh. "I'll rest now."

Braden took a moment to study her, then stood, opened the door a crack and peered out, then left.

Jamie could tell he'd been making sure he'd not be observed. Likely, his path would take him behind the cottage. The lad had a good head on his young shoulders.

Mhairi went to her cupboard and pulled out as much food as she had on hand, as well as three more pitchers. "Bread, cheese, strips of dried venison, fruit, cider, and ale," she said, pointing to each. "This one is water. I'll be outside for a while. Take care of our lass."

"Thank ye, Mhairi. I owe ye."

"Ye owe me nought. 'Tis the least of what I owe ye. Both of ye." She left them, closing the door softly behind her.

Aftyn opened her eyes and pushed herself up onto one elbow. "Where were we?"

Jamie laughed. She'd nearly died. Now, she was fit enough to tease him into kissing her again. He'd never loved his talent more than in that moment. "We," he said and gave her a frown he didn't mean, "are going to eat. Ye will eat a wee bit while I eat more. Then I am going to put ye in a healing sleep for a few hours while I make sure I did enough earlier. Then I'll finish what I must do for ye, like yer shoulder and hands. Ye dinna mind if ye have a few bruises left to prove they truly harmed ye, aye? I can promise ye they willna hurt."

"Very well. Do what ye must. If my father is to consider punishing those men, he will demand proof. They will deny what they did. Bruises should help convince him."

"The color will be on the surface only and will fade in a few days. Yer eye is still swollen, though only a wee."

"Leave it. I can see well enough."

"Brave lass. I was going to suggest that." He helped her to Mhairi's table. They ate in silence for a few minutes, then Aftyn sighed.

"I think that is enough for me."

"Then I want ye to rest until I am ready." He helped her back to the pallet. "If ye fall asleep, that will do ye good."

"I might."

Jamie settled her and returned to his meal. He needed the strength it would lend him to finish taking care of Aftyn and himself. When he felt ready, he returned to her side. "Ye will sleep," he told her when her eyes opened. "And when ye wake, ye will feel better, but ye must act like ye remain in pain."

"I'll do my best. Thank ye, Jamie. I'm sorry for the trouble I caused."

"I'm sorry, too. I'll make up every way I can for my part in causing yer beating. For now, sleep, lass." He laid a hand on her head and lay the healing sleep on her. Then he went to work, making certain he'd missed no injuries in her abdomen, chest, or back. Her knee was swollen, twisted, and bruised, and she had cracks in the bones of one arm, one shin, her right hand, and several toes, confirmation that she had fought for her life, yet she hadn't complained. He was in awe of her determination.

Ignoring his own pain, he fixed everything not visible on the surface, and left the skinned knuckles as they were, a sign she'd tried to defend herself and a small pain that would remind her to behave as if she was in much greater pain.

Finally, satisfied he'd done all he could, he pushed to his feet and limped to the table to avail himself of more of Mhairi's cider. Exhausted, he stretched out on the floor near the door. He wanted to know the moment anyone tried to enter the cottage. Then he turned his awareness inward and dealt with the pains that had transferred to his body. He couldn't fathom how any man could do to a lass what those two men had done to Aftyn. Fury built in him and he let it grow. It would help him heal and give him the power he needed to destroy those two men if the laird refused to punish them as they deserved. And, he decided, despite the consequences, he'd see the laird punished as well, if he let the assault on his daughter go unanswered.

18

Neve arrived later with food sent by Braden. Jamie had rested sufficiently to be ravenous, so what she brought was welcome. He did a subtle scan of Aftyn's injuries and decided it was time to awaken her, so he brought her out of the healing sleep while Neve arranged the food and Mhairi begged a pitcher of cider from a neighbor, saying she'd run out and her son wanted some.

The news from the keep was grim. No one had seen either of the men responsible for Aftyn's beating. Braden had sent men loyal to him to search for them, but the laird's men were only searching for Aftyn, Jamie, and Jamie's missing men.

"Ye willna be safe here much longer," Neve told them as Aftyn sat up and rubbed sleep from her eyes. "But at least ye can eat something before ye have to go."

"Go where?" Aftyn asked, rising carefully as if testing whether her body would cooperate with her intention. "My father must see what those men did to me, so they will be punished."

"Ye heard Neve. Until those men are found, ye are no' safe here," Mhairi replied.

"Ye will go home with me," Jamie murmured, as he took her arm and guided her to a seat at Mhairi's small table.

"No' the keep? They canna get to me there."

"Nay, lass. Ye canna be sure where they can go, and if ye are called to help someone in the village, ye'll be vulnerable. Ye'll go with me to my home. The Aerie."

"Ach, I canna leave. Ye ken why."

"Ye need to be safe," Neve told her, as she filled a wooden plate and placed it before her friend. "If Jamie can take ye somewhere safe, ye must go. I will manage. Hamish can help me. The notes ye are leaving us," she added, turning a solemn gaze on Jamie, "will be a great help in the future."

"I'm glad," Jamie said. "Ye must safeguard them and Aftyn's mother's journal against Aftyn's eventual return. Things will no' always be so unsettled here, and they mean much to ye," he said as he turned his gaze to Aftyn, who was eating quickly. "Yer brother will make a fine laird someday, and in the meantime, once he hears what happened to ye, I hope yer father will see the error of his ways and why I have taken ye away."

Aftyn gave him a look made of a mix of stubbornness and resignation. She swallowed and nodded to Neve. "What if ye are no safe, either? Those men beat a healer. If ye fill that role..."

"I will be well. I can stay at the abbey if need be. In fact, so could ye. Hamish already suggested it. With the work we did after the fire, we would be welcomed."

"I want Aftyn out of the reach of those men," Jamie insisted. "The abbey isna far enough away to suit me. Later, they willna be a problem," he assured Aftyn. "If Braden's men dinna find them soon and yer laird punish them, I'll return with Lathan warriors once I see ye safe, and hunt them down." As much as he wanted to do that, he'd seen the determination in Braden's bearing and gaze. "But I dinna think Lathan help will be needed. Braden was determined to see them punished."

Jamie realized it had been hours since Braden had been here, and the day was waning. His men had ridden out hours before that. And he'd instructed them to wait only until moonrise.

"Neve, ye must go back. They'll be closing the gates soon," he reminded her.

"Nay, the laird ordered them closed after ye went missing. The guards ken me and let me out to visit a sick villager."

Jamie turned his thoughts to how they would escape the Keith searchers. His horse was at the Keith stable inside the keep, as was any mount Aftyn could ride. He couldn't get in and ride out. By now, surely it was known that Bhaltair and Rabbie had escaped the dungeon. He'd be suspected of that, with good reason. Who else would want them freed? The guards would never open the gate for the man their laird hunted.

"They willna find me or my men in the keep," Jamie said. "But if the search keeps Keith's guards busy a while longer, then 'tis good."

Neve took Aftyn's hand. "Dinna fash for me. Hamish and Braden will see me safe. Jamie is right. Ye must go away for a while. But no' forever."

Aftyn met her gaze with tears glimmering in her eyes. "Ye are the best friend a lass could ask for," she said. "I will return to help ye."

"And in the meantime, I have good news," Neve said, releasing Aftyn's hand and giving her a grin. "The reason Hamish can be so helpful is that he has left the abbey and is joining us here. He had some training at an abbey hospital south of Edinburgh. He's eager to prove his worth and to be with me. I mean help me. *Us.*"

Jamie hid his amusement at Neve's flustered announcement. Aftyn didn't seem amused.

"He was to be a priest, Neve!" Aftyn said, and Mhairi's eyes widened.

"Nay, he wasna. We were all mistaken. He was there to help another man who hasna arrived yet start a small infirmary, like the one where he served. He would help train the priests, not become a cleric himself. He doesna have the calling. He can work from Keith for now, and care for both. With me, and when ye return, with us. Or we can go back to the abbey."

Jamie frowned. "Does yer da ken this? If he did, he wouldna need me, and none of this would have happened."

"It wouldha," Aftyn insisted. "He uses what he has in reach. He doesna like to wait for something else, even something better, to come along in the future. Neve's news changes nothing."

Aftyn sighed, and finally smiled at Neve, easing Jamie's concern that they would leave with a rift between the two friends.

Mhairi leaned against the cupboard behind her and crossed her arms. "It seems we will manage quite well without ye, lass. For a wee while."

Jamie returned to satisfying his hunger and thirst.

"Will they let ye return?" Mhairi asked Neve. "If no' ye can sleep here. There's no' much room, but we'll make do."

"They'll let me in, never ye mind. But thank ye. In fact, I'd best be going. Hamish is waiting for me and will worry if I stay out of the keep much longer." She wrapped Aftyn in a hug. "Bide ye well, my friend."

Aftyn returned her embrace. "Ye, as well. Thank ye for helping us."

Neve moved to Jamie, surprising him when she also hugged him. "Take care of her, or ye will answer to me."

"Dinna fash, Neve. I will."

Once she left, Aftyn returned to the pallet. "I will rest until we must leave," she told Jamie. "Thank ye, Mhairi."

"No thanks are needed, lass."

Jamie put a hand on Mhairi's shoulder, reading her fatigue. He gave her what help he could, quickly and without depleting the strength he would need to get them free to safely meet his men. When Mhairi took a deep breath and gave him a smile, he knew his touch had helped, and he nodded.

"I must go find a horse or two," he told her. "But I'll be back as quickly as I can and we'll go."

Mhairi glanced at Aftyn, whose eyes were closed. "Will she be ready?"

"She will."

"Ye can take one from the post house livery. I understand there are several stabled there."

"Thank ye, Mhairi. Ye just relieved my greatest worry."

Someone knocked on the door. Jamie moved quietly behind it, but Mhairi said, "Perhaps they didna let Neve back in as she expected." She opened the door, then stepped back, her gaze full of remorse. Two Keith warriors filled the doorframe. "Ye are hiding Aftyn and the Lathan healer. Produce them or the laird will see ye punished."

"Nay," Mhairi said. "Ye two are mistaken."

Jamie was glad the side of the cottage where Aftyn lay was in darkness, and that Mhairi had found a way to tell him how many men were at the door. They may not have seen Aftyn yet.

"Out of the way," the man said and pushed Mhairi aside to enter. He did see Aftyn then and moved toward her.

Jamie waited for the second man to enter, then shoved the door closed and knocked him out. The first man whirled and drew his dirk. Jamie was unarmed, but unworried for himself. He could handle one man easily. He only feared for the women accidentally being hurt in a fight. He kept his gaze on his opponent and moved away from Mhairi, waving her toward Aftyn. She understood and obeyed instantly.

The warrior took that to mean Jamie's attention was on her

and attacked, but Jamie anticipated him and met his charge with a blow that knocked the dirk from the man's hand. After that, the fight was over in seconds and the second man lay beside the first.

"Have ye anything to bind them?"

Mhairi found a length of rope. Jamie bound them, hands and feet trussed behind them, then gagged them with strips torn from a sheet. "That should keep them for a while. I'll be back soon with a horse."

He opened the door and peered out. The low sun barely penetrated the persistent fog, but there was enough light to see the village was quiet. No one moved about. Most were likely having their evening meal. Jamie slipped out and made his way in the shadows to the post house stables. He picked a mount and saddled it, deciding he'd ride with Aftyn in his arms. Once they reached his men, they'd have the protection of an escort.

But before he could lead the horse he'd picked out of its stall, male voices sounded nearby. More searchers, judging by what he heard them saying to each other. If they entered the stable, they'd find him in the process of stealing a horse and call for help. He didn't know what penalty the Keith might exact for that, but it wouldn't be good. With regret, he left the horse and vaulted over the stall wall, dropping behind the stable and making his way back to Mhairi's in the shadows. Once it was fully dark, he and Aftyn would have to get to the woods on foot. It wasn't the best plan, but it was the best chance they had to find his men.

When he reached the cottage, he found Mhairi and Aftyn outside, being held by Keith warriors, including the two Jamie had knocked out, who gave him glares when he showed himself that promised retribution, and two more.

∼

THE KEITH HAD many reasons to be in a foul mood, Aftyn judged, but not with her, or with Jamie for trying to protect her. They were taken to the laird's solar, where she related the attack she'd suffered and showed him the bruises that were proper for a lass to display. He studied her bruised and swollen eye for several moments, then ordered their escort to wait near the doorway. Apparently unaware that Braden had men looking already, he sent the captain of the guard to organize a search for the men who'd attacked her. Now that she and Jamie were found, he had men to spare for the task. Aftyn kept her silence, not willing to put Braden in jeopardy.

No mention had yet been made of Jamie's men, missing from the dungeon, but she had no doubt he'd get to that eventually.

Jamie stood silently beside her, appearing to brood, but Aftyn could see the tension in his shoulders and the way he balanced his body, ready to move in any direction as the need arose. He was wise enough not to make direct eye contact with the laird. That would only be seen as challenging him, which would not improve their situation. At least Jamie wasn't bound, though she suspected that wouldn't slow him much if he had to fight. He could play the healer, but the warrior lurked just under the surface. She hoped her father did nothing to bring that out.

Once the guard captain left to carry out the laird's orders, the Keith leaned back in his chair and turned his gaze to Jamie.

Hoping to forestall that confrontation, Aftyn spoke up. "What will ye do with the men who attacked me when ye find them?"

"That doesna concern ye, lass."

Heat flared in her body. "How can ye say that? They nearly killed me. I should be allowed to see them punished."

The laird leaned forward, and she thought she might have

caught a glimpse of fatherly concern in his gaze before it hardened again.

"Dinna be daft. A mere lass doesna punish men. I will see to them."

"The question remains."

Jamie's low tone startled Aftyn. He'd yet to speak, and the sound of his voice sent a thrill rushing through her. Then a chill of fear as the laird eyed him.

"Ah, so ye can speak."

"Aye, and I speak for the sake of yer daughter. They did her grievous harm, and she deserves to be certain they will suffer for it."

"Grievous... did they take yer innocence?"

The color climbing into his face nearly stole Aftyn's breath, but she managed to croak out, "Nay. They simply beat and kicked me near to death. When they were satisfied they'd vanquished the useless healer, they left me to live or die as God willed."

"Then how is it ye stand before me mere hours later?"

"I was found and given good care in the time between," Aftyn said, seeing now that her quest for vengeance would make her father even more determined to keep Jamie and put him in harm's way. "But I am not yet well and forbore to mention it, but I would like to sit down. My injuries still pain me. Ye didna see the worst of them."

Surprising her, the laird nodded. "Ye may."

Aftyn moved to a chair under the solar's window and sank into the seat. A guard stepped forward to stand behind her.

Her father turned his attention to Jamie. "I suppose I have ye to thank that the lass is here. My offer stands, despite the fact that among all the other miracles performed this day, yer men have somehow escaped the dungeon. And left behind a saddled horse in the post house stable. Did ye think to leave with them? But stayed to care for the lass?"

Aftyn's heart sank. He was better informed than she'd hoped.

"I have given ye my answer, laird Keith. I must return home before my father sends men to retrieve me—though they may already be on their way. I wouldna wish to put the people of this clan through the conflict that might arise. And since ye dinna choose to answer how the men will pay for harming yer daughter, I deem her unsafe here and will take her with me to be trained at Lathan. At some time in the future, when 'tis safe for her to do so, when the men have been found and punished as they deserve, she may choose to return."

Aftyn winced as the laird surged to his feet.

"*Ye* deem her unsafe here. Ye dare much, Lathan."

"Only to protect yer daughter, which ye seem unwilling to do, even to give her proper standing within the clan and the protection of yer name. She is nay safe. Her bruises are proof."

"Yet her value to the clan is less than that of the men ye say attacked her. A farmer and the stable master from the post house. Why should I punish them when they contribute more..."

"Than the life of yer heir?" Aftyn surprised herself by speaking up in her own defense, but her heart was breaking to hear, yet again, her father's contempt for his illegitimate daughter.

"What have ye done since? Naught more than any goodwife could do."

"Ye are wrong." Jamie's voice rang out, strong and strident. "And if ye willna punish the men who harmed Aftyn, I will. They willna live to threaten her or any other lass again."

Jamie's eyes blazed with fury. He leaned forward, every muscle tense, ready, Aftyn feared, to do battle. His anger frightened her as much as the laird's, especially now that he was already angry and being challenged by his worthless-to-him daughter.

"So ye do care for her. Tell me, how is it that she was near death, yet now she can sit here and argue with me? What did ye do, Lathan?" He pulled a dirk from his boot and drove the point into his desk. "What will ye do if I cut her?"

Aftyn gasped at the threat. Her injuries still pained her, yet her father threatened to draw her blood to test Jamie's skill? Or his resolve?

"Ye dinna want to do that," Jamie told him, too quietly.

The Keith stood and gestured toward her with his blade. "Or if I stab her in the chest? Yer skills are reputed to be miraculous. There's a priest at the abbey who might agree. Saving this lass from such a wound would surely take a miracle. I wonder what the abbot would say to that."

"In seconds, that blade would be buried in yer chest," Jamie told him, quietly. "Do ye truly want to risk her life? Or yers on my skill with a knife?"

Aftyn could see the fury mounting in Jamie. His gaze on her father was narrow and fierce. His fists were clenched and his neck corded

"Dinna threaten me in my own keep." The Keith sat down and leaned back in his seat with a laugh. "Ye are bound for the dungeon until ye can keep a civil tongue in yer head while addressing the chief of clan Keith. And for yer interference in clan matters, since ye insist ye are a Lathan, no' a Keith." The laird nodded to his men, who grasped Jamie's arms and pulled him away, toward the door. "If a Lathan army is on the way, they'll find ye difficult to retrieve from there."

"Nay!" Aftyn tried to stand, but the guard behind her held her arms, pinning her in her seat. "Ye dinna need to do this," she cried. "The abbey will soon have a hospital, a trained healer. Ye dinna need to force Jamie Lathan to serve ye."

"I'll do as I deem best, lass. Now be silent!"

It seemed that Jamie allowed the men to lead him toward the door. Then he erupted, pulling both guards in front of him and knocking their heads together. They fell, but more took their place. When the fight ended, Jamie, battered and bleeding but alive, stood tall. Surrounded by six angry Keith warriors, more drawn from the hall watching from the doorway for their chance to land blows, Jamie gave her one long, intense look as they took him away. She realized he had feared she would be hurt in the fight. She nodded to him, telling him she was unharmed. She wrapped her arms around herself. It wasn't true—she had never felt more harmed. The agony of her beating paled in comparison to seeing Jamie suffer again after he'd taken her injuries into himself. Even her father's betrayal, when he said he preferred her attackers' contributions to the clan over hers, didn't hurt her heart as much.

JAMIE SWORE as the guard slammed shut the door to his dungeon cell. He hadn't meant to lash out at the Keith, but to convince him the threat to Aftyn was real and must be dealt with or it would grow. And the next time, she might not be left with her innocence intact—or her life.

But when her father threatened to harm her or take her life merely to test him, Jamie saw red. Keith had pushed him too far. After his foster father's warnings, Jamie had fought for months to control his temper, but he could not stomach Aftyn hearing her father offer her up to prove his mastery over Jamie.

His first thought had been to go after the Keith, but some sanity had remained, enough for him to fight for his freedom instead. From the dungeon, he could not protect Aftyn.

Yet, here he was. His damned temper had burned another bridge with her father. One he needed to keep her safe, at least for as long as she remained here, until he could take her away. He wanted her. He needed her. He was a fool. He'd let his feelings for her shatter his emotional control. He had to calm down and think.

He collapsed onto the padded bench that served as a sleeping surface and dropped his head into his hands. He knew better! His strategy, his tactics, had flown out the window the moment he realized the Keith would likely not do anything to the men who'd nearly killed Aftyn, and instead threatened the woman Jamie loved. How could the Keith claim they were more valuable to the clan than the man's own daughter? Jamie knew he'd been goading him, but to do so in Aftyn's hearing was cruel.

His hands clenched into fists and tugged at his hair until the pain made him stop. He needed to break out of here. To be ready if and when someone brought a meal. He assumed the Keith would not want to starve him, not if he retained any hope of convincing him to join the clan as its healer. Though, after the fight in his hall and Aftyn's revelations about changes at the abbey, perhaps he'd change his mind.

Nay. The memory of the condition those men left her in sent his blood boiling through his veins yet again. He jumped up and paced the width of his cell. Without his intervention, she'd be dead right now. Then where would clan Keith be?

After the Keith's threats to harm her, did he care? Neve knew less than Aftyn. Hamish might help, or Neve's description of him might be colored by her infatuation. If so, Keith would have been worse off without Aftyn. But his contempt for his illegitimate daughter apparently knew no bounds.

The ringing truth in Jamie's mind was that he would be worse off without Aftyn. She'd given him more than he'd given her. She made him care and taught him that what he could do had more value than he'd ever recognized or accepted.

And she loved him.

That was the only reason he'd trusted her with his ability. He could have taken the risk and put her in a healing sleep before he touched the first of her injuries. But he'd let her see and feel what he could do. Not to prove to her that she'd never be as good as he was. Only to show her that he trusted her with his life. And more.

He loved her. He had to save her.

19

After Jamie was taken away, Aftyn fled to the herbal, the only place she felt was hers in the entire keep. There she paced and castigated herself until Neve and Hamish arrived, breathless.

"We ran up as soon as we heard," Neve told her. "'Tis all over the keep that the laird put Jamie in the dungeon. How is he supposed to do any good from there?"

"I think he's supposed to cool off for a wee," Aftyn told her. "Though I doubt that will work. He got as angry as I've ever seen him when Da said he will do nothing to the men who attacked me."

"What?"

Neve's outrage was evident in her screech.

"That's not all he did," Aftyn said, shaking her head sadly.

"What does that mean?" Hamish asked.

"He threatened me." She shuddered at the memory. Her disbelief, and the outrage on Jamie's face. "To see what Jamie would do, he threatened his own daughter."

"What do ye want to do?" Neve went to Aftyn and hugged her.

Aftyn leaned into her, grateful for her care. Her throat closed up and she couldn't speak around the lump in it.

"Get him out of there, of course," Hamish interjected. "There must be a way."

"From a dungeon?" Neve's tone was incredulous, her eyes wide as she turned to him. "No' without help."

"'Tis my fault he's there," Aftyn finally managed to say. "So 'tis my responsibility to get him out."

"Nay," Braden said as he entered the room, then closed the door behind him. "I heard ye out in the hall," he explained. "Our father threatened ye. If we're to conspire against his wishes, we must do so in private." He hooked a thumb over his shoulder at the heavy oak door.

"Thank ye, brother," Aftyn told him and sank onto a stool, feeling every place the men hit or kicked her, despite what Jamie had done to heal her. Her body still worked to recover from the damage. She was tired, but angry enough at her father to do something to help, no matter the consequences.

She finally accepted that she could not remain at Keith while her father ruled it. Jamie was right. She'd never be safe while he was laird. And her heart was with Jamie, wherever he went. Away from here, surely. Beyond that, she didn't care.

Yet a part of her still felt guilty over leaving the clan, village, and abbey. Then she noticed Hamish reading through some of Jamie's notes made from her mother's journal. "What do ye think?" She asked him. "Can ye and Neve follow those well enough to care for everyone if I have to go away?"

"We already established that ye do have to go away," Neve told her. "We will manage."

"I'm familiar with many of these," Hamish told her. "And can follow Jamie's notes to make anything I havena done before."

Relief that she could leave without guilt eased some of the ache within her.

"Neve is right," Hamish continued. "We'll manage until the abbey's healer arrives. Yer safety is most important."

"My men and I will guard them," Braden said and put a hand on her shoulder. If those men show up, we'll take care of them."

"Nay, Braden."

"Aye, Sister. They tried to kill ye. Do ye think I'll ever rest if they are still free? Now that we've been warned, we can keep Neve and Hamish safe, especially if they stay together." He grinned at Neve after he said that.

"We will be together," Hamish commented, his gaze on Neve, "if this lass will handfast with me. We can stay together, not just all day, but all night, as well."

"Handfast?" Neve's face betrayed her surprise. "The abbey is nearby..."

"And it takes weeks for banns to be read and a wedding planned. We can do all that later, lass. For now, I dinna want ye out of my sight."

"I agree," Braden said. "And I will officiate the handfasting, if ye'll have me."

"Ach, Braden, of course. We're honored," Neve said.

"Now?" Aftyn recovered from her surprise enough to ask the question.

"Now," Hamish said, and produced a length of plaid unfamiliar to Aftyn. "These are the MacNeish colors. Mine. And now, Neve, they will be yers."

He gave the fabric to Braden, who studied it, then smiled.

"Give me yer hands," he commanded. Neve proffered her arm and Braden wrapped part of the plaid around her wrist, then did the same with the remaining cloth to Hamish's hand. "As this fabric binds ye together, so do your intentions and your promises made here and now. Ye will be handfasted for a year and a day. If a child comes of this union, ye will be married, even without the benefit of the kirk. As ye have both stated yer intention to marry in the kirk when 'tis safe to do so, I declare ye man and wife under the old ways, and bless this union. May it bring ye joy and fruitfulness for the rest of yer lives."

Neve had tears in her eyes as Hamish turned to her and grasped her free hand with his. "I love ye, Neve, and I mean to keep ye with me always. Whatever life brings us, I want ye by my side. Do ye accept me as yer husband?"

"Ach, Hamish, ye ken I do, and gladly. I love ye, too. I want ye by my side always. I will be a good partner for ye and do my best to make ye happy all our lives."

"I vow to do the same for ye, lass."

"Blessings on ye both," Aftyn said around the lump in her throat. "I'm so happy for ye!" But their joy reminded her of what she was missing. And who. Jamie was still locked up. If only it had been the two of them here, handfasting along with Neve and Hamish. Nothing could tear them apart then.

"Here, let me help ye," Braden said, and unwound the cloth from their wrists. "Well, I've never done that before, but I'm proud ye were my first."

"Braden, thank ye," Neve cried and hugged him. Hamish took the cloth from him and shook his hand. "Ye are no' losing Neve," he said. "Ye are gaining another healer."

"One we will need, now Aftyn must leave us for a while."

"As to that, who is on guard duty in the dungeon tonight?" Aftyn wasn't sure it would make any difference, but some guards were friendlier than others.

"Graham, I believe," Braden said, and thought for a moment, eyes closed. "Aye, Graham. One of mine."

"Why only one guard?" Aftyn crossed her arms, suddenly worried.

"Da thinks the man who overpowered a guard and let the other Lathans out is now locked up, so he doesna need to waste more men watching him. And he doesna expect any Keiths to help him escape."

"Good!" Neve exclaimed. "I ken Graham well. And his love of whisky. We've been friends for years. I can get him drunk enough for one—or all—of ye to get Jamie out of his cell."

"Nay, better Jamie escapes," Braden said. "Da will be angry, but willna blame Graham for that. If he's drunk, Da will punish him. Let's go."

"Ach, nay, Braden. Ye canna. If we're caught, Da will disown ye. Ye must stay away from there. Once we are gone, ye can be shocked with all the rest when the news is spread."

"And saddened, Sister. I dinna like that ye must leave like this, but I willna let ye do this without me. Hamish, stay by Aftyn. Neve, ye follow and watch our backs. Someone must convince Graham to let Jamie out. Jamie can do the rest.

AFTYN ACHED. She struggled to keep up with Braden and be silent about it, but she'd never been more determined in her life than she was right now to free Jamie and escape. Yes, escape. Jamie never should have been taken there in the first place. She added that to the long list of things she'd never forgive her father for.

Thinking of her father made her wonder if he'd called off the search for her attackers. After he said they were more valuable to the clan, she'd nearly cried, but forced back the tears. She would not give him the satisfaction of seeing how he hurt her. He'd never punish them, not for her sake.

She should not have refused to go with Jamie when he first suggested it. They could have been gone long before those men got their hands and fists and feet on her.

"I see ye fretting," Hamish whispered alongside her, interrupting her spiraling thoughts.

"Aye. I am indulging in wishes."

"Wishes. Such as?"

"Leaving when Jamie first suggested we go. I never would have been attacked, and Jamie wouldna be where he is right now."

"He willna be much longer. Braden willna let our plan go astray."

"Unless we're seen, or another guard is in the dungeon, no' the one Braden expects. Anything could go wrong."

"If he's no' Braden's man, ye being there will raise questions."

"No' if I hit him over the head before he sees me."

"Ye could do that." Hamish grinned. "But if something happens to ye, both yer brother and the Lathan healer will take turns beating me."

He had a point.

Outside the entrance to the dungeon, Hamish caught her arm before she followed Braden inside. "I'll go saddle a horse, and tell the guards Neve and I will soon leave for the abbey. Then ye and yer man can ride out, and the guards will think 'tis me and Neve."

"Ach, Hamish, thank ye. That is brilliant. Please be careful."

"I will. Be safe, Aftyn. Neve will miss ye," he added, as Neve joined them. "As will I." He took her hand and kissed the back, then opened the door for her. She slipped through and heard him close it softly behind her.

Her knees were shaking by the time she reached the bottom of the stairs, but the torchlit hall ahead of her drew her onward. She heard a thud. Then silence.

She reached the guard station in time to see Braden lift the guard's head, then drop it back down onto the tabletop where he'd sat. He glanced up at Aftyn and grinned. "Perfect timing. He's out. Take his keys and get yer man, then go."

"Hamish is saddling a horse and told the guards he and Neve need to go to the abbey. Neve married a good man."

"I ken it. Now, go. We canna be found here. 'Tis why I hit him. He'll no' ken who did it."

Aftyn took the keys and a torch and hurried farther down the hallway. She spied Jamie clutching the bars of his cell.

"I heard Braden and the guard. Then I heard yer voice."

"I'm here to get ye out, Jamie." She put the torch in a holder and rattled the keys, trying one after the other until one finally fit and turned. "Thank God," she breathed, and pulled the door open. Jamie stepped out and took her in his arms.

"For ye, aye, I'll thank him every day."

He lowered his head and claimed her lips with a kiss so sweet, Aftyn never wanted it to end. But they had to go.

"Lass, he's stirring. Get ye gone!"

"The guard!" Aftyn whispered, and led Jamie quietly past Braden, grasping his hand as they went. "Thank ye," she mouthed.

Jamie helped her up the stairs and out into the night air, Braden on their heels. The bailey was quiet. Aftyn hugged Braden and Jamie gripped his arm in thanks.

Hamish stood by the stable entrance holding the reins to Jamie's mount.

Jamie lifted Aftyn onto the saddle, grasped Hamish's arm, then swung up behind her. Hamish handed him a hooded cloak and Jamie donned it and wrapped it around Aftyn.

"Yer sword is rolled up in the plaid affixed to the saddle." He handed Jamie a dirk. "Go with God," he whispered and made the sign of the cross.

Jamie tucked the dirk in his boot, then reached down and clasped Hamish's shoulder in thanks.

Aftyn lifted a hand in farewell and they rode to the gate.

Jamie signaled.

Aftyn held her breath, fearing they'd be discovered, but the guards opened it.

Aftyn couldn't believe they could leave this easily, but whatever Hamish told the guards worked. She prayed they all got back to their chambers without being noticed. They all risked punishment, but Braden had risked his future as laird, perhaps even his life, if their father found out who helped her and Jamie escape.

In moments, they were riding toward the abbey. Once they entered the woods, Jamie circled around to where he said he expected his men to be waiting. A break in the trees showed him the moon just rising. They were on time.

"Jamie!" Bhaltair's voice penetrated the stillness.

"Here. Coming to ye." Jamie turned and rode toward where Bhaltair and Fearchar waited.

"Thank God," Fearchar said. "We saw ye when the gate opened. Now we can go. I'm about to freeze my... ach, Aftyn. I didna see ye there. Good evening."

Aftyn smothered a laugh, her first in days, behind her hand. "And to ye, Fearchar. Aye, let's go."

THEY'D GONE ONLY three or four miles before they met a Lathan war party. "Turn around," Jamie told the Lathan war chief. "We're free and eager to return home." And a show of force would only add to the trouble with Keith. He filled the man in on their escape as they rode into the night.

But they didn't get far before a group of riders intercepted them. Jamie tensed. These had to be Keith warriors. He hoped they were some of Braden's men still searching for Aftyn's attackers.

Then Aftyn gasped in his arms. "Da!" She didn't shout. Her exclamation more closely resembled a mouse's squeak.

Jamie couldn't believe what came of out of the darkness. The Keith and a patrol numbering roughly half of the Lathans' group approached. So much for his hope a peaceful conclusion to this encounter. Jamie leaned down and spoke softly. "Quiet, lass. We dinna want them to find out ye are here." With luck, the Keith had not heard her, and with their greater numbers, they would be allowed to pass without incident. When she nodded, he pulled Hamish's cloak more fully over her and the hood further forward to hide his face and slumped. In the dark, if they were lucky, they'd be mistaken for a fat friar.

"Who goes there on Keith land?" That wasn't her father's voice. One of his guardsmen, then.

"Who's asking?" The Lathan war leader was no fool. As soon as they identified themselves, they'd be in a fight. Jamie wanted to keep Aftyn out of any battle. But he couldn't ride away from the safety of their greater numbers. Nor would he put her down and hope by hiding, alone and small in the dark, she'd stay safe. Nay, he'd protect her with his strength and his weapons.

"A Keith patrol on Keith land," her father's voice rang out.

His sword! It was still wrapped and tied up behind him. He twisted, got a hand on the hilt and gave it a tug. It slid freely. Good. Hamish had anticipated he might need it and kept it accessible. But he wouldn't pull it yet. The Keiths would see the sudden appearance of his blade as a sign of aggression and attack.

"Stay low if fighting breaks out," he murmured to Aftyn. We outnumber them. I'll do my best to keep out of it."

"Aye," she whispered.

"We're passing through," the Lathan war party leader responded. "We mean nay harm. We'll be on our way."

"Answer the question," the Keith's deeper voice rang out. "Who are ye?"

Jamie tensed. His heart beat faster, heating his blood and

readying him for the fight to come. For once, he wasn't eager to pick up his sword, not if it meant he might have to fight—and kill—Aftyn's father. There might be no love lost between him and his daughter, but that didn't alter the fact that he was her father. What sort of legacy would it be for their future children to find out he'd killed their grandfather?

Jamie almost snorted at the turn his thoughts had taken. He couldn't let himself become distracted. If talking didn't get them past the patrol, the fight would begin soon.

"A group of men escorting a friar from Dundee to Stirling."

"A friar, ye say?" The Keith kicked his mount and moved closer.

"Peace be on ye," Jamie intoned in as deep a pitch as he could manage.

"Show yer face, friar," the Keith demanded.

Jamie heard swords sliding from scabbards all around him. *Damn it.* The Keith couldn't help but recognize him. Perhaps he already had. Jamie lifted his head, but left the hood in place.

"Lathan," the Keith barked. "Here they are, men!"

Keith's men charged the Lathan warriors while the Keith made a grab for the edge of the cloak covering Aftyn. Jamie tugged his sword free as her father exposed her.

"Kidnapper! Unhand my daughter."

"*Now* ye decide to claim me?" Aftyn's voice rang out, loud and full of disgust. "Leave me be. I'm going with the Lathans."

"Ye will come with me," Keith demanded. "And him, too," he added, aiming the point of his sword at Jamie. Then he made a grab for Jamie's reins.

Jamie jerked his mount aside with the hand wrapped around Aftyn, wheeled and swung his sword with the other, aiming to miss her father, but to warn him off. Bhaltair rode up on the Keith's other side, sword in hand, ready to protect Jamie and Aftyn.

The Keith's mount reacted to being caught between Bhaltair's and Jamie's horses. It reared. Aftyn ducked and screamed as the Keith fought to keep his seat. Jamie turned his wrist to miss her father. His horse came down too close to Jamie's. Jamie's mount sidestepped and pushed it away, forcing the Keith's hip into Bhaltair's blade.

Blood sprayed. The Keith clung to his mount's mane as Bhaltair's horse danced away, then the Keith slipped to the ground. Someone saw and cried out, "The Keith is down!" Others took up the call. In moments, the surviving members of the Keith patrol threw down their weapons and two ran to their laird.

"Jamie!" Aftyn called.

He leapt to the ground and knelt by her father. The wound bad, but not fatal, as he'd first thought. Without thinking, he touched it and stopped the bleeding. He didn't dare do any more with so many Keiths hovering over him. "Get him to Neve and Hamish," Jamie growled. "Now!"

The Keiths helped their laird and got him back on his horse, another man behind him to hold him up. "Ye havena heard the end of this, Lathan," he growled as they rode off, leaving his men to trail behind him.

Jamie watched him go until he disappeared into the darkness, then turned to Aftyn. She still stared after her father, eyes wide.

Bhaltair's mount stayed close, Bhaltair watching for any Keiths lagging behind.

"Anyone else hurt?" Jamie called out.

"Nay," the Lathan war chief told him, riding up. "Two dead Keiths, but we checked. No injured remain behind. We must leave the two for their clan to collect. I want more distance from here tonight."

"Sorry, lass," Bhaltair told Aftyn. "Ye ken I didna want to..."

"Aye, I do," Aftyn said. "His hide is tough. Ye mustna have hurt him badly or Jamie would still be with him."

"Let's go," Jamie said. The war chief was right. They were still a long way from home. The Keith could send more men after them. But after that unsuccessful show of force, Jamie wondered if he'd bother. He mounted up behind Aftyn, wrapped the cloak around them for warmth, and rode out.

Aftyn slept in Jamie's arms for the rest of the night, and he woke her only when they stopped to rest the horses and themselves. Bhaltair and Fearchar still had the small supply of food and ale Jamie had found in the stable. They consumed it to break their fast once the sun came up.

While she slept, Jamie healed the visible bruises he'd left behind to convince her father the beating really happened, and made sure she had no other injuries he might have missed while they were in Mhairi's cottage. He knew better than to do too much. The ride was taxing, especially with the worry that Keith warriors might follow them, or that they might run across Aftyn's attackers or another Keith patrol looking for them. He didn't want to have to fight again to escape capture.

Jamie had time to ponder the fact that the warrior side of him was eager to avoid a fight. He'd even tried to avoid harming her odious father. And he spent part of the ride continuing to heal Aftyn. She changed so much about him, almost without him noticing. When he first met her, Aftyn mirrored him— untrained and eager to do more, both for her clan and to safeguard her tenuous position there, and with a father who ignored her. Jamie had a miraculous talent he took for granted, a home waiting for him, and a family who loved him. She'd broken through his anger and made him see the good he could do. Aye, he was still a warrior but he was more than that, too. The changes in him were good ones, and he had much to thank her for. The MacKyrie Seer had warned him not to be so certain he knew who he was. She was right. With Aftyn's help, he had found out he could be much more.

Exhaustion setting in, Jamie remained determined to get

Aftyn to the Aerie where she'd be safe. Even with their expanded escort, he took nothing for granted. Despite his concerns, they made it to Lathan territory with no more incidents. Back on familiar ground, they stopped at a stream to rest and refresh. The midday sun high in the sky warmed them. They'd be home before dark, and Jamie was eager to get there.

Aftyn went upstream to wash. Bhaltair and Rabbie stayed busy by the horses, further downstream, while Jamie guarded her. When she joined him, she looked refreshed. Her color had improved and she smiled.

"I'm sorry I didna agree to go with ye when ye first suggested it. We would have avoided so much trouble."

"Ye were nae ready for such a big step. I should have tried harder to convince ye, and I'm sorry ye suffered as ye did."

"I am, too, but at least I got to be a part of Neve and Hamish's handfasting."

"What? When did that happen?"

"While ye were in the dungeon. Braden officiated. He and his men will guard them. Now they are wed, they can be together day and night, so Hamish can keep her safe. They are very happy."

"I'm happy for them," Jamie told her. "And I want to be as happy with ye. Ye have come to mean so much to me, Aftyn. I canna imagine how it would have felt to have left ye behind."

"I wouldna let ye. Nor will I ever again. Ye trusted me with yer greatest secret and ye have cared for me as no other. I'm yers, Jamie Lathan, if ye'll have me."

Jamie's heart soared. "I love ye, Aftyn. I do trust ye, and I honor the changes ye have made in me. I'm a better man for having met ye."

Tears gleamed in Aftyn's eyes. "I love ye, too. I'm sorry I spent so much time being jealous and suspicious of ye. I hurt ye and caused ye so much trouble. I wish we could start over, but I'm glad we've come to where we are."

"We can start over. At the Aerie. We'll start a new life there, and see where it leads us. But wherever that is, we'll go together."

He opened his arms and she stepped into his embrace as if she'd always belonged there. She was his, and once they reached the Aerie, they'd make it official, if they had to hand-fast first. "I'll never give ye up, Aftyn. Never."

20

"Be still, child, and stand straight," the seamstress, Moina, scolded. I've only a little more to hem. Ye are near as tall as Aileanna, but I willna have ye trip on yer way to yer wedding. Ach, ye'll be a beautiful bride for our Wee Jamie."

Hearing that name made her grin and straighten up. Though he was named for his father's best friend, someone she'd yet to meet, she could not picture the man she loved ever being "wee" or answering to "Wee Jamie" past being sent to fostering. There was nothing "wee" about him, from his broad shoulders to the parts she'd spied in his bath, parts she would become more intimately acquainted with tonight. Her grin fled and nervous anticipation took its place.

"Do ye ken I nursed him when he was a bairn? Three were a bit much for their mother, and I with a newborn of me own could suckle one of hers as well."

But of course, a nurse would use whatever name pleased her.

As would a wife, and to Aftyn, he was Jamie, her love. The man soon to become her lover. She knew what happened in the marriage bed. She'd overheard other lasses talking about their experiences, some good, some... not. She hoped tonight would become a cherished memory for both of them. She'd do everything she could to please Jamie. If only she could have more success than she'd had as a healer. The thought made her shoulders slump just as the dressmaker sighed and snipped the last thread.

In the three days she'd been here, she'd been welcomed and provided with all that a lass could need. Aftyn smoothed a hand over the deep green kirtle Jamie's mother had given her to be married in this afternoon.

A healer's color, she called it. "And ye are a healer." she said, giving Aftyn her serene smile.

That recognition, coming from a healer of Aileanna's stature, had brought Aftyn to tears. She could not claim to be a healer like her or her son, but she tried her best and was eager to learn.

"'Tis done," Moina announced. "Ye are ready."

Was she? She took a breath. Aye, she was. "Thank ye," she said as she helped the older woman up from the low stool she'd perched on to take up the length of the dress. Fortunately, the rest fit her well enough, and the lacing of ties in the back made it snug. She wished she could see herself in it. But soon, she would see herself in Jamie's eyes, and that would be enough.

As Moina left, Aileanna entered with her two daughters. Lianna was one of the triplets with Jamie and the heir, Drummond. Eilidh, two years younger, who had a twin brother, Tavish, followed.

"Ach, ye look lovely," Aileanna told her. "And just in time. The priest is with Toran at the kirk."

"And Jamie is there, too, pacing at the doorway and looking impatient," Lianna said with a smile. "If ye are ready, we'll walk with ye."

Aftyn started to nod, then noticed Eilidh's expression. Her brow furrowed and she kept her gaze on the floor. "What's amiss, Eilidh?"

"I'm happy, no' sad. I just realized that now we'll have as many sisters as we have brothers. They'd best have a care."

"They picked on ye two, did they?"

"Aye. Tavish is the worst. Jamie's no' so bad, though. Ye are lucky to have won the nicest brother."

Aftyn thought back to the night Jamie arrived at Keith and what she'd overheard through the door to Niall's chamber. "Nicest?"

"Most of the time," Lianna said. "I'm sure ye've seen his temper a time or two."

"Och, aye."

"Lasses," Aileanna interrupted, her tone firm. "We're expected at the kirk. Now is no' the time to frighten Aftyn away with all yer stories about yer brother."

Aftyn's body went cold, then hot. It was time. She was getting married today. She couldn't help the smile that she was certain shone in her eyes. "I'm ready. Let's go."

The wee kirk was outside the main keep, around the bailey. Aftyn didn't see it until the last moment, but even then it barely caught her notice. Instead, her gaze went to Jamie, pacing in front of the doorway, his kilt swinging around his legs as he strode, first in one direction, then back again.

He must have noticed movement out of the corner of his eye. He stopped suddenly and turned to face the group of women. His sisters snickered, but a glance from their mother put a stop to that.

"We'll see ye inside," Aileanna said and hurried her daughters forward, past her son, though she paused to bestow a kiss on his cheek, and into the kirk. Jamie squeezed her hand, but didn't move. He hadn't since he saw them, his gaze remained fastened on Aftyn.

"My God, ye are beautiful," he told her, once the women of his family went past. He came down the steps to Aftyn and took her hands. "I'm the luckiest man in the Highlands."

Aftyn freed one hand to stroke the side of his face. "I hope ye remember that in the future." Then she grinned. "'Tis a lovely day for a wedding. I'm ready. Are ye?"

"Ach, lass, I've never been more ready. I ken I'm supposed to wait for ye at the front, but I see no reason no' to walk ye in, do ye?"

"Now that we are together, nay. None at all."

Inside, kneeling before the priest, Jamie consumed Aftyn's awareness. His sleeve brushed hers, lending her support without actually touching her until the priest had him take her hand. She smiled up at him as he slipped a gold ring on her finger, barely feeling the metal warmed by his hand. His flesh, his heat, consumed her. She struggled to comprehend anything the priest said until she heard the words, "Now and forever, ye are man and wife."

Jamie helped her stand, then bent to kiss her. Aftyn inhaled his scent and his taste, determined to recall everything about this moment for the rest of her life. Jamie was hers, and she his.

"I love ye, Aftyn," he told her after he lifted his lips from hers. "I'll love ye forever."

"Forever willna be long enough, my husband."

He smiled and turned her to face his family and their guests. She hadn't noticed on the way in, but people she'd never seen before filled the kirk. She leaned toward Jamie and whispered, "I have a lot of names to learn, aye?"

Jamie laughed at that, earning smiles from the gathered crowd. "Ye do, but I'll help ye."

"Ye have been helping me since we met. When do I get to help ye?"

"Freeing me from yer da's dungeon wasna enough?"

"That was too easy. And Braden helped."

"Well, then, wife, if ye want more of a challenge, I'll give all ye want. Tonight, love. Tonight."

AFTYN SAT IN BED, dressed in a beautifully embroidered, borrowed silk night rail, thinking back over the wedding celebration while waiting for Jamie to arrive. She could still hear a low rumbling of voices echoing from the great hall. With food and drink aplenty, the celebration continued without her.

Where was Jamie? She fingered the silk of her gown, hoping Jamie liked it, and liked her in it.

Since she'd left Keith with only the clothes on her back, his clan had been generous with the gifts of clothing and sundries. Her wedding dress and this night rail were the prettiest she'd ever seen. Moina had promised dresses more suitable for every day on the morrow. Not too early, she'd added with a wink.

Aftyn had met Jamie's namesake and his wife, a Fletcher, at the celebration, as well as a host of other Lathan relatives, friends, and allies. She'd gone from having hardly any family to the largest she'd ever seen. They'd all been lovely to her, but she didn't think she'd recall all the names she'd heard. Many of them would leave on the morrow, so perhaps those left behind would be a more manageable, memorable number.

She was doing her best to distract herself. Jamie would be here soon, and then the wedding night would begin. He would make her truly and completely his. Part of her couldn't wait, and part of her was terrified. Not of him, but of what they must do, and of how her life would change forever.

And yes, that made her very happy, but very nervous, too.

The door handle rattled. "Aftyn?"

Jamie's voice warmed her and she called out, "Come in," suddenly eager to see him.

The door opened and Jamie stepped inside, closed and locked it, then turned to regard her. "Ye were a lovely bride, but seeing ye in my bed, ye take my breath away."

She felt her skin heat and knew she blushed. "Where did ye think I would be?"

"I hoped for right where ye are, awake and waiting for me."

She pushed the covers aside, slipped her legs off the bed and stood, then went to Jamie, who wrapped her in his arms. "I'll always wait for ye. I dinna want ye to leave me, ever, but if ye must, ye'll ken where I'll be."

"I never want to leave ye, either, but ye ken there will be times I must fight for my clan."

"Then ye must keep safe and return to me."

Jamie bent his head and kissed her. "Always. I love ye, Aftyn."

Aftyn lifted her arms and tunneled her fingers into his hair. "Then take me, husband. Make me yers forever."

Aftyn slid the pin from his tartan sash on his broad shoulder and set it aside, then unbuckled his belt and let it drop to the floor. Yards of plaid wool followed it, puddling around him and between them, leaving Jamie in his saffron léine and boots.

Jamie untied the ribbon binding her braid and loosened her hair with gentle fingers. He released her and stepped back out of the fabric at his feet, then removed his boots and hose. Left only in his léine, he took her hand and led her to the side of the bed. "I've waited forever to do this," he told her, as he untied the ribbon holding her chemise together. Then he spread it from her shoulders and let it slide down her arms.

Aftyn fought the urge to catch it and clutch it to her chest. Her husband wanted to see her. All of her. And she wanted the same of him. She let the beautiful silk slip down her body, reveling in the cool slide over her hips and down her legs to the floor. She stood, letting Jamie look, enjoying the awe and appreciation in his dark gaze. Deeming he'd seen enough for now, she took the hem of his léine in her fingers and lifted it, skimming his belly and ribs, watching his eyes darken even more as he lifted his arms for her to pull it over his head. He helped her with that, and in a moment, he, too, stood naked.

Aftyn let her gaze drop from his shoulders to his muscled chest, following a line of dark hair down the slabs of muscle on his abdomen to his manhood. She sucked in a soft breath, trying not to gasp at his size. She'd seen him in his bath, but not quite this close and not this aroused.

"Dinna fash," he told her. "Ye will be ready before I breach yer defenses."

She found the will to grin up at him. "Spoken like a true warrior."

"Aye, but the healer in me doesna wish to do ye harm."

"Yet ye must," she objected.

"Only for a moment, and it will pass."

"Ye willna diminish what I feel…"

"Nay, I will let it happen, so ye ken ye are truly mine."

Aftyn nodded and lifted her hands to his chest. "'Tis what I want. And how I want ye, truly mine, as well."

"I, too."

Even after he kissed her mouth and stroked her body to a shuddering climax, she wondered if she'd made the right decision in telling Jamie not to blunt the pain of her deflowering. He was huge, and as he began to enter her, the stretching sensation gave her pause.

"Are ye…"

"I'm well. I think." She wanted this, more than anything, but getting Jamie past her maidenhead seemed impossible. And then he thrust again, a little farther, before easing back. She wanted to love the sense of fullness his presence inside gave her. Was she ready?

"This will hurt, lass, and I'm sorry for it, but..."

Aye, she was ready. It was time. "Make me yers, husband."

Without warning, Jamie thrust, harder, farther. She felt something tear and gasped against the pain. He held still, and when she could breathe again, she asked, "Is it done?"

"Aye. Ye are mine, my love. Does it still hurt?"

The fullness, the pressure, and a little twinge remained, but even that was fading. "A little, but 'tis waning. Did ye...?"

"Nay. I promised I wouldna, and I keep my promises to ye."

"I ken it." She took a breath. "I'm ready for more."

"Then more ye shall have."

Jamie pulled back and thrust again, slowly, gently, until he found a rhythm. She still felt full and tight, but he fit and suddenly she realized she liked what he was doing. Her body seemed to know how to respond to him. She clung to him and lifted her hips, seeking more, deeper, faster. Jamie obliged. She felt herself tightening, filling with a delicious tension until suddenly, she reached the pinnacle again and her body filled with delighted sensations from her fingertips to her core. Jamie plunged into her twice more, then arched, groaning her name as his hot seed filled her with a whole new sensation.

They stayed together, still except for sated breaths, for long minutes, then Jamie rolled to the side and pulled her with him.

"My love, my wife, forever," he murmured into her hair.

"My love, my husband, forever," she answered as she drifted into a lovely, warm haze.

MORNING CAME SOFTLY, pearly light glowing outside their window. Jamie woke first and took his time drinking in the sight of his wife. *His wife.* A year ago, he would not have believed such a thing possible. The MacKyrie Seer's words came back to him. As she predicted, he had found another path, and new

ways to help those he loved. His days as a hotheaded youth
were behind him. The last time he'd lost his temper had been
for Aftyn's sake, not his own. He hadn't accomplished anything
with his anger—another lesson he took to heart.

With Aftyn at his side, he'd learned the value of his heritage
and the control to use his talent—and his temperament
—wisely.

Pleasing his wife had become his favorite way to do that.
Last night, he'd been eager to give Aftyn the pleasure he knew
would ease their joining when he made her his. He loved her,
and he'd wanted her to know exactly what they did together, to
feel the joy in it, all the way to her bones.

It had been magical.

His abilities aside, she was the witch in the family, to make
him feel what he had while wrapped in his pleasure. The unfamiliar, wonderful sensations of her sensual awakening had
added to the power of their joining. Her climax had sent his
soaring to heights he'd never reached before. If only he could
have shared with her how that made him feel.

In a way, perhaps he had. She was not sensitive to him in
the same way he was to her, but he had no doubt she was aware
of every nuance of feeling he possessed. She could please him,
console him, soothe him, make him laugh, whatever he
needed, unerring in her perception of his feelings. More than
once, he wondered if she had a talent of her own, like his. He
was a lucky man.

Exhausted, they'd both fallen quickly asleep, but a new day
meant a new opportunity to please Aftyn. If she wanted more,
he was ready. And if she was sore, he could ease that for her.

Instead, he let her sleep, content to watch her dream. The
changing light painted her skin and made her glow like a pearl.
Her dark hair spread on the pillow around her head. He picked
up a strand near his face and wrapped it around his fingers,

reveling in its silky slip. The sheet had slid down during the night, exposing her breasts. Their pink tips tempted him to taste, lick, and suckle Aftyn awake. But nay, he would await her pleasure for his own.

EPILOGUE

Two months later, Aftyn was still insulted, but not surprised, that her father had not bothered to send for word about her, or to send men to demand her return. But she was glad, too, that her new life with Jamie remained undisturbed. They'd spent a blissful autumn at the Aerie, longer, Jamie told her, than he'd been in residence in years. Since he'd returned from fostering, his father made a practice of sending him out on missions for the clan, or with fighting men to assist an ally such as the MacKyries. He told her he appreciated the respite. And her.

Neve kept her informed. Her news about the happenings in the Keith keep arrived in a new letter every week. She and Hamish were still newlyweds, spending all their time together, which made Aftyn happy for them both. The laird still refused to follow their advice, so his wound still bothered him. And less than a month after Jamie brought Aftyn to the Aerie, Neve wrote to say the men who beat Aftyn near to death had been found beaten and robbed, both dead. She hadn't provided any more information.

Braden wrote to her, too. Usually short missives saying he

missed her and hoped she had found the happiness she deserved. His note around the same time provided no more details than Neve's, which made Aftyn suspect Braden's men made it look like highwaymen had done the deed.

She had discussed the news with Jamie. They both agreed that it was tempting to at least pay Keith a visit. Aftyn could retrieve her belongings and her mother's journal, which she'd left behind in the urgency of their escape, and spend time with the friends she'd left behind. But her father was still laird, and they could find themselves being escorted into his dungeon—if not her, certainly Jamie. So they opted to wait. Her brother would be laird eventually.

It seemed strange to look forward to the day he took over, for that would mean her father had died. She wondered if she would feel anything besides relief when that news came.

She wrote back to both of them, but sent hers addressed to Hamish at the abbey. Her father treated her as if she had never existed, so keeping letters from her out of his hands seemed prudent. He might not care to open correspondence he knew she'd sent, but not knowing how he'd use anything he gleaned from her letters, she refused to give him the opportunity. So far, neither Neve nor Braden had complained the round-about delivery caused problems or delays. Hamish still supported the abbey and visited every few days, since the new healer had yet to arrive, so her replies never waited long.

When she wrote to Neve, she included instructions for making new potions that she'd learned from Aileanna or one of the other healers in the clan. She even noted some that might help her da. None of the other healers had Jamie's or his mother's special talent, but they knew herb lore and shared freely with her.

"Ach, I see ye have a new preparation for Neve and Hamish," Jamie said, leaning over her shoulder to glance at what she was writing. "The evening meal begins soon. Can ye finish that afterward?"

"I could," she told him, reaching up with her free hand to grasp his where it rested on her shoulders. "But I have other plans with my husband this evening." She set aside the quill and covered the ink pot before turning to give him a smile that he could not misinterpret. "If he's no' busy elsewhere, of course."

"I think he can make himself available," Jamie told her with a grin. "If what ye have planned is worth his time."

His grin always breached her defenses, and he knew it. Not that he needed to convince her. "I believe he will agree that it is," she said and stood, coming fully into his arms. "I love ye, Jamie Lathan. And I want ye."

"Now? What about yer letter? Yer supper?"

Aftyn began unpinning and untying, enjoying the process of revealing her handsome husband's body, saying, "They can wait."

Jamie quickly divested himself of the clothes she'd loosened, then turned her around and unlaced her gown. "I canna wait to see all of ye, my love," he whispered in her ear as he slid the kirtle from her shoulders, then turned her and untied her chemise's neckline. "Each time I see ye, I want ye more than the last."

"Then take me, Husband," she told him as she stepped out the puddle of fabric at her feet and kicked off her slippers.

Jamie removed his boots, then pulled her against his hard chest. Aftyn's blood heated as his hands roamed her body, then he picked her up and dropped her on the bed. "In my own good time, wife."

Joy and anticipation filled her. Jamie was a remarkable lover. She supposed his ability to sense the response in her body to his touch made him as unerring at finding her pleasure as if she touched herself. They might miss the evening meal, but she wouldn't mind.

"I ken what ye're thinking, lass," he told her between kisses. "And yes, I can feel yer blood heating, yer heart beating faster, the way ye want me and are ready for me. But that doesna mean I willna take my time and make ye wait."

"I like it when ye make me wait."

"I ken that, too."

"It isna fair that I canna do the same, to ken how my touch makes ye feel."

"Aye, ye can." He took her hand and placed it on his chest. "Feel my heart, my love."

She sighed in appreciation of the massive muscles covering his chest, then lowered her ear over his heart and listened. The deep, slow beat speeded as she trailed her fingers down his chest to his belly. She loved hearing it. It told her Jamie was strong and vital—and hers. Then he lifted her hand to his face and she picked up her head to follow it with her gaze. "I see the flush in yer skin, too," she told him.

"And this?" He said, taking her hand and pulling it the rest of the way down his belly.

"Ach, aye. I ken what that means. Ye want me as much as I want ye."

"More lass, even more."

"Then take me, love."

"Nay, no' yet. Ye havena waited long enough. And I havena touched and tasted everything I yearn for."

She leaned back on the pillows, lifting her arms over her head. "I'm waiting."

∽

A WEEK LATER, a messenger arrived with two letters for Aftyn. One each from Braden and Neve. She settled in the chamber she shared with Jamie at her writing desk and broke the seal on Braden's missive. She read only a few lines before jumping up and leaning out the window to see if Jamie was on the practice ground. Braden's news was too important to wait. She spotted him and went back to the desk to open Neve's note, which contained much the same news.

She dropped it, slipped Braden's note into her skirt pocket, and made her way quickly out to the bailey and around to the practice field. There, she waited for Jamie to notice her. She dared not intrude when the men were fighting. Any lapse in attention could cause someone to get hurt. But in moments, he turned in such a way that he saw her, ended the mock battle he fought with one of the younger lads, and headed toward her.

"What's amiss, Aftyn. Ye look as though ye have seen a ghost."

"An apt description, husband." She handed him Braden's letter and waited with bated breath as he read it. "Ach, lass, yer da. I'm sorry."

"Dinna be. He treated me as though I didna exist. I havena missed him since we came here and I willna start now."

"Braden is now Laird Keith. The men who beat ye are dead. Ye can go back, if ye wish."

"Just me, husband?"

"Nay, we. I meant only that ye will be safe there now."

"Ye, too. My da woulda punished ye. But going back is something for us to think about and discuss. I no longer ken how I feel about it. And as far as we ken, Agatha is still there."

"If we must, we'll deal with her together."

Jamie put an arm around her shoulder and pulled her closer, but not too close. Sweat dripped from him. "Then we will ponder and make a decision together," he told her as he walked her back toward the entrance to the keep.

"Neve sent a letter with the same news. She and Hamish are spending some of their time caring for their first patients in the abbey's infirmary with a Brother Alfonso, the healer we wished at the fire had arrived early. He came long after he was expected, but both Hamish and Neve seem quite taken with him. Still, they appreciate the cures I learn here and send to them. Perhaps the best thing I can do for Keith is to continue to do that."

"Ye have time to decide, lass. If nought else, we can visit so ye can see for yerself."

"That might be useful. They are eager to discuss with us methods they are learning. But ye also have responsibilities here."

"The Lathan laird can call upon many more than me. I would no' be missed if we decided to return to support Braden."

"He will acknowledge me as his sister," Aftyn said. "I wouldna be a nobody anymore."

"Ye never were. And now ye are my wife, and a healer in yer own right. Ye have learned much in the time we've been here."

"Aye, but there's so much more to learn."

"There always will be. No matter how much we ken, we must continue to learn."

"Ye are right, of course."

"Go inside, Aftyn. I'm going to have a tub and some hot water from the kitchen sent up to our chamber."

She looked him up and down, smiling. "I'll be waiting."

IN THEIR CHAMBER WITH AFTYN, Jamie silently blessed Cook for always having a cauldron of water heating in the kitchen. He waited until the tub filled to suit him, then thanked the lads carrying buckets, closed the door behind them and stripped out of his sweat-soaked clothes. At least here, there would be no saucy wench offering to bathe him—other than his wife, of course.

Aftyn dipped her hand in the tub and shook her head. "Still too hot."

He added cold water from a bucket left for that purpose then sank into the tub with a sigh. Aftyn liked him any way he came to her, but he knew she appreciated it when he washed after a long sparring session.

And Jamie liked making her happy. Even better, he liked the way she showed her appreciation.

This, however, might not be one of those times. The news from Keith changed everything there, and perhaps here, as well, for the two of them. They must weigh their many paths forward and decide.

Aftyn took her time with the cloth and handful of soap she rubbed in soothing circles across the top of his shoulders, then down his arms. Jamie closed his eyes and groaned at the pleasure of her touch, then opened them to catch her grinning at him.

"Peeking below the water again, are ye?" He loved teasing her, and that reminder never failed to elicit a lovely blush.

"Just appreciating my handsome husband. I do like all these muscles," she added and ran the cloth down his throat and across his broad chest, "just not so much the sweat that comes from honing them."

She didn't stop there, but rolled up her sleeves, then dipped the soapy cloth down his belly, headed lower. Jamie knew what she was up to and leaned back, giving her access to any part of his body that pleased her. He would like to pull her in the tub with him, but she would shriek and elbow him in the ribs, then haul herself out and drip all over the floor until she stripped out of her sodden clothes. He liked that part very much, but not the cold puddles her dripping dresses left on the floor. He'd learned she enjoyed their play if he undressed her first.

Not today.

His mind had been on Braden's news and the decisions that faced them, and he'd gotten into the tub without thinking about foreplay. She hadn't seemed disappointed, so perhaps, the news distracted her, too. Still, she made him feel very loved with just her hand, a cloth, and a bit of soap.

When he was clean enough to suit her, he stood in the tub and let her dry what she could reach easily, which was most of him. Then she dropped that damp sheet and he stepped out onto it while she readied another for him to finish drying with.

It saddened him that Aftyn could not grieve her father's passing, but he understood why. She'd been ill-treated, and had no reason to love the man. He hadn't told Aftyn, but Braden had written to him a few weeks after they left that his men found her attackers and brought them in for punishment. The Keith released them. Reading that, Jamie had crumpled Braden's letter in his fist, then smoothed it out and read on. Braden's men caught and took care of them. Jamie decided then that he'd let Braden tell Aftyn one day—preferably a long time from now. He'd asked after her, and told Jamie their father never mentioned her, as though she had never existed. Braden was shamed by that, and incensed, and wanted to be certain Aftyn was happy at Lathan. Jamie had been glad to be able to reassure him that his sister was well and thriving.

He would have to write to Braden to congratulate him on his new position. And if they decided to return, even if only for a visit, Braden would deserve to know right away. Jamie had no doubt he'd give his sister a proper welcome.

Finally dry and wrapped in a soft wool robe, he asked her, "Do ye want to go back?"

She settled on a chair by the fire and regarded him. "Am I ready?"

"Do ye mean have ye learned all there is to learn here? Ye ken the answer to that. But consider that Brother Alfonso at the abbey infirmary probably learned many things where he came from that are unheard of here. Perhaps some time spent with him, or with Hamish and Neve, who are learning from him, would help slake your unending curiosity." He smiled and bent down to kiss her, then took the chair opposite, letting the fire warm the dampness from his skin.

"I could work with them. So could ye. And perhaps I could teach Brother Alfonso a few things I have learned here, too," she said, challenge sparking in her eyes.

"Have a care, lass. I dare no' share what I can do with anyone there but ye."

"I ken it. I will be yer greatest defender and keep ye safe."

"*Ye* will keep *me* safe? That sounds like a husband's job, no' his wife's."

She laughed as he lunged for her, picked her up and carried her to their bed.

"But I am no' just any wife," she announced later, when she got her breath back. "And ye are no' just any husband."

Jamie kissed her softly, then looked deeply into her eyes. "Nay, my love, ye are no'. Ye are my wife. And forever isna long enough to show ye how much I love ye."

NEXT UP: HIGHLAND MEMORIES

Lianna Lathan has an affinity for animals, a talent inherited through her mother's line. When a lad her clan fostered broke her heart, that gift helped her heal, even after he returned to his family and disappeared from her life. In the woods near her home, she senses a gravely ill horse's determination to lead her to its injured rider. Stunned by a flood of memories, she recognizes the man before her is the lad she's dreamed of for seven long years and thought never to see again.

David MacDhai recently inherited a troubled keep in the Highlands. As laird, it is his responsibility to put a stop to whatever is sickening the horses his clan relies on for income and defense. When the strange malady spreads to the breeding stock he brought back from the Continent, Andalucians from Spain and Percherons from France, his only hope to save them —and to strengthen his tenuous hold on his clan—lies at the end of a painful journey.

David seeks the Highland Healer's special talents, but her daughter is the one who may hold the key to saving his clan. Seeing Lianna brings into aching existence long-suppressed hopes and desires. For David, his future no longer matters if it doesn't include the lass he has held in his heart and in his memories. Can they heal past hurts and make a future together?

ALSO BY WILLA BLAIR

His Highland Heart

His Highland Rose

His Highland Heart

His Highland Love

His Highland Bride

Highland Talents

Heart of Stone

Highland Healer

Highland Seer

Highland Troth

The Healer's Gift

When Highland Lightning Strikes

Sweetie Pie (A Candy Hearts Novella)

Waiting for the Laird

When You Find Love

ABOUT THE AUTHOR

Willa Blair is an award-wining Amazon and Barnes & Noble #1 bestselling author of Scottish historical, light paranormal and contemporary romance filled with men in kilts, psi talents, and plenty of spice. Her books have won numerous accolades, including the Marlene, the Merritt, National Readers' Choice Award Finalist, Reader's Crown finalist, InD'Tale Magazine's RONE Award Honorable Mention, and NightOwl Reviews Top Picks. She loves scouting new settings for books, and thinks being an author is the best job she's ever had.

Willa loves hearing from readers!
Contact her:
www.willablair.com
authorwillablair@gmail.com

Sign up for my Newsletter
Find links to the rest of my books